THE STEP DAUGHTER

THE STEP DAUGHTER

GEORGINA CROSS

bookouture

Published by Bookouture in 2020

An imprint of Storyfire Ltd.
Carmelite House
50 Victoria Embankment
London EC4Y 0DZ

www.bookouture.com

ISBN: 978-1-83888-940-1
eBook ISBN: 978-1-83888-939-5

For my sons, Reece and Liam. Dream big and work hard.
I love you.

PROLOGUE

Mia

My favorite part of the pool is at the bottom. Not the glint of the surface, or the way my hands slice through the water at the beginning of a dive, but after I jump in, when I can push my hands above my head and drop myself down. My body moving farther until I'm deeper, then deeper still.

I take several breaths before crossing my legs and sinking below.

Down, down, down I go.

And in the deep end, such beautiful colors. The water not looking white or blue, but indigo and gray. Ivory and silver. Shimmers of diamond-like sparkles reflecting off the walls.

My body is suspended. My hair free of a swim cap and floating in all directions, the bubbles escaping from my mouth as I open my eyes wide, taking everything in. I can stay down here for up to a minute, sometimes more.

More often these days, I'd rather be here than anywhere else. A place where it's quiet, where I don't have to talk to anybody. Where the only secrets are my own.

I stare up at the wobbly shape that is my house, the house I've grown up in, and imagine a light coming on in the living room and my stepmother passing by one of the windows. I wonder what she's up to, Vanessa. Probably about to cook dinner. She knows Dad will be arriving home from work soon. I've got time and can stay here a little while longer.

But a shadow appears on one side of the pool. The shape of someone standing above and staring down at me at the bottom—it must be Vanessa. She's come to get me early. Or I've been down here longer than I thought.

I like Vanessa well enough. I know she means well and she makes my dad happy, but I can't help the sadness I feel sometimes. I miss my own mom. I wish she was here with me instead of Vanessa.

I've been thinking a lot about Mom lately. I always think about her, but it's been happening more and more. Consuming me, taking over my heart until I feel the loss of her and how terrified I'll be if I can't remember what she looks like anymore or the way her voice sounds. I see what my other friends have and there are times when I wish I could run to my mom for help. She would understand better. She would know what to do.

I wish she could see me swim. Would she be proud of me and all I've accomplished? What would she think of me now I'm thirteen?

The dark outline of the person towers above. A sound cuts through the water, an echoey call layered over the gurgling of bubbles. The sound is garbled, but I can tell by the way it's repeating itself, the way Vanessa is motioning her hands toward the house, that she needs me to get out.

I hear a different tone this time, the ping of my eardrum, the pressure building inside my head until it hurts. My chest is hurting too, and I know I've been down here for far too long. It's time to come up. If I don't, I'll run out of air soon …

PART ONE

The Day Of

CHAPTER ONE

Vanessa Tanner

Wednesday, The Day Of

There is a strange moment in time after something terrible happens, when you're the only one who knows it's real but you don't dare say anything yet. Because saying it out loud will mean something's happened. Telling someone else will mean it's true.

Mia is missing—my thirteen-year-old stepdaughter. Vanished from the backyard pool.

I didn't leave her for that long, I tell myself. A couple of minutes tops.

She should have been fine outside. She should have been okay alone. I would have heard her cry out—*if* she'd had a reason to.

Shock waves crawl the length of my body. My skin is on fire. I hear a rasping sound and realize it's my own breathing: short, jagged spurts as if a hundred-pound brick has been placed on my chest. Not enough to kill me but enough to make me hurt, a tight knot wedged at the back of my throat; every second that's passing, the muscles are clamping down stronger.

I spin on my heel. Several more steps and I'm pressing hard against the kitchen counter, my eyes making a giant loop around the room, searching for her, looking for something—anything—that that will convince me she's here.

"Mia," I say out loud. "This isn't funny anymore."

But there's no answer.

All the rooms are empty. I yank open closet doors, pull bathroom shower curtains to one side.

Earlier today—was it an hour ago? I can't remember—Mia went out to swim in our backyard pool. I'm not sure if she took the time to tuck her hair under a swim cap. Not positive if I noticed the exact time she went. But she walked out the back door, I'm sure she did, wearing her black swimsuit like she always does, her favorite pink towel draped over one arm, long legs carrying her to the patio as the door behind her clicked shut. Swim practice in the backyard pool, something she does every day after I pick her up. Her practice is so engraved in our routine I hardly notice it anymore. She's a champion swimmer at such a young age. We're very proud.

Mia. Blonde hair. Narrow pointed shoulders on a tiny athletic frame. Blue eyes peeking from behind dark lashes. A smile on her face when she throws a sideways glance, the one that insists she's being playful, the one that makes me think she has something on her mind. My beautiful and clever stepdaughter.

I stare at the back door.

No Mia. No movement.

Only dead air—and the sound of my own breathing.

She should have finished her laps by now …

Maybe if I wait long enough she'll show up—yes, that's it. If I wait just a few minutes more, she'll throw open that door and walk inside as if nothing's the matter, surprised at seeing me standing there, amused curiosity at the wild look on my face. She'll shrug and tell me it's no big deal, it was just a game. She wanted to stay in the deep end a little longer. She'll say, "Scared ya, didn't I?" with that impish grin of hers, and I'll feel a weight drop from my shoulders.

But that's not what happens. She doesn't come out. No shouts of surprise or water dripping down her arms, past her knees. No puddles. No sign of Mia anywhere. And I realize I've never wanted to see my stepdaughter so badly before.

Fear grips the rest of my body, a sickening churning in my stomach as white spots fade in and out, clouding my vision. I blink, forcing myself to get a grip, to understand what is happening. Time is ticking. Every second I stand here waiting is another second no one can help. I'm the only one who knows Mia is gone.

I reach for the phone, my hands shaking so badly I feel as if my fingers could rattle loose from my body. Tears sting my eyes. It's the first time I remember crying, the first time I realize that—*holy shit*—this is happening. When I make that call and Tripp answers, I know I'll be saying the words out loud.

I haul in a deep breath and listen to the phone ring.

Once … twice …

The ratcheting pain in my head …

"I'm five minutes out." Tripp answers as he often does, not giving me a chance to speak first.

"Mia," I hear myself tell him. "I can't find her."

He sounds bemused. Distracted. "What are you talking about?"

"Mia," I repeat, the knot in my throat getting bigger. "She's missing." My words start tumbling out. "I've looked everywhere. The pool. The house. She was swimming, and then she wasn't. Coach told her to get more laps in, she needed the extra practice. We were home—we've been home since school—but then … I don't know. She's gone. I don't know what happened." A sudden realization hits me, my eyes lifting, and for a split second I suck in my breath, waiting for the moment of relief. Tripp will know where she went and this will be over. He's known all along that she's safe and we'll have this solved by dinner time. "Has she called you?"

"No, she hasn't. Vanessa, sweetheart, slow down. What do you mean, you can't find her?"

My moment of hope is gone as fast as it arrived. "Mia is missing!" I'm shouting now, desperate for him to catch up. "She was in the pool and now she's not. She's not in her room. Not answering her phone. This isn't like her—you know it isn't. She wouldn't take off like this, not without telling us first."

"The neighbors …"

"She wouldn't go without saying anything." I stare again at the back door, knees wobbling. "It's like she got out of the pool …" I hear my voice drifting, "It's like she just got out and walked away."

"I'm sure it's just a misunderstanding."

I feel a shooting pain in my head.

He clears his throat. "Let's think this through. Where would she go?"

"That's what I'm telling you. *I don't know!*"

Another long pause. I can picture him: he's driving, wearing a collared shirt, sports coat tossed to the side in the passenger seat. It should have been a regular Wednesday afternoon, Tripp coming home for dinner, except now everything has changed.

It's starting to sink in. I can hear it in the tightening of his voice. "Vanessa, stay right there. Do not leave the house, do you hear me? *Do not leave*. I'm almost home. Stay on the phone …" The urgency is creeping in and I hear the roar of the engine as he speeds up.

I look at my watch. It's nearing 5:30. He'll be here in minutes.

I rush to the living room, my head wrenching left, then right, not sure what I'll find, not certain what I'm searching for since I've covered this ground before. The sofa. A rug. The high shelf against the wall. Some sort of clue. Something she's dropped. Something that will tell me where she's gone. But all I see is a stack of notebooks, her laptop on the ottoman. Her backpack on the hook.

I toss pillows to the floor, nearly trip over the rug, pull back furniture, slam drawers shut. I'm revisiting all the places I might have missed, doing a second run-through of the house, searching for where she might have left a note.

But there's nothing—nothing at all. Nothing that says: *I'll be right back. See you in a sec.* Not a single message left on my phone.

"Have you tried calling anyone?" Tripp asks. "Her friends? Maybe she went to someone's house?"

I slam another cabinet door. "She wouldn't leave, Tripp."

"Maybe she didn't have time to tell you. Maybe she meant to but forgot." His words are desperate. "She has to be somewhere, Vanessa." His voice is guttural, choking. "I mean—you were watching her, weren't you?"

And there it is. Inside my head: a thunderclap and a boom. I stop dead in my tracks. My face flushes hot at his words.

Is this the first time it happens? The first time I think my husband starts blaming me? Or am I imagining things? Am I imagining he thinks I've lost his only child? *Our* child.

But I don't have time to think about that right now. We need to find Mia.

"What about calling her phone?" Tripp asks. "Or tracking it?"

It takes me a moment to answer. "I've tried both. Her last location is in our house."

"Have you searched the street?"

"She was in her bathing suit. She'd be soaking wet. You know she wouldn't go walking around like that."

He's starting to say something, but I cut him off. "Her towel." My eyes shoot toward the backyard, the lawn that spreads out from our historic two-story home, the luxury designer pool at the center. The towel she would have carried outside. The one she may have left behind.

I tear across the house, still holding the phone.

Outside, the temperature is dropping, afternoon shadows beginning their long, wide stretch across the yard. I feel the nip on my cheeks, the slight chill, another reminder that spring is slow to come to Huntsville even though it's mid-March. The humidity of another Alabama summer is just around the corner. But my heart is racing, and despite the cool air, I'm sweating.

I scan the yard, my feet tripping down the steps, the stone patio stretching before me. I reach the pool—not a ripple, no sign of her in the water—and rush to find her towel, plush and oversized, tossed to the ground like an afterthought. It's still dry—she never used it—and something clicks in my head, a particular dread, as I clutch the towel in my hands, crushing the soft material against my chest.

She got out of the pool.

She never dried off.

My heart races.

Something happened. She didn't walk away on her own.

Someone dragged her from this pool.

"It's still dry," I say.

"What is?"

And I startle, not realizing I've said the words out loud, for the moment forgetting I still have Tripp on the phone.

"Her towel," I tell him. "She didn't use it."

"Why wouldn't she …" But Tripp doesn't say anything else. He doesn't finish what he was thinking because something has distracted him, his voice trailing off, and for a moment I think: *thank God, he's found her*. He's spotted her on the street and is pulling over to give her a piece of his mind. For some unknown reason, she'll tell us she went for a walk in her bathing suit.

But that's not what happens at all.

What I get instead is a muffled sound.

"Tripp? What is it?" I'm desperate, my voice hoarse.

I spin to face the house. He's on our street, I know it. Within moments, he'll be bursting through our front door. He'll be here to help, his face red and anguished just like mine as we race through the backyard.

A crack in his voice. "What the hell?"

I squeeze the phone tightly, holding it like a lifeline. "What is it? What's happening?"

"Smoke." His voice grows louder. "Vanessa, are you there? Are you all right?"

My hand braces the side of my head. What is he saying? Why wouldn't I be all right? I want to remind him: *Mia* is the one we're searching for.

"Smoke. A lot of it. Fire trucks." His breath is coming in jagged puffs, and I realize he's gotten out of his car and is running toward me, the words coming in quick bursts. "There's a fire—oh my God, a *huge* fire. The Campbells' house." His voice is frighteningly shrill. "Vanessa—is she … Is she inside?"

And it's at this point I stop moving. My knees and legs lock in position and I stop what I'm doing.

But somewhere in my head, pieces and puzzle parts are cranking into action. Fragments of the day. Memories shredded but slowly coming together, a gradual rise toward clarity leading to this moment, the sheer panic that is taking over my spine.

And I remember what else is happening—the catastrophic event that is taking place next door. The hell on earth that is occurring at the exact same time I've been looking for Mia. The additional nightmare that is so surreal I've been blocking it out.

My husband is shouting. I hear him through the phone—he's running and shouting—and I'm having trouble holding the phone to my ear.

Because when I look to the sky, the evidence is floating down around me: pieces of gray ash cascading through the air and resting on my shoulders. Gray specks landing on my feet. Heavy black clouds and the smell of something on fire.

The terrifying reality that my stepdaughter is missing.

And something else: my neighbors' house is burning to the ground.

CHAPTER TWO

Vanessa

I hear people shouting. Sirens. The slamming of car doors.

But none of this is for Mia—not yet, at least.

It's not that I didn't hear the sirens or firefighters. It's not that I hadn't already run outside to see the fire. But when I rushed back in to check on Mia, to tell her that it wasn't safe and she needed to get out of the pool, she wasn't where she said she would be. My chest filled with panic, my mind turned into a one-track tunnel. And nothing else mattered—it couldn't. My whole body and mind was focused on finding Mia.

Tripp bursts through the front door. "Vanessa, thank goodness you're okay." I hear his voice through his chest as he wraps his arms tightly around me. I'm willing him to keep me safe.

He pulls away. "Are you sure you're all right?" His eyes search my hands and body. "Are you burned?" My voice is gone. He shakes me gently. "Are you hurt? Sweetheart, talk to me."

I look past him to our street, my eyes widening at the noise, the smoke and flames, the two fire trucks that are parked haphazardly and blocking our neighbors' driveway, red lights flashing, enormous streams of water shooting arcs against the Campbells' three-story home. I can see and hear—and almost feel—the spray forcibly hitting the roof in giant torrents, the windows next, puddles of water below. Firefighters yell things I can't understand as they crank another hose to life.

I look down at my arms and legs, touch my face. *Burned? Why would I be burned?* To my relief, my clothes and skin are untouched. I'm not burned. I'm okay. I'm safe here.

But Mia …

My head snaps back to him.

"Mia," I whisper, finding my voice at last.

"What happened?" Tripp asks. "When did you last see her? Did you know there was a fire?"

His questions shoot at me, and all I can do is stand mute. Is this what shock feels like? Is this what happens when you feel like you've stepped out of your body?

Sweat trickles down Tripp's forehead. He waits for me to say something—anything—that will make sense, but I don't know what to say. I don't know what to tell him.

Yes, there is a fire next door. Mia is missing. I don't think these two things are related, but I'm not entirely sure. I do know that we don't have much time. *Tripp, we really must hurry. We have to find our girl.*

"Vanessa! Please." He looks straight at me.

I blink.

My God. Mia. Our little girl is missing.

And I'm starting to remember more. Bits and pieces of information coming to me now: the back door closing, Mia swimming.

But when I open my mouth to tell Tripp, nothing comes out.

He leads me to the couch. "You're in shock. You need to sit down." He squeezes my hand one more time, encouraging me to sit, but then he's off, racing to the backyard. I can't sit still, so I chase unsteadily after him, fired by a small surge of hope that in these last few moments there will have been a miracle: Mia will have returned. We'll find her sitting by the pool.

Tripp is fast. Manic. I can't keep up. He reaches the edge of the pool, comes close to falling in, his body lurching at the edge, the toes of his shoes gripping the concrete lip. I watch him regain his balance, his eyes sweeping the length of the pool, his head pivoting from one side to the other as if I might have missed something, as if he has suddenly developed X-ray vision. But there is no child needing to be rescued. At one end of the pool, the custom-made waterfall built out of limestone gurgles and splashes against the rocks. That sound used to be so tranquil—not anymore.

He stares beyond the pool at the rest of the backyard. The wide stretch of grass that leads to a fence at least six feet tall at the back of the property. The large shed in the corner. A loud *pop* catches his attention and his head jerks toward our neighbors' house: toxic clouds of smoke billowing into the sky, red flames shooting through the roof. Black smoke so dense it's covering the trees.

It's the first time I realize: that smoke is getting awfully close.

Tripp races back toward our house and I follow close on his heels. "Vanessa, where did she go? Did you know there was a fire? Did *she*? How long before you knew—" The sound of breaking glass stops him, and his eyes dart toward our neighbors' house again.

I clutch his arm so tightly I know I'll leave a mark. "The fire," I say at last, finding my voice.

The blood drains from his face. "She didn't … she wouldn't …"

"We need to call 911, Tripp, now." Suddenly my mind is clearing. *We need to find Mia.*

"Wait here, I'll tell them." Before I know it, he is rushing back through the house, knocking over a table, weaving his way to the front door until he is catapulting across the porch and into the front yard. He rushes to the nearest firefighter and begs him to help. My heart is breaking; I feel it in my chest like a deep tearing. I can hear what he's saying, the horrifying realization of where he thinks our daughter has gone.

Then suddenly he's dashing toward the burning house. "No!" I cry and start toward him. But the firefighters are quicker than me. They tug at his arms and pull him back.

A ball of flame shoots from the house and the firefighters turn away, shielding themselves from the heat. But not Tripp. He lunges forward, his brown loafers kicking through mud-soaked grass and water. He is hell-bent on getting into that house.

Someone runs toward him. It's Julia Campbell, our neighbor. The woman who's watching everything she owns, all three stories of it, go up in flames. She's crying—wailing, really—her face red and puffy, eyes swollen, her small hands pushing against Tripp's chest, her own feeble attempt at forcing him away. But Tripp is crying too, and he points to the house and then to himself. I don't need to hear his words to know what he's saying.

Julia's face freezes, her body shaking, legs trembling beneath her as she moves her head violently, her mouth forming a long, mournful word: *Noooo* … Her eyes swing frantically from the house to Tripp to the house again. She takes a step back and lets go of him. Her knees buckle, and I think it's only a matter of time before she'll pass out. I should run to her. I should help, but I don't. I'm stuck here, paralyzed.

Tripp is screaming, while the rest of us are refusing to believe, telling ourselves there's no way Mia could be in there. If she is, it's impossible to think she could survive that inferno. She is too small, too young, too delicate. She'd be gone. And the thought shatters my heart in two.

CHAPTER THREE

Julia Campbell

My house is on fire. My gorgeous, beautiful house. Everything I loved, built and decorated is going up in flames. The whole place: its beautifully shaped columns, stained-glass windows, and one-of-a-kind fixtures that can never be replaced. This home, along with every home on this street, belongs to the historic 1918 registry. It's irreplaceable.

And now Tripp Tanner is telling me something I don't want to hear—that I refuse to hear. I didn't want to believe him at first, thought he'd said something else, had really prayed and hoped to God he'd meant something else, but no, he keeps repeating himself. He keeps saying the words *Mia* and *fire* and *your house*, and it takes everything in my power not to cover my ears and scream.

It's bad enough I'm losing my home, but to know Mia might be in there too … I would never recover. None of us would.

Mia cannot be in that fire. Not that beautiful girl. She's already been through so much. There's been a mistake. A terrible, horrible mistake. She's hiding, or she's in the pool, or at a friend's house. She'll be safe—she has to be; there is no other way. No other explanation. Tripp has it all wrong.

But Tripp is falling apart. And in front of us are only sparks and flames.

The house burns, but I try focusing on my family. They're what really matters. My kids are safe; they're still at basketball practice. My husband is on his way home from work.

And my mom, my sweet mother, she's safe next door. Earlier, I left her at Vanessa's. I was only supposed to be gone an hour—that damn delivery across town, and then that stupid wreck, stuck behind all that traffic. I should have been here. But on second thoughts, thank heavens I wasn't. What if we'd been trapped? What if I couldn't get my mom out of the house in time?

I feel a sickening twist in my stomach. What if *Mia* is trapped?

No, I can't think about that. It's God's plan that no one was home. My mom is safe and my kids, Robert and Kayla, are at the school gym. I remind myself our family is what's most important. We can replace everything else.

Beside me I hear Tripp repeat, "Mia. In there. Help me find her."

But no one was home. And why would Mia go in there? What on earth would she be doing in my house anyway?

My head aches. *How in the hell did this happen*?

I look around. Fire trucks and neighbors' houses blur in and out of focus and I feel dizzy, my legs threatening to give way.

Someone is shouting at Tripp. The fire chief, I think, the man who is hollering above the noise and asking for a description of Mia.

"Thirteen years old. A little over five feet, about five three. Blonde hair." Tripp points urgently. "I think she's in there."

The fire chief looks stunned. "Are you sure?"

"I don't know," Tripp says, choking back tears. "I just need someone to look."

"Did anyone see her go in?"

Tripp yanks at his hair with his hands. "We don't know. We don't where she went. But she's missing and the only place we haven't looked is inside that house, and there could be a chance. If she's in there, we might be able to save her. But we have to look—*please*. Please help me find her."

The chief lunges into action. He orders a group of firefighters to find a way in, telling them to check every point of entry as he repeats Mia's description. "Get in there! There could be a thirteen-year-old girl inside."

The two firefighters who have been holding Tripp back remain by his side, their arms locked tight on his, not wanting to risk him running into the house, even if it's to find his own daughter. Hero or not, he wouldn't last—even I know that. The flames and heat would scorch him in seconds.

I lean against one of the firefighters and we stand clustered together, the group of us, grasping onto one another as people shout and run behind us in the street.

With every passing second, with every pop and hiss and roar from the house, we know we're losing ground. Time is running out. Our chances of saving it are fading. My broken heart is left in a puddled mess. There won't be a single room untouched.

And now Mia ... sweet Mia ... could be gone.

CHAPTER FOUR

Vanessa

"Mrs. Tanner?" I hear a voice. "Were you the last one to see Mia?" Detective Angela Blakely is asking me a question. I turn my head.

I've never spoken to a detective before, never had reason to, and now, with my living room filling with police officers, their loud voices and blaring walkie-talkies, I'm overwhelmed. I just want to find Mia, not answer a load of questions. I think of all of this, but my voice is stuck.

I try zeroing in on the detective's face instead. Staring at her eyes and face is something I can do, at her pristine black shirt that is tucked neatly into matching pants, the gold badge clipped to her waist, the pendant at her neck. She's small and fierce and looks like the kind of person you'd want on your side. Especially when your child is missing.

Seated at our dining room table, I'm a wreck. I usually have my act together: shoulder-length brown hair neatly styled, and I'm usually dressed nicely too. Earlier today, I closed a deal at a fundraiser lunch and wore a gorgeous cream suit with a strand of pearls, along with diamond earrings Tripp had given me for our anniversary. But not anymore. Right now, I could be teeing up for a potential mug shot: streaks of mascara down my cheeks where I've been crying, my hair a frizzy brown ball. I can't help wondering what the detective makes of me.

"Mrs. Tanner," she prompts again.

I try to remember her question.

"Were you the last one to see her?" she repeats.

My mouth feels as if it's been filled with glue. "Yes. Yes, I was."

"What time do you think that was, the last time you saw her?"

"I don't know ..." I can't stop my voice from shaking. "It was before five—maybe four thirty." I sink my head. I'm honestly not sure.

"Mia is your stepdaughter, correct?" Detective Blakely asks.

And I flinch.

Stepdaughter. The insecurity, a stab to the heart. The word that says that Mia isn't really my child.

"Yes, she's my stepdaughter," I answer. "I'm not sure why that matters. I love her and want her found just like everyone else."

The detective cocks her head. She's noted the edge in my voice, the way my body has bristled, how I've had to blink hard to keep my emotions in check.

"That's not what I was implying," she says. "Only clarifying."

Tripp reaches over and squeezes my hand.

The detective holds my stare a moment longer before widening her gaze to include Tripp. "Mr. and Mrs. Tanner—"

"Tripp," my husband interrupts. "Please call me Tripp."

She smiles, briefly. "Tripp, is there any chance Mia might have run away?"

"Why would she do that?"

"Kids run away all the time. They're generally back by dinner."

"Not Mia," Tripp says.

I agree. "Not Mia," I tell her.

"Have there been any fights? Anything she's not happy about?"

Tripp spreads his arms out wide and looks around. "What could she possibly be unhappy about? She has everything she could want right here."

The detective nods, looking around the house. The custom-built curio cabinet filled with Tripp's grandmother's china and crystal.

The brick archway leading to the kitchen with its stainless-steel countertops. Beyond the patio, the pool.

Her eyes return to us. "But could something have happened to her? Something that made her take off?"

"No."

She looks to me for confirmation.

"She's been fine," I say. "Sometimes typical moody teenage stuff, but it's not often."

"She did *not* run away," Tripp says.

He stares out the window. But beneath the table, his knee erupts into a shake. There is a steady beat against the floor. "Do you think she was in the fire?" he asks, and his voice wavers. His chin trembles too. I move my hand to his knee to steady him.

From where we're sitting, we can't see the Campbells' home, can no longer see the smoldering embers or the white wisps of smoke, but we can smell it—thick and wretched, clinging to the air. There's no way to escape it. Outside, we can still hear the firefighters. Someone runs past the window holding a roll of yellow caution tape. In the street, a police car makes a U-turn, brakes squealing, and parks out front.

The detective follows my husband's gaze. "Why do you think she went into the fire?"

"I don't know. But I don't know where else she could be. She was here, and then she wasn't. The only explanation, the only place I can think of"—he shudders—"is the house next door." He blinks at her with red-rimmed eyes, eyes threatening to become a waterfall. "Is there a chance she could have gone in there? Gotten trapped somehow? All that fire, all that smoke …"

"Mr. Tanner—Tripp. I can assure you we are going to search every part of this neighborhood, including making a full inspection of the Campbells' house just to be sure. We'll do everything we can to find Mia."

"Can I help you look?"

"You won't want to do that," she tells him. "We have a team going through the debris. When they're finished, we'll let you know."

"And when will that be?"

She flicks her eyes to the officer beside her for an answer, but there is only a look. "Soon," she says.

Tripp lets his body sink into the chair. His face is red and raw and wrinkled at every seam, his shoulders sagging as he clutches his phone, waiting for the moment Mia will call and say she's on her way, that she accidentally got lost and this has all been a false alarm. But his phone doesn't ring.

I look at the detective. I'm glad she said no. I cannot imagine him treading through what's left of the Campbells' house, burnt wood and sheetrock, not knowing what he's stepping on, not knowing if any of the pieces belong to Mia, the desperate search in case she's trapped somewhere behind the crumpled walls.

Detective Blakely asks for a picture of our daughter and I practically leap from my seat, knowing this is something I can do. I select a photo from a nearby shelf and hand it to her. It's from Mia's eighth-grade photo shoot, taken only a few months ago. She's seated on a bench in her Westminster school uniform, the school gardens in the background, the year in gold lettering at the bottom of the photo. I remember that morning when she'd been getting ready and fighting with her blonde hair, the clip not wanting to stay in place, her hair eventually pulling loose and hanging stubbornly at the side. I'd watched from the bathroom doorway as she'd brushed it back into place.

The detective takes a moment to admire the picture, the way Mia is posing with that cheeky smile of hers, her row of shiny white teeth, her eyes sparkling. The photographer must have told her a joke, something silly that made her happy, eyes lighting up and shimmering, a gentle crinkle above her nose.

Mia is thirteen years old and yet she exudes a confidence that most eighth-graders will never have, that many in adulthood to this day struggle to grasp—including me. For Mia Tanner, the world is her oyster, hers to make of what she wants. She was born into money, since the Tanner family has a legacy of inherited wealth. Her father is an attorney and partner in his family's firm. Tripp's father, her grandfather, is a widely respected judge, with Tripp most likely following in his footsteps one day.

Mia is aware of the sizable trust fund that waits for her when she turns twenty-one. College and graduate school, if she wants it, plus a monthly stipend and any house she'd like, all taken care of. Her father has made sure of this. He's determined she should have everything she wants after enduring those first devastating years.

When Mia was five, her mother, Susannah, died of cancer. After that, it became imperative to Tripp that his only daughter never experience sadness and pain again. He spent most of his days looking for ways to make Mia happy, and soon afterwards, he brought me into the family. We'd fallen in love, and together we've tried to heal everything. It hasn't always been easy but we've certainly done our best.

Detective Blakely hands Mia's photograph to a nearby police officer, who whisks it away, I assume to make copies and broadcast it to everyone involved in the search. She turns back to me. "Let's start with what you were doing before Mia went missing." I lift my head. "You picked her up from school around when? Three p.m., is that correct?"

"Yes, that's correct."

"Where did you go?"

"We came straight home."

"What did Mia do when you got home?"

"She had a snack. Granola bars, some juice." *I think that's right.* "And then she went swimming."

Her eyes widen. "But it's only March."

"We have a heated pool."

"Is it normal for her to be in the pool in March?"

"Mia is a year-round swimmer," Tripp says. "She qualifies for state every year."

The detective nods, her eyes looking quickly across the living room toward the sunroom and the windows beyond. In the distance, the backyard is slightly visible, and I try seeing what she sees: our privileged family, our five-thousand-square-foot home, a brick-and-stone veranda encircling a mosaic-tiled pool. A stay-at-home mom who should have been keeping her stepdaughter safe.

"Were you alone with her?" she asks me.

"Yes, Tripp was at work. She said she didn't have any homework and was going to get a few laps in. Coach told her to."

"Her swim coach wanted her to have more practice?"

"There's a big swim meet coming up this weekend. She knows how important it is."

"And then what happened?"

"I came inside. I don't normally watch her—"

"You leave her alone?"

"Yes, she's very strong in the water. She doesn't want me hovering over her. She usually swims on her own."

"You came inside and then what?"

"I started making dinner. Tripp is usually home around five thirty, so I try to have something ready by then."

"When did you first notice something was wrong?"

"With the fire, or with Mia?"

The detective gives me a funny look. "Which did you notice first?"

"The fire," I tell her. "Clouds of smoke. I could smell it. And then fire trucks. I went outside to find out what was going on."

"You left Mia behind in the pool."

I nod.

"You went outside to look at the fire?"

I nod again.

Detective Blakely doesn't frown, but something in the way she pauses doesn't feel right. There's a strange shift in the room, especially as Tripp's face is coming back to life beside me. He lets go of my hand and the hairs on the back of my neck begin to rise. Something is wrong. I'm not sure what, but it's something they don't like.

"Wait, you mean to tell me you left Mia in the pool?" Tripp asks. "You didn't say this before."

"I thought I did." I look around.

"You knew there was a fire … and you left her?"

"Mr. Tanner—" The detective tries to interrupt, but he cuts her off.

"What were you thinking?"

I shoot him a hurt look. "She was fine. I was going back to get her."

"She couldn't have been fine. She's gone missing!"

"I didn't know … I didn't think she would leave …" I hear my voice cracking, feel the blood rushing to my cheeks. "I thought she'd be okay, I really did." I'm choking on my words.

Am I imagining things, or is the room around me caving in, everyone glaring, even my own husband?

"I only left for a few minutes."

And then the sobs begin, the ones I didn't want the police to see, especially the detective. The crushing blow. The guilt and condemnation rising to the top. The unjustified fear in my heart that they were going to want to blame me eventually—the fear that they would try to go after the stepmother. They suspect I can't possibly love her as much as I say I do, which is wrong. I shake my head. Those few minutes I went to check on the fire are coming back to haunt me.

But the finger-pointing is only just beginning.

*

Being a stepmother. Where do I begin?

Did I ever think it was going to be in my cards? No, not really. I didn't think much about having children—I mean, one day, sure. Maybe after building a career and settling down, when my job was in full swing and I felt secure and competent enough, I could try balancing work and family life with a child of my own. I'd meet someone and we would get married. We'd be in love and start a family. I always thought that was a good plan.

But I didn't think I would have stepchildren—not that there's anything wrong with stepchildren, but I always thought I'd have my own children first. Not raise someone else's daughter before I had the first clue as to how to parent.

Being a step-parent means going full throttle into a child's life. A child who already knows their own mind: what kind of snacks they want, how they like their hair to be done, how they *don't* like their hair to be done. And yes, temper tantrums and crying fits too. You don't get any run-up. There is no chance to gaze at them as a baby first.

But as we know, life throws unexpected curveballs. Plans can go up in the air, like a fruit basket turned over in an instant.

And with Tripp, it was as if I'd skipped four entire steps before finding myself with an instant family.

"We're a package deal," he always says to me.

Don't get me wrong, it's not that I don't like children. I just thought kids were down the road, one of the things I wanted but didn't need to think about every second of the day. I imagined my future husband would be kind. We'd love each other. We'd sit down and decide to start a family, and it would be a mutual decision, plain and simple.

In the meantime, I'd finish college. Work every internship possible. After graduate school, I'd land a great job and seriously kick ass at it for the next ten to fifteen years before settling down.

First comes love. Then comes marriage. Then comes a baby—*right?*

But not with stepchildren. Not when your beloved was married to someone else before you came into the picture. Not when there is already a child waiting in the wings.

Before all that happened, before my world changed, before I met Tripp and Mia, I did what I'd set out to do: earning degrees in economics and business administration, and an MBA too. I did everything I could to focus on my career and get ahead in the finance world, working one sixty-hour week after the next, never once considering what I needed to do to settle down and find the right man. I knew he was out there. We would meet in due time, so I wasn't even looking.

And then I met Tripp.

We fell in love fast—me especially. My emotions, my need to be around him at all times, hit me from out of nowhere. The feelings were so intense, I couldn't imagine *not* being with him, couldn't imagine a world without Tripp Tanner and his beautiful, kind face. Everything else that was important came screeching to a halt.

My best friend Janie, who remains single and is just as career-driven as I was, teased me about swooning over Tripp like a schoolgirl. My weekends sipping martinis with her and flying around the country for consulting work were replaced with dinner and movie nights with Tripp. Sunday brunches staring into his eyes and feeling the joy and happiness of finding someone I'd connected with. Janie told me she was happy for me—she meant it. She also knew I was in for a ride.

Because Tripp wasted no time and told me his story on our first date. Staring at me from across the table with those heartbroken eyes, he told me what it was like to lose his wife and the effect it was having on their daughter. I immediately knew I needed to help him, that he was someone special, that I could see myself falling in love. I could repair this man, piece by broken piece. He was a project I could tackle, and although caring for him would be more challenging than anything I'd faced at work, with no numbers to quantify and no spreadsheet telling me how it could be done, I was ready for the challenge. I knew I could heal this family.

Because after all that Tripp had been through, here was someone who would cling to me and never let me go. I could be his everything. We would be in this together, I believed that.

But things changed.

CHAPTER FIVE

Charlotte Sinclair

Earlier, The Day Of

There is a giant burst of orange and red, and I watch the colors lift up and out and then sideways, higher into the sky, big jagged spurts of flame. Loud popping sounds.

I must be imagining things.

I was just humming a song, one of my favorites. What was that song again? A radio was playing it for me, but now I can no longer hear the tune. What happened to it—the music? What happened to my song? I twist my head from side to side but can't see the radio, can't find the speaker. There's only white carpet and a lamp I've never seen before.

Another loud pop, and I jump.

I look down at my lap and don't recognize the blanket across my legs. I inspect the chair next. The armrests are covered in green felt—this isn't my chair. This isn't my room. Where am I? And why have I been left all alone?

I'm starting to panic, but then I remember Julia—my Julia. My daughter with the beautiful blonde hair and lovely smile. She brings me biscuits and tea in the mornings and lets me watch the frost disappear from the grass while the sun shines on the garden, a golden sheen that lights up the driveway and warms the house. And in the afternoons, she takes me upstairs to the landing, a makeshift sunroom where I can look out and enjoy a different view into the backyard, the clouds rolling across the sky, with hours of watching and dozing and napping again until it's time for bed.

I saw a hummingbird today. At least I think it was today. The recycling truck barreled down the street—or was that last week?

The popping sound outside the window gets louder.

I look out the window. I'm facing the downslope of a mountain, its darkening shadow creeping along the grass and into the backyard. But it's blurred. Hazy. Is that smoke?

Something about this view is familiar. I've seen that tall fence before. I recognize the alleyway running behind the yard too. The single pear tree. But something about it is different, as if I'm coming at it from a different angle.

I try pushing myself up to see if I can find my daughter. Maybe she's outside. If she's in the garden, I can shout for her. And that's when I spot the pool. The very edge of it. I can't believe I missed it before, with its beautiful tiles and water turning a dark gray in this fading light. But it's empty. That's funny, because I usually see someone swimming in there, usually a girl.

If I'm sitting here, if I'm looking down at that pool … that means—

The sound of shattering glass startles me to my core. The house. Next door. That burst of orange and red is flames. *That house is on fire.*

I know that house. The burning window, the one with the burgundy drapes. The sloping roof with the double chimney. I remember the day the drapes went up. I've had breakfast looking out that window.

That's where we live.

I'm sitting at the neighbors' next door while the house I share with my daughter and grandchildren is on fire.

Julia must have brought me here to stay safe. Which means she's out there. I need to get to her.

Julia. She needs me.

But I can't move. I can't get up on my own. My legs are stuck. My damn worthless legs. And I'm terrified. Alone—more alone than I've ever felt before.

But there *is* someone. Someone has come into the room, come to my rescue. It's not Julia, but someone else. She stands before me, her hand touching my shoulder gently before kneeling at my feet. And when she does, she is backlit by the sunlight coming through the window, beaming through her dark hair until she looks like an angel, gorgeous and heaven-sent.

"Don't worry, Charlotte," she says. "Everything is going to be all right."

I gaze at the woman and blink. Her hand is so soft and smooth and warm, caressing my skin with one finger, and the movement is so lovely I stop worrying about where I am, just for a second.

But the stroking stops. The woman gets up to leave.

I don't want to see her go—I cry for her to stop—but she tells me she needs to hurry. She's looking for someone and she's worried.

She's backtracking to the door. I keep calling to her, but it's no use. She's gone.

CHAPTER SIX

Vanessa

We're still at the dining room table and I'm glancing anxiously from Tripp to the detective, and back to my husband again. "I thought Mia would be fine. I really did …"

But Tripp looks stunned. "There was a fire burning next door and you didn't think to get her out of the pool first?" He's trying to control it, the shake in his voice.

I stare at my husband—my loving, thoughtful husband. Is that the second time I note an accusatory tone?

"I didn't …" I stammer. "The fire … At first I wasn't even sure where it was coming from."

"It was next door," he says quietly.

"I was coming right back." My hands start to shake. "It was only for a couple of minutes, I swear. I saw the fire and then I rushed to the pool to tell her to get out."

"But she wasn't there." Tripp turns his body from me—not an abrupt turn, but enough of a shift to show that he's angry.

My voice is rushed, wobbly, filled with a thousand excuses. "She had so many laps left I thought she'd still be there. Coach told her to get more practice in, I didn't want to cut her off. And when everything started happening, it happened so fast. I was confused. I had to go outside and check for myself. But I was coming right back. I wasn't gone very long."

I pause to look at the detective. *What is she thinking?* She's remained quiet the last few minutes, taking this in, possibly deciding I'm a shitty parent when I know I'm not. The other police officers are looking at me strangely too, their arms folded. They have to believe me, right? They should put themselves in my shoes: I love Mia. She's my child. We're family.

I try looking at it from their point of view. I was the last one to see her. I left her to check on a fire. They think I didn't care enough to protect her; therefore I must be the one to blame.

Mia. Where could she be? How could she have left? Where did she go?

Where did I go wrong?

I hear voices growing louder behind me. More officers are arriving at the house by the minute, searching every room as if my own inspection wasn't good enough, the front door opening and closing, the room where we sit growing heavy with anticipation. Detective Blakely is looking at me, her face blank, waiting for me to continue talking. But then I realize tears are spilling down my face.

Tripp turns back to me. He's had a moment to think, control himself, calm himself down. He's looking at me, his eyes red and forgiving, and he reaches his hand to squeeze mine again. "It's okay," he says, and I let my breath out, the weight in my chest subsiding, the pain in my heart lifting. "It's okay," he repeats. "You didn't know."

I sob with relief at his words. The understanding. His love for me. He's terrified too. He didn't mean how he acted before.

I grip his fingers, *thank you.*

Across the table, the detective is watching. She's letting us have our moment, but the look on her face can only mean she wants to keep questioning us—questioning me. She thinks I'm ready, even though I secretly wish I had a few more hours to calm myself down.

She clicks her pen. Round two. Here we go.

"Would you say you have a close relationship with Mia?" she asks.

But Tripp cuts in. "Look, why is this necessary? Can't you see Vanessa has told you everything she knows? You need to go and do your job: find our daughter."

Detective Blakely gives him a steady look. "Mr. Tanner, we have officers searching the neighborhood. Every household. I know this is really hard for both of you, but we need to get a picture of Mia's life. This will help us to find her."

He frowns, but doesn't say any more.

"Vanessa, how would you describe your relationship with Mia?" she asks again.

"Close," I tell her. "We're together almost every day."

"Would she say the same?"

"Yes. She knows how much time we spend together."

"Do you fight?"

"No. I mean, there are things she's not always happy with. Tripp and I have rules. A way of doing things." My voice is calming down. "I try to discipline her when I can. She's thirteen, she's starting to push back; she's at that age. She's not always happy with what we say, but we do the best we can."

"Would you consider yourself strict?"

"We both parent her." I look to Tripp. "We take turns."

"But you're the one who's mostly home with her?"

"Yes."

"Does she behave?"

"For the most part. She doesn't act up more than other kids her age."

"Does she listen to you? Does she do what you ask?"

I think of this morning, Mia sitting on one of the kitchen bar stools eating breakfast, me leaning against the counter waiting for her to finish her oatmeal, mindful of the clock, of when she would need to head for school. I watched her patiently, my hands wrapped around my coffee mug, the final countdown until she and Tripp would be on their way.

"Look," I tell the detective, "Tripp works a lot. His job is very demanding. I'm the one who mostly takes care of her. Tripp takes her to school but I pick her up. I make sure she gets to swim practice. I make sure she studies for her tests."

"Vanessa is a wonderful mother," Tripp adds.

I look at the detective. "I know what you're thinking. I'm only her stepmother. She's not my flesh and blood. I don't have my own children so how could I possibly care for her? But I do. I *do* care. We make this work. This family. Do we always get along? No, but that's what happens with kids. She wants her independence. So when she swims, I do my own thing. I don't hover—she doesn't want me to. But it's not like I left her today on purpose. I never wanted her to get hurt, if that's what you're thinking, if that's what you're *implying*. I never would have left if I'd thought there was a chance something might happen. I was coming right back."

I look for some sort of reaction from the detective, but she doesn't give one. She turns to Tripp instead. "Would something like this scare her?" she asks. "Would she see the flames and run?"

"That fire was huge. It would have scared anyone."

"But would she have run off to hide? Is there somewhere she likes to go to get away? A safe place, perhaps?"

"She would have gone to her room."

And I know Tripp is right. It's her favorite place in the world: lavender-and-white-patterned wallpaper, her favorite books lined up on a shelf. She keeps the flower-embroidered blanket her mother made for her on the bed. She would stay in her room for hours if we let her. When she isn't in the pool, she's there instead.

But there's no sign she ever came back into the house, let alone to her bedroom. No indication she returned.

"Is she the kind of kid who would go looking for someone to help? A grown-up, perhaps? Another friend?"

"She would have looked for Vanessa," Tripp says. "Or she would have tried looking for me."

"And she was still in her bathing suit, correct?"

"Yes," I tell her. "One of those swim-team racerbacks. A black one. But she didn't use her towel. It was left on the ground, dry."

This interests the detective. "Then if she ran, she ran straight from the pool."

"Yes, but where? Where would she go?" Tripp asks.

The detective's eyes zero in on mine. "Mrs. Tanner, when you went out to the fire the first time, what did you see?"

"Julia's house ... the whole house was in flames. I knew no one was home but it was still terrifying. I've never seen a fire get so big and so quickly. Somebody had already called 911 because I could hear the fire trucks coming."

"How long do you think you were out there on the street?"

"Not long. A couple of minutes."

"And then what happened?"

"I came back here. I wanted to get Mia out of the pool, tell her to get dressed. I figured she was still swimming. Maybe she hadn't seen the smoke. Couldn't hear the sirens under all that water. I was going to get her out of the pool and bring Charlotte downstairs too."

The detective frowns. "Who's Charlotte?"

"Julia's mother. Sometimes I watch her while Julia runs errands."

I glance over my shoulder and point to the woman sitting in the living room, to the paramedics who brought her downstairs and are still tending to her. The detective scribbles something on her pad.

"And Julia wasn't home yet?"

"She hadn't returned, no."

"So you were going to get Mia and Charlotte, and then what?"

"I checked for Mia, but she wasn't here. Not in the pool or the backyard. Every room in the house was empty. I couldn't find her anywhere."

"And Charlotte?"

"I went to check on her. She was half-asleep. Once I saw she was okay, I left to keep searching for Mia. I knew Charlotte would be safe in the guest room."

"How long before you called your husband?"

"A few more minutes, I think. I'm not sure. I wanted to check all the rooms first, check the backyard again. But pretty soon everything was chaos."

"Did it ever occur to you that Mia might have gone next door to the fire?"

"No, I never thought that. The fire would have scared her."

"Is there any reason she would have tried going into the Campbells' house?"

"She knows the family," I tell her. "She used to go over there when she was little, but she doesn't go anymore."

"Why's that?"

I lift my shoulders. "Julia's kids are older and play basketball. Mia would rather swim instead."

"Do you think she could have gone over thinking there were people trapped?" the detective asks. "Or a cat or dog that needed rescuing?"

"The Campbells don't have any pets."

"Mia wouldn't have gone without thinking there was something she could do to help," Tripp tells her. "There must have been something … some reason."

"Did she have a thing for fires?" Detective Blakely asks, and the question jolts us both in our seats. But she doesn't miss a beat. "Did she like to watch flames? Light candles?"

I feel the tight shift in Tripp's body. "What are you saying?" Each syllable comes out slowly.

"We have to explore all options."

"My daughter did not have a *thing* for fires."

"Would she have seen the flames and been drawn toward them?"

"*No.*" Tripp's face flares up, and I don't blame him. The question is so ridiculous, I'm speechless.

But the detective eyes us both. "I'm sorry, but I need to cover all bases. You understand that, don't you?"

Tripp shakes his head. "She doesn't have a thing for fires," he repeats.

"I still have to ask."

"That question is offensive." The attorney in Tripp barrels through.

Detective Blakely takes a breath, still maddeningly patient. "The problem is, Mr. and Mrs. Tanner, no one has come forward and said they saw your daughter. There hasn't been a single phone call or report. We've got police out there asking, knocking on doors. We've called the homes of all the kids in her class. Neighbors three streets over. And with all this commotion, all this traffic, it's hard to believe no one saw her leave this house. They didn't see her trying to run away or get help."

"Then what the hell happened?" he asks.

"Until we can rule out the fire—and it doesn't sound like she would have any reason to be over there—we can't know for sure. She may have run away. She may have gone somewhere to hide. A friend's house we haven't reached yet. But in the meantime, I have to consider all the possible scenarios."

"Your scenario about her liking fires is wrong." Tripp lowers his voice to a mumble. "Don't ask that one again."

I wait to hear how the detective will respond. But someone else enters the room, another police officer, and strides toward her. He leans down to whisper something in her ear. It's hard to tell what he's saying—her face remains stone-cold blank, a mirror of calm—but when he finishes, her eyes lock hard with his and she swivels toward us once again.

"There's a gate behind your house," she says. "Did anyone check it earlier?"

I'm confused. Tripp looks to me and I look at him. I can't remember.

"Someone's opened the gate," she says. And my chest constricts like someone is squeezing the air from my lungs. "The gate to your backyard has been left wide open."

CHAPTER SEVEN

Charlotte

The paramedics who brought me downstairs keep asking if I can breathe okay. Do I need oxygen? Do I want a mask? But I wave my hands, desperately wanting to clear them away from my face. I want to find my daughter.

One of the paramedics tells me she's going to check my eyes. I protest, but it's too late; she's already flashing a light. I'm temporarily blinded, and I scowl, jerking my head away. If I could, I'd knock that flashlight right out of her hands.

"Mrs. Sinclair," she says. "We need to check you over." I flinch again at her touch and she presses a stethoscope to my chest. I want to run but I know I can't. I wouldn't get very far—not with these useless legs.

I never used to be this way: stuck in a chair with a body that refuses to move. Once upon a time I could glide through music effortlessly, as if the notes and my body were one and the same. If only these people could have known me before, could have seen me, the beauty I was before turning into this tired old lady with thinning white hair, ugly swollen ankles, and a mind that goes fuzzy at the drop of a hat. I'm unrecognizable from the girl in my twenties. If they could see me, if they could picture it, then they'd know who I was, what I used to be. They would be in awe.

When I was a young dancer, I never dreamed my lessons would land me auditions, principal ballet roles that would take me all over the world to the finest stages. What a whirlwind it was. Performing first in New York, followed by Paris and Cairo. The long, mournful piano pieces. The rousing applause. The smack of my teacher's cane, my tired legs giving out when I failed to do an arabesque, my partner unable to lift me, my teacher erupting into screams. But the highlights were worth the pain: starring roles as Cinderella, Giselle. Sold-out shows of *Romeo and Juliet.* The champagne parties that followed. The diet pills we pretended not to take. The sponsors we never told anyone we were sleeping with.

But when the nights faded and the crowds went away, everyone else asleep, my favorite times were spent alone in the studio, just me with a single lamp and the moonlight. Shadows stretching across the floor hiding years of scuff marks. Ballet barre hinged to the wall. A large bank of mirrors and a room to myself where I could dance with no one watching.

In the studio, there would be no music—only silence. Or only the music I wanted to hear in my head. Mendelssohn's *A Midsummer Night's Dream*, the pull of the violin, the yearning overture, and scampering fairy feet. It was quiet: only my gentle movements, the extension of my neck, the soft flutter of hands over my body. And then the leaps. I was the principal dancer. The only audience. The first critic—the one that mattered.

Now I stare at these people in uniform. Do they know who I am? Can they imagine what I used to be?

But they're talking about a missing girl. Is my daughter missing? My heart drums a fast staccato against my chest.

"Mia Tanner," the female paramedic says. Not Julia, thank goodness. Not my daughter. I try to remember if I've met a girl called Mia. I catch another part of the conversation—"She was in the pool."

"Mia?" I say out loud.

Surprised, the police officer looks at me. "Yes," she says.

"I saw her."

She nods. "She was here after school, but now her stepmother doesn't know where she is. She's gone missing."

"She's not missing."

One of the paramedics pats my arm. "It's all right, Mrs. Sinclair. They're looking for her."

"But she's not missing."

I have no idea why I'm saying this; even the police officer seems mildly amused. The other paramedic looks sympathetic. But something inside me knows it's true.

"Mia," I say again.

But is it real? My mind grows hazy, threatening to play tricks. Shadows moving in, a fog in my head threatening to blur the parts I remember. I rest back in my chair. I can't be sure of anything anymore.

CHAPTER EIGHT

Vanessa

It takes me a moment to realize which gate Detective Blakely is talking about. Tripp, too. But then it registers.

"The gate was open?" Tripp says. "But it's behind the shed. Way in the back of our yard. Mia would never go there."

It was just after Mia's eighth birthday when Tripp had the fence installed. We'd been dating a few months and would spend weekends on the back patio watching her play on her long green slide and swing set. But soon she was everywhere. She'd run around the backyard, the large stretch of grass, zigzagging this way and that until Tripp feared she would take off down the alleyway. He added a gate but had it placed behind the shed. Out of sight, he told me, where she wouldn't think to explore. It was fitted with one of those heavy-duty locks bolted at the top. Out of her reach.

"Someone left the gate open," the police officer tells us.

"Is it possible one of you opened it?" Detective Blakely asks.

"I haven't been back there in ages," Tripp answers.

She turns to me. "When you were searching for Mia, do you remember the gate? Was it open?"

I try to think. The empty pool. The mad rush around the yard. But I never went behind the shed.

My heart pounds furiously. "I didn't check."

"Does anyone else know about the gate?"

"All the neighbors have one," Tripp tells her. "The gates lead to the alley behind our houses. But we hardly go back there anymore. We don't use the alley either."

"Why is that?"

"This is an older neighborhood. People used to park their cars in smaller garages behind the houses, but now everyone has built garages up front."

The detective thinks this over. "Do you have security cameras?"

"No, but there's an alarm. We set it at night."

"Do you think it's possible somebody came in?"

"Came in where?" Tripp asks.

"Through the gate. Into your backyard."

"What do you mean? You think somebody came in and *stole* my daughter?"

"Mr. Tanner, remember, we have to take every scenario into consideration."

"But the lock is on the inside."

"Yes, but people have been known to jump fences. They could have climbed over yours. They could have …" She pivots to me again. "When you first saw the fire, did you leave your front door open? Any chance someone could have rushed into the house while you weren't looking?"

"I left it open, but only for a few minutes …"

Beside me, Tripp's knee is shaking again. "You think somebody came into the house when Vanessa went to check on the fire? You think they kidnapped Mia and dragged her out the back?" The word *kidnapped* rings heavily in our ears. "How? Why?"

"The chances of it are slim, but we have to check every possibility."

"Screw your possibilities!" Tripp explodes.

Detective Blakely doesn't flinch.

How do detectives do this? I wonder. How do they walk into other people's homes and propose the unthinkable, the brutal images and circumstances they've witnessed in other cases, imposing this line of questioning on everyone?

But the detective is calm. She nods to the other officer and gives him a knowing look as he heads for the back door.

"If my daughter has been kidnapped, you need to find the person who took her," Tripp says.

Someone here in our house. Watching us. Picking the right time to take Mia. It can't be true. None of this is true. This can't be happening.

"But the fire ...?" I ask, my thoughts jumbling. "How would they know that was going to happen? How would they know to come in?"

"She could have simply run away," the detective says. "There's a chance she's at someone else's house and we'll find her within the hour. But"—and her mouth settles in a firm line—"we also have to start assuming the alternatives. Maybe someone saw her. They know she goes swimming. The fire was the perfect opportunity to take her while no one was looking. It's a stretch, a huge risk on their part, but it could have happened. The fire department will investigate the source of the blaze. They'll check to see if it was arson. And then we'll know if someone purposely set the fire so they could kidnap Mia."

CHAPTER NINE

Julia

I will never forget the expression on my husband's face when he saw our burned-out home. I was standing in shock waiting for him to arrive, and when he did, he leapt from his car, a wildness to his eyes I'd never seen before, then ran over and wrapped me in his arms, stunned. I collapsed against his chest. The first time I'd felt safe since this tragedy began.

Now Thomas is at the end of the drive with Fire Chief Hendricks, his mouth and eyes stretching wide as a thousand questions pour out of him. The fire chief listens and struggles to keep up. *How could this happen? How can we fix this?* Of course, Thomas is already leaping into fix-it mode. My husband the protector. Suit and tie and secret cape, arriving straight from the office. Ready to step in and save the day with a spreadsheet and a plan.

On a daily basis, Thomas deals with more stress than I could ever imagine: long hours as the chief financial officer at an aerospace and defense contractor, keeping their multimillion-dollar budgets in line. From certain angles, especially when the light shifts and places him in a gray shadow, I can't help noticing how much he's aged. The years flash before my eyes. Sometimes it's hard to remember the man I first married. The boy I snuck into the woods with at night for cigarettes. The make-out sessions in the back of the car in college. The beach where we swam naked on our honeymoon. But I know he's in there somewhere.

"You and me," he always said, and there was a playfulness in his eyes. Spontaneity and devotion. Time for us. Time for fun. But over the years, I know we've grown apart.

These days, his evenings having a cocktail or cooking dinner with me have been replaced by cigar nights with guys from work. And when he's not working, he's zoned out in front of the TV, ESPN Sports or something equally loud and consuming. Our children are hardly at home anymore, always at friends' houses, always another basketball tournament. The next stop: driver's permits. Over the years, everyone in this family has stopped needing me and I've been left sitting around the house with nothing to do. No one coming to me unless it's for food or money or picking up dry-cleaning or driving them to their next game.

It's one of the many reasons I turned to photography—I needed something of my own before I lost my mind, before I gained thirty pounds mindlessly eating bags of potato chips on the couch and bingeing the latest Netflix show. There are only so many times I can shop the mall, visit the salon for highlights or facials, or attend another tedious ladies' luncheon. I couldn't bear the thought of signing up for another school fundraiser. No, I needed something that belonged entirely to me, something I could do on my own.

But right now, with the house ruined, I'm going to need Thomas more than ever. He can take care of things. He can deal with the fire chief and insurance claims while I mourn our lost home.

"Everyone is safe," he kept telling me when he first arrived. He pushed the hair back from my face and checked to see if I was hurt, hugging me close. "The kids are safe. There's nothing we can't fix. We'll move away. We'll build a brand-new home."

"But I don't want to move," I told him, the pain raw at the back of my throat. "I want *that* house."

Thomas was reassuring. "We'll be fine. We'll rebuild. Our family is intact. That's what matters."

And I nodded. "I know," I said.

I was reminded of how often Thomas sounds like this: cheerful and optimistic, uplifting and almost irritatingly calm, even when in the pit of his stomach he knows this is a train wreck. But he'll never let on. He'll know what to do—he's always known. He'll fix this house or find us another one. Either way, he'll save me the grief of dealing with insurance and leave me out of the worst parts. He will take care of me and the kids. Right now, that's exactly what I need.

He folds his arms and leans in to hear what the fire chief is saying. A minute later, a pivot on their heels, and both men walk toward me at a steady pace. My shoulders stiffen. Thomas motions for me to come closer, to meet them halfway, but I don't move. I've already given a statement. What else am I supposed to say?

"Ma'am," Fire Chief Hendricks says, closing the gap between us.

I wipe the tears from my eyes.

"How are you holding up?"

"Not good. It's overwhelming."

"As you know, we're still trying to determine the cause of the fire. I was explaining to your husband we're not sure if it was an electrical problem, or arson."

I laugh nervously, thinking it's a bad joke. "Arson?" I glance at Thomas, but he nods slowly, the corners of his eyes pinching tight. "You're kidding me, right?"

"We're not sure yet," the fire chief says. "But there's also a chance it was an accident. The homes in this neighborhood are more than a hundred years old and something could have happened: an electrical short in the basement, bad wiring, a spark that could have shot up through your house."

My house. I stare once more at the smoldering heap. Firefighters are coiling hoses and returning to their trucks. Another team works to clean up debris left in our yard. But there's a third group, a new crew that is wasting no time spreading out on our property: police officers in high rubber boots and thick work gloves, dogs on short leashes. They poke and prod the outskirts of our home, searching, pointing, the dogs treading carefully around a section of exposed brick. On one side of the house, the terrace has crumbled. Several more areas are too unstable to cross. They step cautiously and search where they can. With a sickening roll in my stomach, I know they're looking for Mia.

The fire chief follows my gaze. "There's been a development," he tells me, nodding at the Tanners' house. "A reason to believe the missing girl may not have been in your home after all."

Thomas reaches for my hand and squeezes. My heart beats wildly in my chest.

"Have they found something?" I ask. "Is there a chance she's safe?"

"Someone may have used the fire as a distraction."

"What do you mean?"

"Police officers found the back gate open. Word is someone may have come into the Tanners' yard when no one was looking." He pauses to let the words sink in. "Someone may have used the fire to kidnap the girl."

When I hear those words, I tear across the street to the Tanners' front door. I burst into the house, nearly colliding with a police officer at the base of the stairs, my feet skidding to a stop. The officer glares at me but I don't care. "What's happening?" I shriek, pushing past him so I can search for my neighbors.

I find Vanessa and Tripp at the dining room table. They're sitting with a woman, her dark hair pulled back, a badge clipped at her waist. She must be the lead detective; several more officers stand by her side. Her face turns in my direction as soon I enter, my arms flapping, and I have the distinct feeling I have interrupted her, that I'm an unexpected intruder, flying through the door without an invitation, my hair reeking of smoke and ash.

She eyes me. "Mrs. Campbell, right?"

I stop in my tracks. She knows my name.

"I'm here to check on my mom," I tell her. This part is true, but I also need to be here for the Tanners.

She nods, and I swivel my head, locating my mother in the living room. Other than looking annoyed at the two paramedics fussing over her, she's safe and accounted for, and I breathe a sigh of relief.

"I'm so sorry for what happened to you today," the detective says. "Your house."

I turn again. But instead of looking at the woman, I focus my attention on my friends. Tripp is sitting motionless, eyes down. Beside him, Vanessa's face is streaked red and blotchy. She pulls repeatedly at the sleeves of her gray pullover, nervously twisting the material until it's stretched past her hands.

"Vanessa … Tripp …" I say, taking a step forward. "I'm so sorry. What's happening? Is there anything I can do?"

Neither of them answers—they're so lost in their own thoughts I'm not sure they've even registered I'm in the room—but the woman eyes me carefully. Thinking, deciding, and wondering if I can be of any use.

"I'm Detective Angela Blakely," she says. "We believe Mia went missing around the same time as your house fire started. There's also a chance she may have gone out the back gate. Do you know anything about that?"

My knees feel weak and I take a step back. "So it *is* true," I whisper. And for the first time, Tripp swings his head in my direction. "She was kidnapped?" I ask.

Every part of my body feels unsteady. The detective stares at me from across the table while I grow faintly aware of the police officer nearby with a gun on his hip. There is so much noise in this house, it's making my head hurt, but the detective's voice rings loud and clear.

"Did you see Mia today?" she asks.

I look at Vanessa, then slide my eyes to the detective. "I saw them coming home from school. I was getting my mail, saw them park in the driveway."

"Did everything seem all right?"

I remember how Mia threw open the car door and sprinted for the house, her stick-thin arms pumping wildly at her sides. She looked pissed and Vanessa looked frustrated. She rolled her eyes and gave me that look that said *teenager* before dragging Mia's backpack from the car.

I could tell she wasn't in the mood for a chat and I didn't have time either, since my cell phone had buzzed in my back pocket. As I checked the message—the Kirklands were asking for their daughter's senior portraits to be delivered— I noticed what Vanessa was wearing: a gorgeous cream suit, matching pearls, and beige pumps. She'd been to the salon, her brown curls recently highlighted and blown out straight. I assumed she'd been out somewhere fancy, a steak and Chardonnay lunch downtown, a meeting for an upcoming fundraiser.

I don't say any of this to the detective. The fact that Mia was pissed doesn't mean anything. Children throw fits all the time—just look at my own kids. Vanessa is doing the best she can dealing with a teenager.

A police officer enters the dining room, interrupting my thoughts, everyone else's too. "We found a shoeprint," he announces. "Possibly a man's. It's in the alleyway."

The blood drains from Tripp's face, the skin across his temples shifting from red to pink before turning a sickening pale color. Vanessa's eyes pinch shut.

"Any sign of Mia? What about her prints?" the detective asks.

"No, but whoever he is, it looks like he dragged something along the ground."

The detective clicks her pen. "Right." She faces Vanessa and Tripp. "We're going to issue an official missing persons report.

We'll ramp up the search and do everything we can to track that footprint. Someone may or may not have used the back gate to take your daughter, but I assure you," she says, standing, "we'll follow every lead until we locate her."

The detective's words set several people into action, particularly the police officers gathered in the dining room. Someone barks an order into their phone while more officers rush for the door.

"I need you both to stay here," Detective Blakely tells the Tanners.

Tripp chases her into the foyer. "I can't stay here while my daughter is out there somewhere."

"You need to be at the house in case Mia returns—in case anyone calls."

"Vanessa can stay." He looks at his wife. "Is that all right, Vanessa? You can stay, can't you?"

Police officers are moving past him so quickly there's a traffic jam at the front door. Someone is rushing in from outside and collides with them at the steps—it's Thomas. He catches my eye before approaching Tripp, his hands spread out before him, offering to help.

"Tripp, what can we do?"

But Tripp shakes his head. "You've got enough to deal with. Your house. The fire."

"Forget about the house. We can take care of that later. We've got to find Mia."

Tripp glances at the detective and she nods.

"Okay, you can both ride with us," she tells them.

Thomas steps toward me and the dread twists in my heart. I don't want him to go; I hadn't planned on him taking off like this. "Can you stay?" he asks. "Stay and look after Vanessa?"

I glance at my neighbor. I know she doesn't have any family in Huntsville and it will be hours before her parents drive up from Mobile. They'll probably want to wait until morning.

I nod, and both my husband and Tripp look relieved.

Tripp puts a phone to his ear. Within seconds, he's saying, "Dad, something's happened. Mia …" His voice cracks. "Mia … We can't …" His hand rakes hard through his hair. "Can you get Mom on the phone?"

I turn to my husband, trying to squash down my anxiety. "What about the house, Thomas? What should I do if you're not here? I don't know what to tell the fire chief."

He squeezes my shoulders. "There's nothing we can do right now. They'll be picking through it for hours. The kids are safe at their friends'. Plus"—he glances toward the living room—"your mom is here. There's no sense in moving her." He softens his voice. "Vanessa needs you here, okay? Stick together. Stay here and keep your mom safe. I'll text you with updates."

"But the house …" I try again.

"We'll get a hotel room, a suite for the kids. I'll file everything with insurance." He kisses me on the cheek. "Everything will be okay, Julia, don't worry. Right now, what we're going through pales in comparison to what the Tanners are dealing with. Mia has to be the number one concern."

I kiss him back. I know he's right. Mia needs to be the priority.

Tripp shoves his phone in his pocket. "My dad is going to meet us."

Detective Blakely peels her eyes from a police officer she's been conferring with and says, "Okay, we're sending several more teams to canvass the neighborhood. Another group will search the woods." She takes a good look at Tripp and Vanessa. "Mr. and Mrs. Tanner, once the missing persons report goes out, the media will be notified, which means they'll be here soon. They'll want to ask questions and interview you." She looks pointedly at Vanessa. "Are you prepared for that?"

I see Vanessa's shoulders stiffen, her fingers trembling against her belly.

"Lock the door," Tripp tells her. "No one comes in but the police. We'll put together a formal statement tomorrow." And then, instructions for both of us: "Make sure you answer the phone if anyone calls. Keep the phone nearby. If you hear anything, call me."

Everyone leaves except for one police officer, Officer Donahue, who Detective Blakely says will stay behind to help.

Car doors slam and walkie-talkies fade. Someone's tires screech as they take off down the street. Even the paramedics are finishing with my mom and heading for the door.

One by one, engines crank, and I realize everyone leaves without saying goodbye.

CHAPTER TEN

Julia

Someone has put up spotlights in my front yard, the bright beams shining on my house. Through the window I can see a search team poking around in what's left of the first floor, parts of the house smoldering, and I turn away, unable to look.

I check on my mom. It's the first time I've been able to speak to her since the fire, and her eyes water as soon as I approach, her head lifting slowly from her chest.

I cup her cheek with my hand. "It's all right," I tell her. "We're safe."

She nods, her face wobbling slightly as it does when she's tired or on the verge of tears. I feel terrible. I'm grateful I left her with Vanessa and she came to no harm, but I regret it's taken me this long to get to her. She must have been so confused. She must have been scared, with no idea where I was.

"Let's go to the kitchen," I tell her. "We'll make some tea. Tea makes everything better."

It takes great effort to lift her from the chair, and after getting her steady on her feet, I slowly lead her across the house to the kitchen. Vanessa is already there. She's pacing, wringing her hands. I persuade her to sit down with my mother.

"Are you hungry?" I ask her. I'm standing by the counter, ready to find the tea kettle. "Do you want me to make you anything?"

She shakes her head.

"Are you cold? Do you need a blanket?"

Another shake of the head.

"Or hot?" I glance at the ceiling fan. "I could turn on a fan?"

She gives me a look. "It's okay, Julia," she says. And then, more softly, "*Please*."

I nod, my hands fidgeting.

"Tea," I announce.

Vanessa jolts, and stands up quickly, motioning for me to sit instead. "I'll take care of it." She pulls several mugs and a bag of ground coffee from a cabinet, her motions jittery. "Forget the tea," she says. "We're going to need caffeine."

Somewhere in the background, the police officer lingers—I can feel it. He's standing guard in the foyer, possibly by the front door, his black hair cropped short above his ears, a wide, heavy belt and a gun at his hip. His presence sets my teeth on edge.

Vanessa sets a container of sugar on the table. She pours milk into mugs, not asking how anyone wants their coffee, her mind a million miles away, her previously blown-out hair now turned into frizzy curls around her head.

I watch her. She's no longer in that gorgeous suit either. The strand of pearls long gone. But at least she was able to change when she arrived home—I'm still in my jeans and silk top from earlier, an ugly line of ash smeared down one of my sleeves, my shoes soaked from having stepped in overflowing water.

I rub at the ash but it only makes the smudge worse. Even if I wanted to change, everything I own, I realize, wincing, is charred and burned.

The coffee pot puffs and steams, cranking to life, the slow drip filling the pot to the brim. Vanessa shuffles in the direction of the front door and offers coffee to Officer Donahue. I hear him saying something in response, a *no thank you*, perhaps, before she returns to us at the table.

We sip our coffee in silence: my mother, Vanessa, and I. One incredibly long minute followed by two painful minutes more.

I stir my coffee unnecessarily, my nerves getting the best of me, the awkwardness of not knowing what to say, not knowing what words will bring comfort.

"Who would want to take her?" I finally spit out. Vanessa jerks at the sound of my voice, yanked from her own worries, her forehead lined with creases. I don't care. I feel the need to fill the empty space, to talk about it out loud so I can process it in my head. Otherwise the silence is too deafening for my ears. "She's so innocent," I continue. "So sweet. Only thirteen, just a kid. Do you think someone came through that gate?"

"I don't know."

"Is the gate normally locked?"

"Yes, usually."

"Wouldn't she have screamed?"

"I didn't hear her."

"But wouldn't *somebody* have heard her?"

Vanessa shudders. "We don't know anything yet."

I change tack. "What was she doing earlier today? The last time you saw her?"

"Swimming. More practice."

I prattle on, my nerves in overdrive. "Thomas and I are always saying we're going to see Mia at the Olympics one day. She'll take the gold for breaststroke and be a star on the relay team, we just know it. She's so strong, Vanessa. All those laps and strong kicks. She'll be able to fight whoever's got her, whatever they've tried to do. She'll be fine, you'll see."

She nods faintly.

"Remember that party last summer at the neighborhood pool? Those high-school kids who challenged her to a race? She kicked every one of their butts. It was amazing." I smile again, and finally Vanessa does too.

We were gathered at our neighbor's fiftieth birthday celebration. Bill and Donna Jenkins invited us to the clubhouse, where they tied large balloons to each chair with additional balloons attached to the diving board and an enormous cake set out in the shape of a yacht—Bill's retirement dream. The kids swam while the rest of us milled about sipping sangria. I remember one of the older kids shouted and challenged Mia to a race.

And that was all it took. The girl didn't back down, even when she peered down the line at the rest of the competition and each kid was at least three years older than her. I stood next to Tripp and Vanessa and we cheered loudly; I remember them looking so proud. I was impressed. It was my first time watching Mia compete—all the stories I'd heard about my neighbors' daughter, the powerhouse swimmer who was smashing times at every meet, and I was finally getting a chance to see her for myself. She beat the high-school kids by two intense seconds.

"She's a fighter," I say to Vanessa now.

Her eyes redden looking at me.

I reach over and squeeze her hand. "Whoever's taken her doesn't know who they're messing with."

I honestly believe this. Mia is strong. I picture the defiant girl kicking her way to freedom, pushing past whoever is trying to harm her. She'll escape.

That day, when I watched her on the starting block, I saw that grit—we all did. Over the years, I've watched her grow and fend for herself, always thinking, outsmarting others, stopping to analyze people first. Realizing that without her mom, her life will be different: she'll have to learn who to depend on, who to trust, figure out who to get close to. In my eyes, Mia is as self-aware as they come. Besides being strong, if any thirteen-year-old can think her way out of a difficult situation, this girl is the one.

Several years ago, Mia must have been about nine, I invited her and Vanessa to the house for a photo shoot: nothing serious, no money involved. I only needed the practice—a moving subject, a young girl with lots of energy to spin in front of the camera. I thought it would be fun and a great way to get to know Vanessa. She hadn't been married to Tripp for very long, and if she was going to live next door, and no disrespect to Susannah's memory, the best thing I could do was be friendly.

I'd picked up photography a year earlier, my kids posing for me first. When they grew bored, which didn't take long, I moved on to my nieces and nephews. It turned out I had quite the eye for photography. I could play around with lighting, get my subjects to pose the right way and relax too. This small hobby of mine turned serious when I began charging for sessions, and soon I had clients from church. Eventually my calendar filled with school portraits too.

Thomas was quick to convert a space at the back of our house into a studio—he was thrilled I had something I was excited about. We didn't need the cash, but he could see that it made me happy.

I have the time for it anyway. Mom sleeps a lot, and except for the occasional doctor's appointment, she's not that much trouble. Robert and Kayla are hardly around these days, spending most of their time at the basketball court or with friends. Being typical teenagers. And when Robert gets his driver's license in a few months, he'll be gone even more. Thomas is saving a car for him, my old 4Runner we keep in the small garage behind the house. Eventually he'll hand that car down to his sister.

So with most of my days free, it seems natural to for me to be doing something, and how lucky I am to have found a hobby I excel at. The photography is fun; my days would stretch endlessly without it, and to be honest, I'm grateful to be doing my own work; it's my extra spending money.

I remember Mia loved having the photos taken. During the shoot, she was a natural star, a little light bulb coming on inside of her and shining brightly in front of the camera, something we hadn't seen much of since her mother died. She giggled and twirled, not minding the flash, not caring that both of us were watching. I played music while she danced, flipping her hair this way and that, her eyes a dazzling blue as I zoomed in, the tiniest crinkle appearing over her nose.

I took at least a hundred pictures that day, all the while thinking how heartwarming it was to see this little girl laughing again. Vanessa was beaming with pride too.

"She's a delight, isn't she?" I said.

Vanessa smiled. And then Mia burst into laughter—about what, I have no idea. Her own private joke, her own way of cutting loose in front of the camera. She jumped up, a little hop followed by a twirl, the hem of her dress flipping as Vanessa rushed over to fix it, taking a moment to smooth a strand of the girl's hair. The move so intentional. So delicate.

Mia turned to me. "This is so fun. I feel like a movie star."

"A movie star for a day," I laughed. "And in the future, an Olympic champion."

I looked at Vanessa. "Thank you for bringing Mia today. Looks like she's enjoying it."

"Thank you for inviting us," she said. But then a glance at her watch, as if wanting to make sure they hadn't taken up too much time, not wanting to overstay their welcome.

"Relax," I told her. "I've got all day."

She slid her eyes to Mia. "I should probably get her back for lunch."

"I'm not hungry," Mia said, planting her hands on her hips.

"You know you need to eat before practice."

But Mia still wanted to dance to the music. "I'm not ready to go."

Vanessa sighed. "That was the deal, remember?"

The girl didn't answer.

I watched them both, possibly one of their first stand-offs, and offered a compromise. "Five more minutes, okay? A couple more photos and then you, young lady"—I looked directly at Mia—"are listening to your stepmother and going straight home for lunch."

"*Fine*," Mia said, dragging out the word. She looked at Vanessa. "But only if I get to pick out what I want to eat first."

Vanessa looked away, but conceded.

I decided right there on the spot that we'd invite Tripp and Vanessa to dinner that weekend. We'd make it a monthly affair. My way of getting to know Vanessa while also imparting little bits of advice when I could. I didn't know what it was like for her not having children of her own and suddenly finding herself with a stepdaughter, but I thought I could help. After all, I had the expertise. And I was right next door.

After Susannah died, I was devastated along with everyone else. That beautiful woman leaving such a young family behind. I tried to give Tripp space. He had more than enough family members to come over and take care of him. But when they eventually left, I asked if I could help. I offered to watch Mia while he worked. But he said he was going to take some leave, that it was important for him to be home with her the first few months. Mia kept saying she was terrified he was going to go away and she would lose him too.

When Tripp started dating (I caught wind of it through one of the ladies at the gym), I tried to stay out of his business. Especially when everyone—and I mean everyone, including me, I admit—said he was marrying again too soon. It was just over three years; couldn't he take his time and wait a little longer? But men don't like to be lonely. That's been my experience, at least. Especially when they're grieving.

I watched Vanessa move in—I couldn't help myself; the moving trucks were literally outside my door. I heard she was leaving her job to stay home with Mia, which was surprising because she was a senior planner for a wealth management group downtown. But she had decided to become a stay-at-home mother.

She came in and out of the house with boxes and clothes from her former home, with additional shipments arriving too: pots and pans, new sets of bath towels, an abundance of clothes, some furniture. Tripp said she was studying cookbooks and desperately wanted to learn how to be a gourmet chef. She wanted them to sit down for dinner every night, and play board games too. From what I could tell, she seemed intent on being a good wife and mom, finding all kinds of ways to fit in with her new family.

But then more delivery trucks started showing up. More furniture was carted in. A dressing table and matching wardrobe—things of Susannah's, I realized—went out. It was slow at first. Subtle. But then quicker. Susannah's furniture packed up. The painting I remember her bringing home from San Francisco gone. The pottery from Chile. Her late grandmother's bedspreads and quilts. It was hard for me not to think it was wrong. Those were all memories of Susannah, a woman so many of us had loved. But there was a new wife and she clearly didn't feel comfortable being surrounded by her predecessor's things, especially when the first wife had died.

When I asked Tripp about it, he was dismissive. He was also in a rush to get into his car, one arm struggling to slide into his suit sleeve while his other hand fumbled for the key fob. "Everything's fine," he said. "It's all going into storage for Mia to have one day. Vanessa is taking care of everything." And that had been that. I didn't need to worry.

At the kitchen table, my mom is slumping in her chair. I pat her leg. She's still awake but staring at something in her hands: a tissue one of the paramedics must have given her. She holds it tightly between her fingers. Vanessa has finished her coffee and is getting ready to pour another cup.

My mother makes a small noise. She's clearing her throat, wanting to say something, her eyes watery and red-rimmed from fatigue, the smoke from earlier not helping either.

"Mia. Good girl," she says.

I stroke her arm. "That's right, Mom. Mia is a good girl."

Her jaw is shaking. "Good girl," she says again. "Swimming."

"Yes, swimming."

"Swimming today."

"Yes, always swimming."

"Swimming *today*," Mom repeats.

Vanessa immediately sets down her coffee cup.

"She gets her days mixed up," I tell her. "Think nothing of it."

"Swimming today," my mother says again.

Vanessa leans close. "Charlotte, did you see Mia?"

Mom nods.

I squint my eyes. Is she rambling, getting her dates and memories mixed up like she often does? Or did she really see something?

Occasionally, she'll surprise us. She'll remember where Kayla's jersey is when no one else in the house can find it. She'll ask if she can have eggs because I've brought her toast three days in a row and she wants something else. If Thomas goes out of town, she'll tell us his flight time and note the date he's coming home. But then there are other things, other facts she confuses: forgetting Robert is a teenager and talking to him as if he's five years old. Or asking for her ballet shoes when she hasn't danced in twenty years.

But today? Could she have seen Mia while staring at the Tanners' backyard? From the guest room upstairs, could she have seen the pool?

"Mom, did you see Mia today?"

She bobs her head. "Always swimming."

I sweep my eyes to Vanessa.

"Charlotte," Vanessa says gently, "did you see something happen to her?"

But my mom doesn't answer, her eyes going still as if her mind is drifting. She's already starting to think about something else.

I rub her shoulder, coaxing her for an answer. "Mom?" Nothing. I look at Vanessa. "I'm so sorry. Her thoughts are easily jumbled up. She could be remembering seeing her swim a year ago, and we'll never know."

But then Mom whispers the girl's name. "*Mia.*"

Her voice is shaky, hoarse. She sounds scared. I glance at her face. She looks petrified.

CHAPTER ELEVEN

Charlotte

I don't understand why I'm sitting in this house. This isn't my home. This isn't where I live. I don't recognize anything on these walls.

Julia is talking to someone, and when I blink, I see her face, her brown hair so unlike the bright honey-blonde of my daughter and grandchildren. But when she tucks a curly section of hair behind her ear, my memory stirs.

She's the angel, the one who saved me. The one from earlier. She held my hand and knelt beside me. She told me everything was going to be all right.

And then I remember.

Mia . . .

Something about her swimming today.

"Did you see Mia?" Julia asks.

I try to remember. I try so hard. But my mind goes spongy again, parts of it wanting to stay in the present, other thoughts swirling and going down the drain.

Like water in a pool.

A pool . . .

Didn't I see her swimming laps earlier? But then she stopped. Something made her. But I'm having trouble remembering . . .

Who is this other person I'm seeing? Why do I feel like they're not watching but waiting—but waiting for what? It's hard for me to know who it is; I can't tell from this distance, my memory not always connecting the dots. But something tells me I know this person. I've seen them before.

They're waiting for Mia to get out of the pool.

CHAPTER TWELVE

Vanessa

Somewhere in this house, I feel as if the ghost of Tripp's first wife is blaming me for what I've done, for what is happening. For losing her daughter. Her one precious gift. Right now, she must be judging my every move, cursing me from every shadow.

If I were alive, this would have never happened.

You're not fit to be a mother.

How could Tripp have chosen you?

With everything that's going on, I hear her. I see her. This will always be her house. She will always be the first wife who lived here. She would have never lost her daughter. It's my fault.

I glance across the kitchen table. Charlotte is still mumbling about the pool, and I'm staring past Julia's shoulder to the hallway beyond, the dark corner where a table lamp sheds a patch of light on the floor, the rest of the hallway covered in darkness.

I almost expect to see her—I'm *that* freaked out of my mind worrying about Mia. I'm looking for an apparition in a draped white gown, rushing through the house, her hair falling down her back like her daughter's, screaming at me that I've lost her child.

I'm losing it. My hands are shaking around my coffee mug until I'm afraid it will spill.

I search the hallway, and to my relief there is no one there, and certainly not a ghost. No frightening apparition. No sounds except for whatever Charlotte is murmuring in the background.

The reality of today hits me—*my God!*—and I stare at the kitchen counter. Mia was here only a few hours ago. She ate a snack *right there*. Left her pink hair tie on that table.

If only I'd known …

When I picked her up after school, she was all smiles and waves to her friends. Nothing in the world seemed to be bothering her. She had no way of knowing what was to come. I sat in the pickup line as I always did, my nails tapping on the steering wheel, the car moving forward an inch every few minutes until it was my turn.

I spotted her blonde hair first, her backpack looped over one shoulder, a skip in her step as she laughed about something with her friends. "See ya," she said to them as they waved goodbye, but as soon as I approached, her smile faded—and why was that? What happened?

I'm not Susannah. I'm not her dad. I struggle every day to be a good mom, one hard lesson and pitfall after another, but I am trying. There are days I hit it out of the ballpark, but then there are other days when Mia shoots me a look like she's wondering where I'm coming from. But I know I'm being too hard on myself. I'm an overachiever—I excelled in school and was hailed supreme at my job—so it's no wonder I've set the bar so high for myself as a parent. I don't want to fail miserably at this job; I'm not allowed to, and never have before.

But I'm not Mia's real mother, and her look of sadness and disappointment lately has been boring holes into my heart. I tell myself it's hormones. The older she gets, the more she questions things and reflects on memories. She's comparing herself to her friends and mourning the fact that she lost her mother. But her actions, her words, what she says to me … she doesn't mean to hurt my feelings. I haven't been meaning to upset her either.

She's only a child, I repeat to myself. *Only a child …*

Julia is sipping her coffee. Something buzzes and she jumps. She pulls her phone from her pocket and immediately hits the decline button.

"You can take that if you want," I tell her.

"No," she says, placing the phone face-down. "I'm sure they only want to know about the fire. I don't feel like talking about it. Especially not with Mia . . ." She doesn't finish her sentence.

I nod, thinking of my own phone stashed in my purse. I'll only answer if Tripp calls. And like Detective Blakely said, I'll wait for the house phone to ring too.

"Do you think we'll hear something soon?" Julia asks.

I grip my mug. "I hope so."

She stares out the window at one of the fire trucks still parked outside. "They should be finished searching the house by now. If there was any chance she was in there . . . I mean, they should know soon, don't you think?"

I don't answer.

"That footprint. Someone must have come in and taken her." Her widening eyes take up nearly half her face. "She didn't end up in that fire. I know she didn't. Someone must have taken her out the back gate, that's why it was open. It's so scary. Terrifying. My God, Vanessa, who do you think it could have been?"

I want to beg her to stay quiet. I know she means well, but I want to tell her the endless rambling is hurting my head, that it would be best if she took her mother to a hotel; she needs the rest. They don't need to stay and help me; my own parents will arrive tomorrow.

But I don't get the chance to speak, because the house phone begins to ring.

CHAPTER THIRTEEN

Julia

Vanessa is leaping from her chair. The phone rings once, twice as she sprints across the kitchen, arms extended, legs stretching to reach the other side of the room. I've never seen her move that quickly before: it's pure adrenaline and fear.

"Yes? Hello?" she answers breathlessly.

In an instant, the police officer appears in the kitchen too.

We watch as Vanessa listens to whatever is being said on the other end of the line. The pause is so long, the suspense so crippling, I'm practically on the edge of my seat, waiting to hear what she'll say in response.

Is it the kidnapper? Is it Tripp saying they've found her?

Is it terrible news?

The corners of her mouth turn down. "I don't have a statement at this time," she says, and hangs up the phone. She stares at the wall for a moment longer before saying out loud to no one in particular: "The *Huntsville Times*. They received the missing persons report."

"You can expect more of those calls," Officer Donahue tells her. "Don't give them anything. Get off the phone as fast as you can and keep the line clear."

Outside there is the distinct sound of squealing brakes, a van door slamming. I crane my neck and spy a news truck out the kitchen window. It's followed by a car, and then another truck.

Two men jump out and set up a tripod. They run some cables. Someone else climbs out the passenger side holding a microphone.

The doorbell rings and Vanessa bristles. My mom lets out a gentle moan.

Officer Donahue holds up one hand to say he's got it. I hold my breath as he moves to the foyer, pulling the door open just a crack.

"News Channel Nineteen," I hear someone say. "Any sign of the missing girl? Any updates?"

"No comment," he says firmly.

"Anything you can tell us? Any leads?"

Thankfully, Officer Donahue remains steadfast. "The family is not available to speak at this time." He shuts the door.

We watch as another news van pulls to the side of the road and parks, the men on the sidewalk setting up their camera and swiveling it toward the house. That's when I realize that anyone can peer in through the kitchen window and see Vanessa. They can film us at the kitchen table, coffee mugs half empty, their cameras zooming in on us literally as we speak.

The house is a virtual fishbowl.

"We need to close the curtains," I tell her.

She gives me a stunned look.

"We need to get you out of sight, move you to another room. We're too exposed."

Somewhere in the house, a cell phone rings.

CHAPTER FOURTEEN

Vanessa

It's the phone in my purse that's ringing. I rush to answer it and see that it's my best friend Janie.

"Vanessa. Are you all right? *What's happening?*" She is frantic. "What's going on? Have they found her?"

I press my hand to my aching head. "No, not yet."

"Where are you? Where's Tripp?"

"I'm at home." I glance at Julia, who is hurriedly yanking the curtains shut, closing every blind. "Tripp is out with the police."

"Holy shit," she whispers.

"Where are you?" I plead.

"I'm in Orlando, remember? I only arrived a few hours ago. Of all times … of all times not to be there with you." I close my eyes. I'd rather have Janie here than anyone else. She's the only person I feel comfortable with. "I'm so sorry, Vanessa," she says. "I can catch the next flight. I'll head to the airport, take whatever I can and get back." She's moving around, gasping into the phone. I hear her knock something over and imagine her rushing around the hotel room, hurrying to throw everything in a suitcase.

I look at the time. "You won't find anything tonight. Not to Huntsville."

"I can fly into Atlanta. Take a rental car and drive over."

"You'll be driving at three in the morning. That's crazy."

She curses. A long pause. "I'll be there first thing in the morning," she promises. "The very first flight."

"Thank you."

"Vanessa?" She sounds panicked. "Are you going to be all right?"

"I don't know." I feel like I'm hanging on by a thread.

"Were you the last one to see her?"

"Yes."

It takes her a beat to respond. She says, "Hold tight. I'll be there as soon as I can."

Officer Donahue steps into view and gestures toward the phone.

"I've got to go," I say, not wanting to hang up so soon. "They want me to keep the phone lines clear."

"Who's with you?"

"A cop." Another sideways glance. "And Julia."

"Okay," she says. "Be brave, Vanessa. Don't give up hope. They'll find her. I bet she's down the street watching a movie with a friend. False alarm. You know kids these days …" She's trying her best to reassure me, to protect me.

"It will all be a big mix-up," I agree, but the words feel hopeless and empty on my tongue.

I end the call.

The police officer looms in the doorway and I take a look at him, wondering how long he'll be staying with us.

"Are you sure you don't want any coffee, Officer Donahue?" I ask. "Or something else to drink?"

"I'm good. Really."

"We're in for a long night. I want you to be …" I'm flustered. I don't know what I'm trying to say. "… comfortable."

He tilts his chin, and for the first time I catch the small semblance of a smile. "Thank you, I appreciate that." He adds, "You can call me Philip."

"Okay, Philip," I say slowly.

He looks compassionate. "Ma'am, I'm really sorry about what you're going through. If there's anything I can do …"

A chasm breaks open inside my chest.

Find Mia. Make this nightmare go away. Let morning come so we can start over.

Tell me this isn't real.

But I only nod.

Another small smile and he backs from the kitchen, resuming his post by the door. Within seconds, I hear him answering a call on his walkie-talkie—my ears prick up—but it's about a break-in across town and unrelated to Mia.

In the living room, Julia has moved her mother to the couch and is propping a pillow behind her back. Once her mother is settled, Julia asks me, "How many other phones are in the house?"

"There's the main one in the kitchen. And another one upstairs by our bed."

"What about Mia? Doesn't she have a cell phone?"

"Yes. But her cellular is off, we can't track it."

"Where is it?"

Our eyes instantly meet. My heart does a double beat as I go running for Mia's backpack. It's still on the hook. I can't believe I didn't think of this before. I tried calling her number, but I never thought to look for the phone itself.

I rummage through the front pocket but find only pens, a pair of earbuds, a granola bar. And then my fingers wrap around something smooth, something rectangular: her cell phone in its pink glittery case. I zip back to the living room.

Julia's eyes widen. "Most kids wouldn't leave without taking their phone. Which means …" She doesn't finish her thought.

She doesn't have to. I'm already attempting to figure out Mia's password, trying her birthday, Tripp's birthday, her mom's. Nothing works.

Think, think. What kind of password would she use?

The phone buzzes with each failed attempt and I know I'm getting close to reaching my max. I stare hard at the screen, aware of Julia hovering behind me. I can only think of one other date: 1-5-12. The day Susannah passed away.

The screen clears, and I suck in my breath. I can't believe I got it. But then again, it shouldn't have been that hard. A series of numbers reminding Mia of the most important person in her life, and the painful day she lost her.

There's a family photo on the home screen. Mia must have been around two, her mom and dad hugging her in front of a Christmas tree.

I focus my attention on several rows of apps: Instagram, YouTube, Snapchat, a couple of games. Her text messages—ten in total. All of them left unread.

A message from Stacia, one of her eighth-grade classmates. *Whatcha doing?* she asks.

Three messages from her coach about the meet on Saturday.

9 a.m. warm-ups.

UAH pool.

Heat sheets to follow.

Nothing out of the ordinary there.

Weather alerts, something her dad must have set up for her.

But then something strange: a series of texts from Tripp.

I love you.

I'm sorry you're upset with me.

You know I still love you and your mom.

The messages came in one right after another, but Mia never bothered to open them. She didn't respond either. I peer at the timestamp: 8 p.m. last night.

What was Tripp apologizing for?

I read the messages again. *I'm sorry you're upset with me.*

Did Mia seem upset last night? I try to remember, but it was late when I got home. I was at Janie's house stuffing runners' packets for the next Race for the Cure and Janie was flying out to Orlando the next day. Tripp stayed home with Mia.

I read the messages for a third time. *You know I still love you and your mom.*

What was that about?

Julia is still hovering. "What is it?" she asks. "Have you found anything?"

An unsettling feeling rises through my gut and something tells me not to let her know about Tripp's texts—not yet. "Nothing much. The usual stuff on a kid's phone."

"Any messenger apps? Or anything that looks like an app for something else?"

I give her a strange look, but then I'm reminded that Julia has older teenagers. She would know all the tricks, all the ways kids try hiding stuff from their parents: hidden apps, messages that disappear.

I swipe through multiple rows of icons. I find a Facebook message, but it's from a cousin in Georgia, a birthday greeting from six months ago. Snapchat is harder to navigate. I see a bunch of stories and I'm not sure where to look. Then I click on WhatsApp.

I spot several chat groups, including one called Flippers. I scroll through the list of phone numbers and names, recognizing them as kids from Mia's swim team. There's a picture of the swimmers, one of Mia on the starting block, Mia with her arm around another teammate. Coach leading them in warm-up. Messages with reminders and start dates and times. One of the boys asking if anyone found his goggles.

Another group chat is labeled *Unicorns* and is made up of girls from her school. The messages are filled with heart emojis, exclamation points, and stars.

OMG.

Candice thinks Philip Parker is hot.

Math class is sooo boring.

Nothing out of the ordinary here.

But as I scroll through the messages, I notice something else. For whatever reason, Mia has decided to leave each group. She hasn't ignored the messages or saved them for later. She hasn't shut down the app. Instead, she's opted out of each thread as if she can't be bothered to keep in touch anymore, as if she no longer wants to talk to anyone, has no need for future chats. I look at the time for each dismissal. Last night: 8:10 p.m.

Shortly after Tripp's text messages.

She's known these kids for years—some of them since kindergarten. One of the girls from school just came for a sleepover. And the Flippers group is the main communication tool the coach uses for upcoming meets.

What's going on? Is there something she doesn't want to tell us about? She loves her swim team and her friends. Why would she make a point of leaving their chat groups? And she was already practicing for this weekend's meet; she had every intention of being there. Why would she want to cut those messages off too?

I stare at her phone and click from one app to the next.

What else has she deleted?

CHAPTER FIFTEEN

Julia

"Vanessa, shouldn't we tell the police we've got her phone?" I ask, glancing anxiously in the direction of the dining room. I can't see what Officer Donahue is doing, but he's moved away from the front door. I can hear him switching to a different channel on his walkie-talkie, the heavy sound of his boots pacing against the floor.

"I will," Vanessa says. But she doesn't get up. She's still staring at the screen, eyebrows scrunched together, deep in thought.

My mother lets out a yawn: a big one that shakes the sides of her cheeks. Her energy is waning.

"I should get her to bed," I say, feeling a stab of guilt. "Any chance she can go back into the guest room?" Vanessa doesn't answer. "Vanessa?" I lean forward. "My mom. She's tired. Is it all right if I put her to bed upstairs?"

"Hmm?" She finally looks at me, and something clicks. "Yes, of course." She adds, "Do you need any help?"

"It's okay, we'll manage."

I take Mom by the arm and ease her toward the stairs. We climb one careful step at a time. She'll be wondering why we're returning to the guest room. She'll be looking around wanting her own bed.

"We have to stay here tonight," I tell her. "Just for tonight. You'll be comfortable here, don't worry."

The door to the bedroom is open; the chair where my mother dozed earlier is by the window, the blue quilt hastily dropped to the floor. I take her to the bed instead.

She looks at me, her eyes watering.

"It's okay," I tell her. "We're helping Vanessa. But you need to go to bed." I think about myself, not sure if sleep will be an option. I can't imagine things quieting down until we find Mia. I'll be waiting up with Vanessa until we know something for sure.

"Mia?" my mom says, and again I'm surprised that she's trying to piece events together.

"That's right, Mom," I tell her. "Mia."

A knock on the door; it's Vanessa. She's brought a pair of pajamas for my mother, as well as a toothbrush and washcloth.

"Thank you," I say, amazed by her thoughtfulness at a time when her own world is falling apart.

She pats my mother on the shoulder, Mia's phone still clutched in her grasp, and leaves. I help Mom into the bathroom.

When we're finished, I put her to bed and fold the comforter back so it doesn't cover her face. Wisps of gray hair curl gently against her forehead, above her long eyelashes, and I'm reminded of how she was once a great beauty. The long, slender neck and high cheekbones. The dancer's grace, the exquisite ballerina. And then there's me, born with two left feet. This woman has danced all over the world, while I have stayed in Huntsville most of my life.

She reaches for my hand and stops me in mid motion as I smooth the blanket across her chest. "Mia," she says again, and her eyes lift. "Swimming."

Here we go again.

"Yes, Mom. Always swimming."

"I love watching her."

"I know."

"Vanessa was helping her," she says.

I pause. What an interesting thing to say. I search Mom's face. I'm not sure why, but a nervous feeling takes shape in my stomach. Maybe it's the way she keeps bringing up Mia's name, or the way she's describing her swimming—or more importantly, the fact that she was looking out Vanessa's second-floor window and could have seen everything.

"Mom, did you really see Mia in the pool today?"

She gets a faraway look, and I can't tell if it's because she's thinking, or because her mind is drifting somewhere else. I nudge her gently. I can't afford to lose her to sleep right now.

"This is important, Mom. Mia is missing. You may have been one of the last people to see her. You might be able to help." I keep the urgency from my voice—I don't want to frighten her—but I can't let this memory slip, not if she holds a clue of some sort. I shake her gently. "Did you see Mia?"

The faraway look takes over her face and she says, "Mia loves to swim."

CHAPTER SIXTEEN

Vanessa

I'm amazed Julia is here with me. She's trying to help when she has literally lost everything she owns. Personal items destroyed. Baby photos burned. Every stick of furniture melted to black.

She's known Mia since the day she was born, helped plan the baby shower with her mother. Attended Mia's first birthday. I've seen every single picture in Susannah's albums.

Julia started our couples' dinners not long after Tripp and I were married. We still try to do them, getting together every few months when our schedules allow, taking turns cooking or going out to dinner at the new steakhouse downtown. Nights where Thomas and Tripp will talk about football or the stock market, or both, and Julia and I will talk about the kids or the fundraising committee—football too, if our favorite teams are winning.

But if I'm being completely honest, Julia and I have never totally gelled. We've tried, we really have. Thomas and Tripp get along great—they've known each other for years, before we were neighbors. But Julia and me? We're friendly enough. I watch Charlotte for her when Julia is in a pinch. We have dinner conversations and laugh and have a good enough time. But it's never developed much past that, not in the way Janie and I are when we're around each other. Our conversations flow from a faucet. But my friendship with Julia has never felt completely natural.

I used to think it was because she didn't like me or thought me unworthy of Tripp. She deemed me incapable of filling Susannah's shoes. After all, she'd known Susannah first and was devastated when she died. Here I was, the replacement wife, only here because Susannah wasn't. For Julia, I would never compare.

The Campbells are old-money Huntsville, just like Tripp's family. I'm different. I'm a Chisholm. My family is of no great importance. We grew up in Mobile, Alabama, with no direct connections to north Alabama. I only moved to Huntsville for a job. My granddaddy isn't one of Huntsville's founding fathers the way Tripp's family and Julia's are.

Janie is like me. Originally from Atlanta, she moved here for a job too. She remains my most steadfast friend. The one I prefer.

And it's Janie who's been trying to help me lately. She knows how much I miss work, how much I miss being in the office, my days and weeks filled with Mia's activities instead. I've involved myself in charity events here and there, but Janie knows what I really want, and that's to return to my career.

In the beginning, I willingly stepped away from work. Before Tripp and I were married, we had long conversations about our future, about Mia. The decision was made for me to leave the office and stay home with my stepdaughter. She was still young, only nine, and we knew it would be better for her.

That was five years ago.

A couple of months ago, I started looking at jobs. Janie has been sending out my résumé too, talking to old bosses, convincing them I'm serious about returning to work. But no one believes me. Why go back full-time when I'm married to a rich attorney who says I can stay home? They think I've won the jackpot. They think I want it this way.

But I have a master's degree and I want my own life again. Mia is old enough to take care of herself and doesn't need me with her every step of the way. She would tell everyone the same.

Tripp remains overprotective, as if the sky is always about to drop. When I first brought up the subject of going back to work, he looked concerned.

"We need to do what's best for our family," he said. "Mia's care must come before everything else. She needs you here." He looked at me, his eyes warm and expectant. "You know that's important. I thought we'd agreed."

"We did." I tried my hardest to keep my voice level, to keep my emotions at bay, to not sound accusatory or ungrateful. "But it's been long enough. She's finishing middle school and she's always at school or practice these days. There are so many hours in between."

"But if you're at work, you won't be here for her. You won't be able to get away. You'll be stuck in a meeting and I'll be stuck in a meeting. I'm about to start putting in more hours; there's a big case coming up." He shook his head. "It would be better if you stayed home. We need you. Mia needs you." He smiled and reached for my arms. "Don't you want that for her? The security?"

I pulled my arms from his, but gently. "Of course I do." I tried a different approach. "But maybe we could start off slowly. I could work part-time. Baby steps. Just a few hours here and there and I'd always be ready to pick her up."

Tripp frowned. "But you're so good at what you do. They'll start asking for more hours; I know how this works." Another smile. "That's what I would do. Someone like you, I'd talk them into moving to full-time within weeks."

"Maybe we can ask Mia," I suggested. "See if she's okay with it. A lot of kids her age are latch-key, and she's so independent. She'd love it, in fact."

But Tripp turned serious. "I do not want her to be a latch-key kid." He looked me over, softening his voice, a hurt expression on his face. "I thought you were happy. You and Mia ...?" He gave me a hopeful look. "Me ...?"

And I hugged him, deciding to end the conversation. We didn't have to talk about it anymore that day, but I didn't want the topic to be over, not if I could help it. I'd brought it up, and he could take the next few weeks to mull it over before I would mention it again. I'd find a way to reason with him.

There is a sound behind me now, the footsteps of someone moving through the house, light and gentle, sneaking into the kitchen.

Mia?

I spin around, but no one's there: only an empty hall with doors that remain shut.

I catch my breath and peer into the shadows. Nothing.

But I could have sworn I heard her—didn't I? Coming to the kitchen for a glass of water. Raiding the pantry for a late-night snack. Socks on her feet to keep her toes warm along the kitchen tile.

It's *not* her, I tell myself. As much as I want it to be, Mia isn't here. She's not in this house. It was only a figment of my imagination. And yet my hands have gone cold. My mouth dry. I let out my breath.

Where is she?

I'm seeing things—hearing things—ghosts and footsteps: Susannah, my stepdaughter too.

Outside, coyotes are calling.

My eyes dart toward the patio. The base of the mountain is only a quarter-mile from our house. If there's a chance Mia went out the back gate and wandered in the direction of Monte Sano, she'll get lost in the trails, turned around in the thick brush, confused and frightened, particularly in the dark.

Last year, a group of teenagers lost their way and had trouble returning to the trailhead. With no cell service, their phones went dead, and before they knew it, dusk came and went, each clump of birch trees looking the same as the next. After more than six hours of huddling in the cold, they were found near Three Caves, an off-limits rock quarry, rattled and bruised, but relatively unharmed, their parents' sick worry soon transformed into relief.

They were the lucky ones …

My heart lifts. Why shouldn't something like that happen for us too?

CHAPTER SEVENTEEN

Vanessa

My cell phone rings, the jolt of it nearly causing me to drop Mia's phone to the floor.

It's Tripp. I feel my heart racing as I answer. "Yes? Anything?"

"Nothing yet." My heart sinks. "We haven't found her … but … there is some great news." He takes a deep breath.

"What is it?"

"They didn't find her in the fire." And there it is: the unrelenting sound of relief, his muffled sob. "They've searched most of the Campbells' house and it doesn't look like she was in there. Vanessa …" There's a long pause as he tries to get a hold of himself. "She's going to be all right. She's still alive somewhere."

I nod furiously, a rush of air leaving my mouth.

"Listen," he says. "I need to ask you something about Mia."

I lift my chin. "What?"

"Do you know if anything was going on at school? Did she seem okay to you?"

"She seemed fine. Focused on the usual stuff. A test. The next swim meet." I pause. Does he know something I don't? "Why?"

"I don't know. I just …" He chooses his next words carefully. "Did you notice anything that was different about her? The way she was acting toward you?"

"Toward me? Not really."

"Anything at all?"

I stare hard at the wall, my heart thudding in my chest. Where is he going with this? Is Detective Blakely getting to him?

"Tripp, what is this about?"

"Look, I know you're not as close as you used to be. You and Mia. You've both been trying, I know you have, but she's growing up. She's changing and you didn't want me to notice." Somewhere in my brain, something sets on fire. "I started reading between the lines," he continues. "Over the last few months, and more so recently, the two of you have been drifting apart."

My cheeks flash red. The shock that he's turning against me.

Can Detective Blakely hear him? Are they riding around in the car and Thomas can hear him too?

Tripp pushes on. "I just wonder if anything happened recently, anything specific. Do you think she would have talked to you about it? I mean, do you think you would have noticed?"

The thunderclap boom inside my head returns.

Would I have noticed?

My ears feel as if they're on fire too. The heartache makes me tremble. I've done everything for Mia. *Everything*. She's been the focus of my life the last five years, and this is how they're going to repay me? The detective convincing my own husband to question my relationship with my child. To make him ask if I'm a good enough parent to know if something was going on with my stepdaughter.

What happened to us, Tripp? Only yesterday you kissed me goodnight. This morning I made you coffee-to-go in your favorite stainless-steel mug. We were going to have dinner tonight, the three of us, like always.

Earlier you clutched my hand and cried. We cried together, worried sick about Mia.

We're still crying now.

"Would you have noticed?" he repeats.

I'm breathing hard into the phone. "Does this have to do with me asking to go back to work?"

"Back to work ... *What?*"

I squeeze the phone. "Me asking to go back to work," I repeat. "Are you upset with me about that but didn't want to tell me before? Is that what this is about?"

He makes a sound—a sigh, a stammer. "No. You working? No, that's not what I—"

"Well then, what?"

"Is there anything she could have been upset about?"

My voice drops cold and flat. "No."

"Wasn't she upset about something from a couple of weeks ago? Something at school?" He sounds strained.

My mind scrolls back over the last few days: Mia studying for her math test, the afternoon I dropped off a check for the school fundraiser, the last swim meet, where she crushed the competition. Everything seeming normal. Mia killing it the same way she does with everything.

"There was an event organized by the homeroom moms, right?" Tripp continues. "A mother–daughter tea. She asked you to go but you never showed up."

I squeeze the phone until it almost cracks. I *cannot* believe he would betray me this way.

I lower my voice. "I already apologized."

"Yes, but—"

"We've already gone over this. It happened. I felt terrible. She was upset. She forgave me. It's over now."

Of the two of us, I'm the parent in attendance for most everything: every swim meet, PTA gathering, slumber-party drop-off, school supply pickup, last-minute projects, routine dentist appointments. Tripp works long hours and leaves it to me to get things done. I'm the one who takes care of Mia. I do everything I can. This engine doesn't run without me.

"I think it crushed her," Tripp says into the phone.

I squeeze back the tears.

"I told you already," I say. "I didn't mean for it to happen."

But it happened. I know it did. And he knows it too.

An invitation had arrived from school on heavy cardstock, ivory tones with scalloped edges, someone taking the time to write our names on the front of the envelopes with a gold felt-tip pen. Mia insisted we buy new dresses for the event.

"All the girls are buying something," she told me. "We have to look perfect."

I nodded, a nervous roll of guilt in my stomach at attending an event that Susannah should have been able to do instead of me.

"I like that one," Mia said. We'd been in the store less than five minutes and she'd already found a dress for herself in green with velvet trim.

"It's pretty," I told her, running my hands along the three-quarter sleeves.

Her eyes lit up. "Now we can find something for you." And we did: a gorgeous cream suit that she had spotted.

I knew she wanted this day to be perfect. She wanted *me* to be perfect. Her real mother was gone and couldn't be here, and I was the next best thing.

But that Wednesday afternoon came and went, and I blew it. I'd put it on my calendar, looking forward all week long to wearing the new suit, showing up to the school and sitting beside Mia as we enjoyed petit fours covered in flowers made with pink and white icing, the ladies taking photos for the girls' scrapbooks. But I'd made a terrible mistake: I'd put down the wrong time.

It was so unlike me that to this day I still don't know what happened. The tea was to begin at two o'clock, but for whatever reason I had it marked for four. I spent the afternoon at the art museum in a closed-door meeting with a brand-new donor and kept my phone on silent inside my purse, missing every one of Mia's calls—ten total. Tripp's too.

By the time I reached the school, my first thought was that I must be early, since I didn't see many cars in the parking lot. And then a sinking feeling. The hallway quiet. The room where the tea was to be held already cleaned up. The organizer, Helen, packing up the last of the decorations.

When I tried calling Mia, she refused to answer. She was no longer at school; Helen told me, eyes averted, that one of the other mothers had driven her home.

When I arrived, Tripp's car was already in the garage. He'd rushed home early and was in the living room with Mia. Her eyes were swollen with tears, her hair coming loose from its ribbon.

I felt sick to my stomach.

"How could you?" she cried. I felt her pain cutting through me so viciously I had to close my eyes.

Her own mother would never have done this—it wouldn't have been possible. She would have made things perfect. She would have been there early. Hell, she would have been the one organizing it all.

Mia ran from the room, her feet carrying her out the front door and down the steps as fast as they could until I worried she would trip and fall, the door slamming closed behind her. She sat under one of the magnolia trees until dinner and refused to speak to me for days. But that weekend, we forged a truce. I knocked on her bedroom door and begged for a chance to talk things over. I apologized over and over, to both her and Tripp, until she finally relented and hugged me. I thought we'd be okay.

Now, as I lean against the kitchen counter, my head throbbing with the memory, Tripp waits for me to say something.

"This has nothing to do with Mia disappearing," I whisper.

"Vanessa ..." he says.

I stand up taller. "Is that what this is? I admit it again, I screwed up royally. Unforgivably. But now you think it's my fault she's gone? She's mad at me about something from two weeks ago, so she ran away?"

"I'm not blaming you—"

"That's how it sounds."

"I'm just trying to think of every possibility. I know it's not your fault. It was an accident. It happens."

Then why bring it up? I want to ask. Instead I say, "I went through her phone."

"Her phone?" I hear something in the background—someone speaking. They're cutting in and Tripp's voice goes quiet, and then muffled, his mouth moving away as he tells someone, "Yes, her phone." I can only imagine he's telling Detective Blakely, can only imagine the look on her face. The thing she forgot to ask, the thing she's overlooked.

"Where is it?" Tripp asks. "Do you have it?"

"Yes, I have it."

More voices in the background.

"Tripp!" I shout, trying to get his attention. He makes a sound, his mouth moving closer to his phone. "You texted her last night. Something about her being upset with you." I wait for him to explain, but he doesn't. "What was she upset about?"

He sounds distracted, clears his throat. "Last night?"

"Yes, last night."

He's trying to think, twenty-four hours feeling like a lifetime.

"She said she wants me home more. She misses spending time together."

"So why didn't you say something? When Detective Blakely asked if she'd been upset lately, why didn't you bring that up?"

"I didn't think it was a big deal."

"It sounds like a big deal." I hate that I'm sounding this way, but the hurt of what he brought up, the mother–daughter tea, is burning a hole in my chest.

He goes silent.

"And what about the part about still loving her and her mom? What was that all about?"

He sighs heavily. "She's been really sad about Susannah lately."

The more subdued moments. Mia spending increased amounts of time in her bedroom. The way she refused to let me wash the blanket her mother had made for her.

I seize on this moment. "Do you think that has anything to do with it?"

"She's been sad about her mom, but that wouldn't have made her run away. We've already checked Susannah's grave site, just in case."

I shiver thinking of Mia walking there.

But in a bathing suit. In the cold. That wouldn't have made sense.

We're quiet again. Then he says, "It's the footprint outside the back gate I can't stop thinking about. The single footprint. They think it belongs to a man." His voice shakes. "What I don't understand is where are Mia's prints? Why didn't anyone see them? Why is there no evidence of her walking out on her own?" His sobs fill my ear and I close my eyes, the pain raw and real. "I don't understand it. What happened to our girl?"

CHAPTER EIGHTEEN

Julia

Vanessa is nowhere to be found when I come downstairs, and I don't bother looking for her straight away. She clearly doesn't want me looking at Mia's phone, even though I'm positive I could navigate that thing faster than she can—I'm constantly snooping on my kids' devices; I know what to look for.

I wander past the sitting room with its priceless Japanese vases, the curio cabinet with sixty-four pieces of china and crystal on display—I should know, I took the time one day to count—and into the sunroom. I push open the French doors and step out onto the patio. It's dark, my eyes taking a moment to adjust, but farther ahead I can make out the gray outline of the pool.

I smell smoke, too. And something else—something damp, like it's just rained. I realize it's the gallons of water the firefighters have dumped on my lawn next door, pieces of hardwood and roof tile soaked in a puddled mess. There are loud thuds and the sound of metal scraping; it feels odd standing next door while strangers are combing through my home—what's left of it, anyway—going through everything I own, tossing aside pieces left unrecognizable.

I take a few steps toward the dark, shadowy pool, and it dawns on me how creepy I feel being at the last place Mia was seen. The surface shines a metallic gray with hints of blue. Not a ripple, not a sound. Even the decorative mosaic tile appears jet black beneath the water.

I stare at the pool, picturing Mia moving swiftly up and down its length.

How many laps before she noticed my house was on fire?

What made her look up?

I imagine her last moments, the way she might have kicked and screamed as someone pulled at her.

A chill takes over my body, my thoughts getting the best of me, the darkness tricking my mind. Then I remember the pool-house lights and reach for the switch. A brilliant white glow illuminates the water, and my heart calms a few notches. That's better. The pool no longer looks so menacing.

But a flash of something at the bottom catches my eye. I crouch down and reach into the water, but my hand only cuts through the surface, making ripples and causing the image to go hazy. I pull back and wait for the water to clear again. When it does, there's something familiar about the size and shape of the object. It's shiny, too.

I roll up my sleeves and touch the water again.

Is it a ring? I bend closer but can't be sure. Something round. Something golden. Something that doesn't belong at the bottom of the pool.

CHAPTER NINETEEN

Julia

"What are you doing?" Vanessa asks.

I rise quickly to my feet, wiping my wet hands across my pant legs. I was mere inches from falling in, the water shimmering a little too close for comfort as I dug my toes against the pool lip, my shoes gripping the concrete until I fought to stand upright again.

I take another look at Vanessa: there's something different about her. She looks like she could burst. "You okay?"

Her words come out quickly. "They didn't find Mia in the fire."

"Oh, thank God."

"I just got off the phone with Tripp. He said they've searched most of your house and she's not in there."

We stare at the fence, the smoldering heap next door.

I turn back to Vanessa, the rush of relief moving through my chest, rippling to my fingers and toes. "This is great news." I clasp my hands together. *Thank you, Jesus.* The tears spring up, a huge knotted piece inside of me subsiding. "There is hope. This means she's still alive."

"Yes," Vanessa says. "Tripp is … We're both …" She's having trouble with her words. "It was a terrifying thought."

I am nearly light-headed, my hand clamping over my chest to feel my pounding heart. "Yes, it was."

But Vanessa's mouth is trembling. "The thing is, if she wasn't in the fire, where is she? Who took her?"

I stare again at the backyard, the far end of it out of reach of the pool lights and draped in darkness. Behind that, the gate hidden behind the shed, where police officers found a man's shoeprint in the alley.

But Vanessa's eyes remain locked on the pool. "I don't understand," she says. "She was here—*right here*. I was only gone a few minutes. She's taken care of herself plenty of times before. She's always made the right decisions." She bites her lip. "But it's right, what the detective is saying. I shouldn't have left her. I should have been here. I would have been able to protect her."

"Someone did this," I insist. "You couldn't have known. They'll find this person soon. They'll bring Mia home."

Vanessa shakes her head.

"Have you noticed anyone lurking around?" I ask. "Anyone strange?"

She cuts her eyes toward me. "No—have you?"

"No, but maybe this person had seen her before, knew her routine, was really good at going unnoticed. They watched you come home. They knew that she swam every day. They knew she'd be in the pool."

Vanessa is crying. She's pressing her arms tightly against her chest and letting the tears fall. "I should have stayed," she says again. "I should have sat in a chair and watched her. Checked on her from the window. If I had, I could have stopped it. I should have grabbed her from that pool as soon as I saw the fire, too. She'd be safe right now."

I rub her shoulder. "Don't start blaming yourself, understand? Mia swam every day. She didn't need somebody watching over her. There's no way you could have known this would happen."

"But how could I have been inside my house and not known she was being taken?" Her eyes dance nervously around the pool. "*Kidnapped*, for God's sake. What does that make me?"

"The fire distracted you. You panicked."

"I ran outside. And what? *That's* when they took her? I was so close—hell, I was in front of the house—and someone grabbed her?"

It does seem crazy that anyone would steal Mia while Vanessa was only a few feet away. She could have heard Mia scream. She could have run outside at any moment. Whoever did this, whoever they are, was brazen. Ballsy. Who would risk something like that in broad daylight?

"There's something down there," I tell her, remembering what I was looking at in the water. "At the bottom of the pool. Do you see it?"

She steps to the edge and leans forward, then crouches down, swishing the water with her fingers as I did. "What is that?"

She steps back and searches for something behind her: a net. She plunges it to the bottom, nudging the item with the net's metal bar until it moves to one side and then drops inside. Lifting the net, she brings the object closer, only a foot away, then a few inches.

I can see it more clearly now. Gold. Shiny. She pulls out the net, a cascade of water dripping and landing at our feet, and plucks out something small and round.

A ring, just like I thought.

A thick gold band, wide enough to be a man's.

She turns it over in her hand and holds it close to her face—she's checking to see if there's an inscription. Her face blanches. Her lips quiver. I fight with every fiber of my being not to take the ring from her hands and read it myself.

She finally speaks. "All my love. 8.22.2015."

"Whose ring is this?"

She pauses. "That's my wedding date."

The air catches in my throat. I'm not sure I've heard her correctly. "What—you and Tripp?"

She nods.

I stare at the ring, the pool, and back to her hand again. But there it is. A man's wedding ring yanked from the water, and it belongs to her husband.

"What's it doing in the pool?" I ask. None of this makes sense, and she's not helping by not answering. She's gone very still. "Did it slip off when he went swimming? While he was cleaning it? Maybe it fell off when he was walking across the patio, and bounced in."

I'm blathering, rattling off every conceivable type of circumstance, and I'm not sure why I'm so nervous, the scenarios popping in and out of my head so that Vanessa can have an explanation. But I know she isn't listening. Her eyes are locked on the ring, her mind elsewhere.

She keeps it flat in her palm, holding it steady. And then my brain clunks into action: she didn't *know* it was missing.

I probe her gently. "Vanessa?"

Still she doesn't speak.

"Vanessa, what are you—"

She cuts me off. "Tripp ..." she says, her voice drifting. She's no longer looking at the ring but staring at the water instead. "Why would his ring be in the pool?"

"There are a million and one reasons."

But she's looking at me now with fear in her eyes, the pool lights shining an eerie glow across her face. "Why didn't I know he'd lost his ring? Why hasn't he said anything?"

We both turn and stare at the water.

"Unless it happened today," she says. "Today," she repeats, and her eyes widen. "Do you think ... Does he know what happened? Did he see something?"

"You mean, did he see Mia?"

"Was he here?" She steps closer to the edge of the pool.

Goosebumps cover the length of my body. I don't like where she's going with this. I don't like what she's suggesting. "Vanessa, you know he wasn't here. He was at work. You would have seen him."

Her head jerks toward the fence. "Maybe he came in through that gate?" Her voice trails. "The one shoeprint ..."

"That's impossible, Vanessa. There's no way. He would never … He would have said something." I step beside her, forcing her to turn so she'll meet my eyes. "Look, you're tired. You're devastated. You don't know what you're saying."

"But the ring, Julia." She juts her hand out to me. "*Tripp's ring.* How do you explain it?"

"It's a coincidence."

"It's in the pool."

"Coincidence," I say again.

But she doesn't want to hear me. She's reaching forward, grabbing my arm. "Do you think he's the one who dragged her from the pool?"

CHAPTER TWENTY

Charlotte

I see Mia dressed in a wedding gown, walking across the grass. A soft veil flowing down her back, a crystal-embroidered skirt sweeping the floor. How lovely to have an outdoor wedding. Her arms are wrapped in beautiful lace, crystal beads shimmering along a sweetheart neckline.

But the material is long and heavy. Cumbersome. She struggles with every step, the Chantilly veil dragging to the ground. She can barely stand, can barely hold her head up.

In her hands, there is no bouquet.

I look to see if there is anyone who can help, because with every step, she falters, the dress far too heavy as she buckles beneath its weight. Where is the groom? Where is her father?

But Mia is alone. The wedding guests are nowhere in sight. There is no one in attendance. No one has set out the flowers or chairs—not yet, at least. But surely, I think, someone will come along soon.

Mia stands beside a pool. A fountain at one end with cascading water flowing down some rocks. It's so beautiful, the setting she has chosen for her wedding, the splashing water from the fountain creating lovely background music.

She looks radiant, the satin skirt clinging to her waist and draping against the ground. The water shining behind her.

Now someone is approaching her. She doesn't see them at first; she's looking the other way and gazing at the water. Whoever it is, they must be here to surprise her.

My heart does a pitter-patter. Is that the groom? Or a wedding guest?

I lean forward to get a better look. I'm waiting for the moment Mia will face them, the happy smile on her face, her eyes lighting up with joy.

I'm hoping they'll give her a kiss on the cheek. They'll find her bouquet for her. They'll tell her how beautiful she looks. How she looks just like her mother did on her wedding day. Her blonde hair shining and hanging beneath that veil. Her whole life ahead of her.

But when Mia turns around, she is no longer smiling.

CHAPTER TWENTY-ONE

Julia

I can't believe the words coming out of Vanessa's mouth.

"Vanessa, you can't possibly—"

She thrusts out the ring again. "Then how do you explain it being here?"

"I don't know. It fell off—think about it. It's just a ring. Finding it in the pool doesn't mean anything. It doesn't mean he *did* anything either." I want to shake her, slam some sense into her.

But she is already recreating the scene. I can practically see it in her eyes, her thoughts flashing from one ghastly image to the next. "She must have been fighting him *here*, in the pool. And then she pulled the ring off his hand as he was tugging at her. He didn't have time to go back and get it."

She has absolutely lost her mind.

"You can't be serious."

"Mia was upset about something. I'm not sure what, but something happened between them. I found text messages on her phone. He was apologizing."

"Do you even hear yourself right now?"

Her eyes are wild. "She must have learned something. Seen something. He must not have wanted anyone to know."

"So he would hurt his own kid?"

"I know it sounds crazy—"

"It *is* crazy! And so what if she was upset? She's a kid. It happens. Tripp apologized. But he wouldn't do something like this. He wouldn't hurt Mia."

Vanessa stares at the ring. "But … does he even know it's missing? If he lost it a few days ago, wouldn't he be looking for it if he knew it was gone? He would have said something to me, right?"

"Maybe he didn't notice—"

"He would have said something by now." She stares at the pool. "Unless it happened today."

"Or it could have happened last week. Over the weekend. It doesn't have to be today."

"But it's in the pool. Mia was in the pool …"

The patio door opens, a rattling creak as Officer Donahue steps into the light, his large frame hovering at the top of the steps. Our eyes race toward him. "You ladies doing all right?"

Vanessa quickly shoves the ring in her pocket.

I try smiling and pray she doesn't say a word.

"Detective Blakely called," he tells us. "Someone reported seeing an old pickup truck driving around the neighborhood. They're not sure if it's someone looking to collect old junk, but they're considering it as a possible lead."

Vanessa doesn't respond.

Officer Donahue clears his throat. "Mrs. Tanner, did you hear what I said? About the truck?"

She gives a weak nod. "Yes."

"Have you seen it? Light blue, white trim. Early Ford model. Spare tire on the driver's side."

"I don't think so."

"Mrs. Campbell?" I jump at the sound of my name. "Anything about this truck ring a bell? Seen anyone suspicious driving through the neighborhood?"

"No," I tell him.

He looks from one of us to the other, his eyes narrowing, "Do either of you have any information you'd like to share? Anything we need to discuss?"

My heart is pounding. I keep one eye trained on Vanessa, hoping—pleading—she won't say anything. Please let her keep her mouth shut. If she shares her fears about Tripp, all hell will break loose. I hold my ground, wanting the officer to go away before it's too late. She doesn't mean to jump to conclusions about her own husband.

"I've been trying to think," Vanessa says. I hold my breath. One second, two. "But I can't come up with anything right now."

I exhale quietly.

Officer Donahue studies us, unconvinced. "We'd better get back inside."

I re-evaluate: Mia is missing. Tripp's ring was at the bottom of the pool. And for whatever reason, Vanessa is now questioning her husband's whereabouts earlier.

I follow them into the house, my insides gnawing at what's happened over the last few minutes.

"The news is about to go live from the front yard," the police officer tells us. "I'm not sure if you want to watch the report, but you should be aware of what's happening."

Vanessa immediately heads for the dining room. She pulls back the curtain and peeks outside.

I race to the coffee table and find the remote. Scrolling through the channels, I find WAFF 48 just as the opening credits are launching the newscast. The female anchor wastes no time announcing breaking news: "Tonight the search is on for a missing thirteen-year-old girl named Mia Tanner." I watch, my heart sinking, as Mia's picture fills the screen. Vanessa gasps and steps slowly toward the television. My knees buckle until I'm seated on the couch. This is all too real now, with Mia's disappearance officially on the news.

"Mia was last seen at her home on Ripple Lane in the affluent neighborhood of Twickenham. A student at Westminster school, she is a member of the school's swim team and was practicing in her home pool when she vanished just before five o'clock this afternoon. Police are asking members of the public to contact them if they have any information about her disappearance."

The next image is a picture of a light blue Ford pickup truck. "Police also want to know if anyone has seen a truck like this one driving around the Twickenham area. If so, you're asked to call this number."

A phone number appears on the screen.

I shut my eyes and whisper a silent prayer.

My cell phone immediately vibrates. Vanessa's house phone rings simultaneously. I pull my phone from my pocket to see multiple messages flashing.

Tracy from three streets over: *I can't believe this is happening. On top of everything else. Let me know if you need anything.*

Coach Eric from basketball: *Just heard about the Tanners. Don't you live next door? We'll be thinking about them.*

And then the ones digging for info. Heather from the fundraising committee: *Are there cops surrounding your place? It's all over the news. They've been up and down our street. What do you know?? Tell me!!*

I ignore all the messages, especially Heather's. I don't want to talk to anyone. I don't want Vanessa to see me tapping away on my phone, telling people God knows what. I need to calm her down first.

The phone in the kitchen continues to ring.

"You need to answer that," Officer Donahue says.

Vanessa looks up. She moves toward the phone, slow as molasses, her feet dragging with every step.

We wait for her to answer. Who is it this time?

CHAPTER TWENTY-TWO

Vanessa

"I'm calling from WHNT," the caller says.

"No comment," I tell them.

The moment I hang up, the phone rings again. "AL.com—"

This time I'm ready. "No comment."

And then again. I'm about to launch into my standard answer when someone says, "Vanessa, we need Mia's phone."

It's Detective Blakely.

"Can you ask Officer Donahue to meet us on the street?" she says. "When the newscast is over, wait for the media to pack up and then have him walk out with the device."

I share the information with the police officer and hand him Mia's phone. There is a surprised look on his face, eyebrows arched, possibly wondering why I waited this long to show him, why I didn't say anything to him before. But I don't explain myself.

He waits by the door.

After a few minutes, the newscast moves to commercials and Julia switches off the TV. She stands wide-eyed, arms crossed, the minutes ticking by with the steady beat of a drum. I can feel her staring at me. What is she thinking? Is she horrified by what I've said? Does she understand how Tripp's wedding ring is burning right through me?

Headlights flash across the drive and I know it must be Detective Blakely. Officer Donahue waits another minute before opening the door. The last of the news vans are pulling away, and he takes his chance heading to the patrol car.

As soon as he steps outside, Julia is already trying to talk me off the ledge.

"I'm sure it's not what you think," she says. "Tripp loves Mia. He loves you. There's got to be another reason."

I feel lightheaded, sick. "But why would we find his ring today of all days?"

"Tripp did *not* do anything to Mia. You have got to get that out of your head."

I hate the way Julia is staring at me—the shock on her face.

"There's got to be another explanation."

"Then what is it?" When she doesn't respond, I say, "Should I ask him about it?"

"What would you say? Good news, I found your wedding ring? But I also think you know what might have happened to Mia?"

"Or I could tell the police. Detective Blakely needs to know. She can figure it out."

"Vanessa!" Julia snaps. "Get a hold of yourself! This is your husband you're talking about. He would never hurt his daughter. You're losing it."

The nausea hits my stomach.

"Let's stop for a second, okay, and think differently. Do you think there's a chance Tripp could have thrown the ring into the pool instead?"

"Why would he do that?"

"Have you guys …" She pauses. "Has everything been okay between the two of you lately … your marriage?"

The question—the very audacity—makes my heart want to leap from my chest.

"Why would you say something like that?"

"I'm just wondering."

"Our marriage is *fine*, Julia." I spin away, desperate to put some distance between us.

How could she? Our marriage is rock solid. We haven't been fighting. I mean, little squabbles here and there, but what couple doesn't have those?

I take a deep breath. "You think Tripp threw his ring because he doesn't want to be with me anymore? Is that what you're saying?"

She opens her mouth to protest, but I stop her short.

"You think he threw it there on purpose?"

Julia's voice grows weak. "I just had to ask."

"To get out of our marriage? Because he's sick of me?"

"I'm sorry ..."

"I can't believe you!" I glare at her.

My voice is loud enough that Officer Donahue, returning, hears me. He slams the front door and enters the house, the heat of the moment thick and heavy in the air as he stares at us, Julia's face dropping, her mouth hanging open. Panic rising in her eyes.

"What's going on?" he asks.

I'm still staring at Julia. I can't stop now. "You want him to get rid of me; I knew it. You've never liked that he married me. All these years, acting like my friend when really—"

"Vanessa ..." A worried glance at the police officer.

"Admit it," I say. "It's true. I've never been good enough. Can't hold a candle to Susannah, could never compete with her. I thought we were friends. But maybe you've been secretly waiting for my marriage to fall apart all this time. You and everyone else; I should have known it. You never thought we'd last this long."

"That's not true!"

"Yes it is."

Julia's cheeks flush red. "At least I'm not the one thinking he might have done something to Mia!" she screams. "The fact that you can even think he would hurt his own daughter ..." Her face crumples—it's too late, she's said what she said—and she's clamping a hand over her mouth, glancing in panic at Officer Donahue.

But the officer is approaching fast, stepping between us as if ready to break up a fight.

He stares down at Julia. "What are you talking about?" He spins to face me. "What is this you're saying about your husband?"

CHAPTER TWENTY-THREE

Julia

Officer Donahue towers over Vanessa. "Mrs. Tanner, what is going on?"

But Vanessa is shaking her head, her eyes barely able to meet his. "I need to speak to Tripp. I need to speak to him now."

"Is there something Detective Blakely should know?"

She repeats, "I want to talk to my husband first."

Officer Donahue pauses before considering her request. I watch him, my mind reeling, as if all the air has been sucked from the room. I've never seen Vanessa look so angry and frightened at the same time. The horrible accusations she made. And me—I can't believe I blurted out everything I know. Now Officer Donahue will have to tell Detective Blakely, and it's my fault. I messed up and they'll be questioning Tripp. This has gone terribly wrong.

But one thing—Officer Donahue doesn't know about the ring. Vanessa has kept it hidden in her pocket.

She steps away, insisting on making her private phone call, and heads down the hall, leaving me alone with the police officer. I feel ridiculous and exposed, the heat smoldering in my cheeks, the intensity of those last few minutes hitting me all over again. I sink into the sofa.

I know I've upset Vanessa. It was difficult telling her those things. I felt awful even bringing it up, but I had to do it. I had to say it. It was the only way I could think of to get her on a different track, to consider other reasons for his ring ending up in the pool, before she accused her own husband of kidnapping his daughter. But turns out she dishes it out too. All those things she said about Susannah. About how I hoped her marriage would end. I don't know what to think.

Does she really think Tripp could have done this to his daughter—pulled her body out of the pool, tugging and fighting until Mia got a good grip of his hand and slipped the wedding ring from his finger so that it fell—*plop*—right into the water?

No way. All of that commotion would have gotten Vanessa's attention. She would have heard. She was here. She would have known if Tripp had come home early. She would have seen them fighting by the pool. She would have stopped them too.

But she said she didn't see Mia after she told her she was going swimming. If Tripp had come in and taken her, then maybe it really did happen like Detective Blakely said, when Vanessa ran out to check the fire.

Stop it. *Stop this.* I shake my head furiously. Look what's happening—even to me. There's another explanation for this. There's got to be. The ring fell off, it was an accident. Or Tripp and Vanessa got in a fight about something and he got super pissed and threw his ring in the water. It must have happened recently; it could even have been last night. The timing is awful, but I know he would never lay a hand on his daughter. She's all he has left of Susannah. She's his own flesh and blood.

My phone rings. It's Thomas.

"How is everyone holding up?"

I swallow down the shake in my voice. "We're okay." For a second, I consider telling him about the ring, but then reconsider. What if he tries to play the hero and says something to the police? Or worse, what if he thinks he's doing the right thing and springs it on Tripp? "How are you?" I ask instead. Better yet, "*Where* are you?"

"Tripp is heading back to the station, but I got pulled away to join a different search team. We're on the mountain."

I think about what Thomas was wearing when he followed Tripp out the door. He's in no shape to be searching the woods at night: no proper boots or socks, only his dress shoes and a thin button-down shirt from the office. It's March, the temperature dropping fast on the higher elevation of Monte Sano.

"Can I bring you a jacket?"

"I'll be all right." His voice gets quieter. "I don't care about being cold. The part that worries me is who took Mia. Is she really up here in these woods? She'll be freezing."

I nod, a sickening feeling spreading through my stomach.

"I can see our street from up here," Thomas continues. "The Tanners' home. I can see the lights. I feel good knowing you're safe there."

I look out the window and try to picture my brave, loyal husband standing among green kudzu, the perennial vines climbing and twisting around rocks, Thomas shivering but not complaining, holding a steady flashlight beam against a backdrop of trees, ignoring the random coyote call. Thomas the protector. Searching for our neighbors' daughter, but also taking the time to call and check on his wife.

"Everything that's happened today has made me realize how important family is," he says. "How much we mean to each other. How much I want to hold you and the kids in my arms and be thankful for what we have. I don't want to let any of you go."

"I know," I say, feeling myself melting with his every word. "It's terrifying. What if this had happened to one of our kids?"

I shudder thinking about Robert and Kayla, how my phone calls to them earlier found them safe and cared for at friends' houses, albeit with dozens of scared questions about Mia as I tried to assure them the police would find her and everything would be okay. The kids asked if they'd be able to see me tonight, but I didn't have a clear answer.

"I love you, Julia," Thomas says.

"I love you too," I tell him, and really mean it.

A thump comes from above. It shakes the ceiling.

Oh shit. Mom.

"I've got to go."

"Julia? Are you all right?"

But I'm already hanging up the phone.

I race up the stairs two at a time, my legs carrying me down the hall until my shoulder is pushing against the door of the guest room. I flip on the lights. My mother is curled in the bed, sheets twisted and pulled to her waist, one arm outstretched.

Something lies on the floor. It's heavy, an ornate box that must have been by the bedside. Mom has knocked it over, her arm raised at an awkward angle.

I search the length of her body. Her eyes are open and she appears startled, but thankfully she's unharmed. I pick up the box; there's nothing inside. Nothing is cracked or broken. I close it before returning it to the table, moving it further away from the bed.

"Did you have a bad dream?" I ask, guiding her arms under the covers, but she doesn't answer. "It's okay," I tell her. "It's over now." I sit at the end of the bed.

"Mia," she says, and her voice is weak, coming at me like a whisper.

My heart does a somersault—she *does* remember.

I stroke her face, soothing her. "They'll find her. It will be okay."

But she shakes her head. "I saw her. Her wedding day. So beautiful …" Her lips are trembling.

My heart sinks. The confusion is back again, darkness and mismatched thoughts swirling around in her head.

"There was a wedding. Mia in a dress."

I smooth the covers at her shoulders, hating when this happens to her, when the demons of dementia plague her mind. After everything she's heard today, what she's seen—the fire and smoke, police asking about Mia, her whole turned world upside down—it's no wonder things seem distorted and strange.

I pat her hand. "Shush now," I say. "You woke up. You don't have to dream about that anymore."

Her eyes well with tears, the lids red, eyelashes brittle. She gazes at me, wanting so badly to make sense of what she's seen.

I'm reminded how tiny and fragile she is during these moments. The mother who raised me, the glamorous dancer, now small and quiet and weak, slowing down and diminishing with each passing year, sinking into this confused state, desperately needing my help.

"It's all right, Mom," I tell her. "Go back to sleep."

Her eyes flutter. She's tired, I know she is. She doesn't want to be in this strange house. She doesn't want to sleep in someone else's bed. She wants her favorite nightgown with her favorite pillow surrounded by her familiar things.

"Mia . . ." She tries again, her eyes opening and closing. She's battling sleep. Her voice grows softer. "The veil . . . Chantilly lace . . . So beautiful . . ." She takes another deep breath, settling down and relaxing. "She fell in."

CHAPTER TWENTY-FOUR

Vanessa

I feel the ring in my pocket, the heavy thickness of it, as I dial Tripp's number. Taking a seat at his desk, I close the study door for privacy, keenly aware of the stares I've left behind.

The police officer, Philip. What is he thinking? How soon before he tells Detective Blakely what we've said?

And Julia. She's gone too far. Why would she say that about my marriage?

And what about me? Have I gone too far as well, thinking my own husband may be capable of the unthinkable? That there's something he's not telling us? Rushing to conclusions only because he hasn't had a chance to explain about his wedding band?

I hear him picking up.

"Tripp," I say.

But he interrupts, cutting me off like he always does. "I was about to call you. Something's happened—a development. An accusation."

I stop short.

"Someone has made a complaint against Coach Jacobs."

I drop the ring to my lap.

"There may have been some inappropriate behavior toward the girls."

"That can't be right."

Coach Jacobs. Mia's beloved swim coach for the last eight years. A kind-looking man in his late forties with floppy brown hair. Practically Mia's favorite person in the world.

I've seen him walk the length of the pool countless times, monitoring a succession of flip kicks before blowing his whistle, shouting at the kids to pull, kick, beat their times. He hugs the kids after every swim meet, poses for pictures, and rallies the parents for final instructions as we get ready for the next week.

It can't be. Not Coach.

"They don't know what they're talking about. Why would they say something like that?"

"One of the parents from the team called the police when they heard about Mia. He's the first person they thought of. They said they don't like how he is with the girls, that they've noticed things …"

"What things?"

"I don't know everything yet."

"Coach wouldn't hurt anyone."

"I don't want to believe it either."

"It's not true."

Tripp releases a heavy breath. "If I find him, I swear I'll kill him."

"But we don't know anything yet. No one knows for sure."

I remember Mia's phone. Didn't Coach send her a bunch of messages? Didn't he add pictures to the chat group?

But that's what he's supposed to do. He's the coach. He sends the same messages to the other swimmers, the parents too.

They've got it all wrong.

"Have they talked to him?"

"No."

"Why not?"

"They can't find him."

"What do you mean? He was at school today, wasn't he?"

"He left early."

"Have they tried his house?"

"He may have left town."

"But he has to teach in the morning. There's another swim meet this weekend. He wouldn't just leave."

"Another reason why he's getting their attention."

"Can they track his car?"

"They're trying, but they're going to his house first. They're on their way now."

My mind is spinning. I see Coach Jacobs driving students home when practices run late. He's brought Mia home numerous times.

"Vanessa, you know him better than I do. Have you noticed anything? Has he ever paid too much attention to Mia?"

I squeeze my eyes shut. "No, I don't think so."

Then I remember how he gave her a huge hug after last Saturday's meet, pressing her body close to his.

My God, I feel like I'm going to throw up.

I see the clipboard in his hands, the way he leans over each swimmer and explains what they need to do, the way they look up at him. The way he speaks to Mia before she heads for the starting block. Hugs at the end of the swim meet, messy wet ones where he doesn't care if his tracksuit gets soaked.

No, I refuse to believe it.

"He wouldn't do something like this. He wouldn't hurt her."

"Did Mia ever say anything to you?"

"No." I would have remembered.

"They're checking her phone to see if he made any calls that would seem strange—late at night, times when he shouldn't have been texting the kids."

"Is there anyone else he may have gone after?"

"The parents who spoke to the police said Jacobs was acting strangely when he dropped off their daughter last week. He said some things to her that freaked her out."

"Like what?"

"I don't know yet. Everything is coming out in pieces."

In the background, I hear voices. A door slamming. Where is he?

His voice is muffled. "Vanessa, do you think this could be it? Do you think he's the one? Detective Blakely thinks there's a chance: Coach going missing the same day as Mia, him knowing Mia's routine, when she would be in the pool. He knew exactly when to time it."

"But why her? It doesn't make any sense."

Tripp doesn't want to hear my doubt. "They'll have everyone searching for him. They'll track down his car in a few hours and bring her home."

"But if he did take her, where on earth would they go?" I think of what we know about Coach Jacobs. Did the school ever bother to run a background check? And why take her? What does he want? Where would they hide?

Mia trusts him. She looks up to him. Is that why she went with him so readily?

"Tripp, I looked through Mia's phone. There are swim team chats, chats with kids from her school. She left every single thread last night."

"What do you mean?"

"WhatsApp. Group texts. She left each group last night. She didn't want to follow their messages anymore."

"Was he already coming after her?"

I sit up straight. "You think that's why she left the chats?"

"I don't know. Maybe she was trying to find a way not to hear from him anymore."

My head jumps ahead, filling in the gaps. "And then he got angry. Came for her today at the pool."

Perhaps Mia hadn't left of her own volition after all. Maybe she'd fought and kicked when Coach pulled her from the pool.

I slip Tripp's wedding ring back into my pocket.

And then I realize how easily, in the space of a few minutes, in my grief and terror, I have switched from turning on my own husband to accusing the swim coach instead. Just like that. My loyalty cracking in every direction.

CHAPTER TWENTY-FIVE

Julia

Vanessa has returned to the living room, her skin five shades paler, disbelief mixed with shock as she tells me the news. She makes a sound and I realize it's air escaping from her mouth. She's terrified, her hands shaking. It's one thing not to know where Mia is, and another to hear about a suspicious truck in the neighborhood—but to know that the kidnapper might now have a face and a name, and for it to be someone we know . . . It's punched her right to the core.

I watch as she sinks against the sofa, her body going limp, as if that one motion has sucked the last of her energy. She looks like a wreck, and I'm not sure how she's going to make it through the rest of the night if Mia isn't found.

"Can I get you something to eat?"

She doesn't answer.

"Vanessa?" I prod.

She doesn't look at me. "I don't know if I can manage food."

"Can you try? It's getting late. Neither of us has had anything." I go to squeeze her hand, but at the last second decide against it. "It might help."

"I don't think so," she says.

I head to the kitchen anyway. I can understand why she doesn't have an appetite, but I'm getting hungry. I search the fridge first. I find juice, several bottles of cooking wine, some hard cheese. Eggs. Butter. I could make omelets.

I decide on soup instead, and grab a can and pour it into a bowl. As the microwave rotates in slow turns, I take inventory of the rest of the kitchen. Spotless. Nothing left on the cutting board. The sink is empty. No cups or pans or plates.

Doesn't Vanessa usually cook dinner before Tripp comes home? Isn't that what she said earlier?

I peep in the dishwasher. Only a couple of coffee mugs and some Tupperware. No sign she's been cooking anything.

The microwave dings and I pull out the bowl, bringing it to the table to eat alone. But to my surprise, Vanessa walks into the kitchen. She looks once at the soup and then away again, as if the very thought of food makes her ill. She's shuffling toward one of the cabinets, and as she reaches up for a glass to fill with water, the arms of her pullover slip down. For the first time, I notice a bruise just below her elbow the size of a lemon, the haunting blue color bright against her skin.

And then I see I'm not looking at one bruise, but five, with one of them wrapped beneath her arm, like fingers. Like someone has reached around and squeezed her tight. As if they've tried to stop her from getting away. Or grabbed her in anger.

I stop eating, my spoon frozen in mid-air, a strange feeling working its way across my chest.

She was so quick to wonder about her husband when she saw the ring. If their marriage is so great, why would she convince herself he knows what happened?

I stare at her. My neighbor. The woman I've chatted to on numerous occasions in the driveway. Our longer conversations at dinner with our husbands. The woman I thought was a friend.

But how much do I really know about her?

How much do I know about this family?

I push the bowl away. I'm not sure I want to stay here anymore.

PART TWO

Vanessa

CHAPTER TWENTY-SIX

Vanessa

Her name was Susannah. Mia's mother, Tripp's first wife—the wife he should have loved and cherished forever. She died of an inoperable brain tumor, but I don't know any of that yet. Not on that day we first meet at the coffee shop.

I'm paying for my coffee when I hear the soft splash of something falling to the floor, the gush of liquid followed by someone uttering the word "Damn." And it's the way he says it: not angry, just weary and defeated, as if this is another let-down in a long line of monumental disappointments. The sound of a man getting used to setbacks.

I drop to the floor beside him instinctively, blotting at the mess with a stack of napkins I've pulled from the counter. We don't say much as the two of us sop up the spill, only a few mumbled words from him now and again about being clumsy. But I'm too busy making sure the coffee doesn't seep toward his shoes.

He glances shyly at me, a wave of blonde hair falling across his eyes—blue eyes, I notice, with shades of gray. The color of rainwater. A handsome but tired face. He wears a hooded sweatshirt and it appears he hasn't shaved in days. He seems vulnerable. I can feel it instantly, that sense of a wounded animal, a broken spirit. Someone who has already gone through hell and back.

When we stand, he reaches forward with his hand. "Tripp Tanner," he says, and there is an awkward handshake, followed by the shuffling of cups, a wad of wet napkins dripping coffee to the ground.

I manage to say, "My name is Vanessa," but nothing else. I'm already late for work. I don't have time to chat.

We bump into each other several more times at the coffee shop after that. During one of those encounters, he jumps up to stand in line and offers to buy my coffee. Conveniently that day, my first meeting isn't until nine. He reaches to pull out my chair before taking a seat of his own, and I realize I've been secretly hoping all along that this will happen. I've been waiting for one of us to make the first move.

He looks better than the first day I saw him. Color in his cheeks, and to my relief, the beard—odd in this summer heat—is gone. Today he's wearing a suit and tie rather than the jeans and hooded sweatshirt of before. Whatever he's been through, whatever mid-life crisis he appears to have endured, is over.

At the end of that first coffee, Tripp asks me to dinner. He's nervous, out of practice. At the restaurant, one of those pristine-white-tablecloth places where they make a great show of telling us about the wine, he is focused too earnestly on rearranging the silverware, inspecting his napkin closely for a microscopic tear. I'm not sure if he's always so awkward, or if it's been that long since he's been on a date, but he's fidgety, his eyes darting around. He seems uncomfortable, as if there's something on his conscience, as if he feels guilty for being there.

I'm prepared to talk about the weather, another scorching Alabama summer, anything to get the conversation moving, but then he surprises me.

"I was married before," he says.

Ah, there it is.

"She died."

I force a sip of wine. I'm not sure I've heard him correctly.

"I'm a widower. About two years ago."

"I'm so sorry," I tell him. I don't know what else to say. Because I'm at a loss, really. I mean, how old is this man? He seems so young to be widowed.

I don't know much about him other than that he likes vanilla lattes and reads *Time* magazine. Another day, to my amusement, he was flipping through the latest *Rolling Stone*. I assumed I'd learn more over dinner: what he does for a living, places he's traveled, but we haven't gotten to any of that yet.

"I have a seven-year-old daughter," he continues. He pokes at something on his plate. "Do you have any children?" he asks.

"No."

"Ever plan on having any?"

I remember thinking that was a pretty forward question for a first date.

"One day," I tell him.

"As you can imagine, the loss has been unbearable for both Mia and me. My daughter—she's been through a lot." He sets down his fork. "She still asks for her mom. It's hard on her, always wondering who's going to be there to pick her up, who's going to put her to bed."

"Of course," I say, nodding. "She's so young. It hasn't been that long."

"No, it hasn't. Although sometimes it feels like an eternity." He looks away, and I feel for him, I honestly do. This isn't what I was expecting. I never thought in a million years this was what he'd be telling me. "I'm sorry," he says, sitting back in his chair. "This is a lot for you. I can understand if you don't want …"

"No, it's all right. Really. I just feel sorry …" His eyes flick up. Wrong word. "I'm trying to think about all you've been through."

And there's a child, I remind myself.

"I wanted to tell you right out of the gate," he says. "I hope you understand. Before we get too far along and you decide …"

"What? That I can't handle it?"

"Whether you want to be a part of this."

"I don't even know what *this* is."

I'm not sure why my words are coming out this way. Maybe it's the wine, or the culmination of all my previous dates ending in disappointment—many of the men egotistical, insensitive. But this date feels different. Tripp seems different. There is no false bravado, not that I can tell. And he seems more emotional, receptive. More concerned about how I will react. Now I know why.

"I can understand if you don't want to see me again," he says.

"Why would I not want to see you?"

"I'm a widower, raising a young daughter on my own. I work long hours. I've tried getting a nanny, but Mia refuses. That's why I've been staying home, spending time with her. The last few months, her life has been in upheaval. She struggles. Every day she has the look of someone who expects her entire world to bottom out, over and over again. I can't bear it." He looks at me sadly. "I'm not sure if that's something you want to be a part of."

This is only the first date, I want to remind him.

But I hear what he's saying. He comes with baggage. If I want to date him, he and Mia are a package deal. And he's giving me an out; he's telling me directly. I can say I've had a lovely evening, and we never have to see each other again. He'll understand.

But I don't want that. To my surprise, I don't want this to be the last time we're together. It's not so much about his daughter, although that's undeniably one of the saddest stories I've ever heard. It's more my feelings toward him. I can't shake them. They're already budding, an incredible desire to protect him, a chance for me to help him be happy again.

"I'd like to give us a try," I say.

Tripp's shoulders relax. He looks categorically relieved. Whatever he may have imagined would happen when he told me about his family, sharing something so personal, I didn't cut and run. I might be the first woman he's dated since his wife died, and I'm still here. I may be topping up my wine glass for the third time, but at least I didn't bolt.

In the back of my mind, I wonder what on earth I've gotten myself into. I wonder what Janie will have to say about the situation. She'll tell me I'm in way over my head. Why can't I date someone less complicated? Someone who plays golf, someone who's divorced but doesn't already have children. Someone who is not a widower.

But this isn't drama, not in the traditional sense. This is tragedy, something Tripp shouldn't be punished for. He didn't ask for his wife to die. He shouldn't remain alone for the rest of his life.

Janie will meet him, I think, and she'll see what I see, and she'll understand. Tripp is someone who will love me. He's already suffered loss once. He won't want to go through that again.

I don't ask any more about his wife that first night, although I'm tempted. I'm not sure how to go about asking someone how a person died. But Tripp eventually offers the information. He starts off slow, during a road trip to Nashville. We're spending the weekend together, our very first, and he chooses this time to tell me about Susannah. With his eyes on the road, he doesn't have to look at me when he speaks. He can just talk. It's easier this way, I suppose.

It started slowly with migraines, which turned out to be a brain tumor. Once they found it, there was ten months of chemotherapy; they weren't sure she would make it through Christmas. She passed away shortly after New Year's. There was a large funeral, since both their families were from Huntsville, their family lineage tracing back to the original settlers in Twickenham. Afterwards, months of trying to explain to Mia where her mother had gone, why the cancer had taken her, how she no longer felt pain and was dancing with the angels above. Why Mia didn't need to feel sad anymore.

But it didn't work. She was only five. It was hard for her to comprehend and she continued asking for her mom.

"In the beginning, bedtime was the worst," Tripp says. "She had these dreams and would come into my room crying and wanting Susannah. It was enough to tear me up inside."

But in the last year, he tells me she's been seeing a counselor, sometimes twice a week, and he thinks it's working. She's starting to accept the loss. She wakes up every day and knows it's just her and her dad, and she's learning to cope. Time, over everything else, he hopes, will be the truly great healer.

I stare out the window, interstate signs and billboards flying by. I try to understand what it must have been like for Tripp to watch someone he loved transition from health and happiness to lying in bed day after day, her movements and voice growing weaker over time until it was hard to hear what she was saying, not sure if in the last few days she could understand what he was whispering to her.

How he managed to get through that ordeal, I don't know. He must have thought he had everything. He's a successful lawyer, partner and majority stakeholder in his family's firm, the son of a long line of judges and attorneys. There was never any doubt he would excel at doing the same. He married his college sweetheart—a beautiful woman, I imagine, although I haven't seen a picture—and they were happy. They had a little girl born with bright blonde hair—this fact I know, as he's shown me several pictures of his daughter when she was an infant, swaddled in pink blankets with a dancing bear mobile above her crib; as a toddler with her arms reaching to greet him when he arrived home; posing with her backpack on her way to elementary school.

But then Susannah got sick. And fourteen months later, she was gone.

"We're making progress, but there are days when Mia thinks every time I leave the house I might not come back," Tripp says. "I had to lie about where I was going this weekend, leaving her with her cousins so they can distract her for a while." He stares straight ahead. One look at the side of his face and I can see his eyes squinting behind sunglasses, the lines etching toward his cheeks. "It's a terrible feeling knowing she doesn't have a mother. That I couldn't prevent that from happening."

"It's not your fault Susannah got sick," I try telling him.

"I know," he says, glancing at me. "But I can fix it. I think I know a way to make things right again."

CHAPTER TWENTY-SEVEN

Vanessa

Less than two years later, at the beginning of the summer, Tripp asks me to marry him. In my heart, I know we're rushing things, but I can't say no. I don't want to. I've fallen for him, head over heels. Mia and I have been for ice cream several times. I've watched her dance recital. We've seen *Charlotte's Web* and had picnics. She's cautious with me, and in turn, I have trouble knowing what to say. I want so desperately not to mess this up. Tripp looks happier than I've ever seen him, holding both our hands, bringing us to the zoo, to the park, introducing me to his extended family.

We're in the courtyard of one of our favorite restaurants when Tripp gets down on one knee, his eyes shining bright, his face full of hope for a new beginning, and I know what my answer will be. Everyone will think we should have waited. Janie will tell me to slow down. People will whisper that Tripp is being irrational. He's moving too fast, simply filling the void left by Susannah. But I don't think he is. I'm convinced it's the strong and steady love he feels for me.

And then he brings up another idea—an ideal of sorts, a way for us to become a stronger family.

I've already said yes. I've already made plans for the wedding. The date is set. Whatever he's asking will be another yes, I'm almost sure of it.

"I need for Mia to never feel alone," he says. We're on the couch; it's late afternoon. Mia is upstairs playing in her room and the pair of us are reading, my feet crossed lazily in his lap. "I need her to know she's cared for, that someone will always be here. When she wakes up, when she comes home."

"We'll take care of her," I say.

"I want someone in the house with her at all times."

I don't think anything of it at first. In fact, part of me is still reading. I turn the page.

"Vanessa," he says, and the way he says my name—slowly, deliberately—gets my attention. "I want you here with her."

"I'll be here as much as I can. We'll hire a nanny."

"No," he says, softly. "I'd like *you* to be the one that's home with her. She needs the stability."

I close my book, suddenly understanding what he's trying to say. "You want me to quit my job?"

He nods and gives me a long, heartfelt stare, gazing into my eyes.

I don't know what to say. I'm speechless. Maybe I should have seen this coming—he's been hinting at it, hasn't he? How Mia won't want a babysitter. How she prefers it when I pick her up from school. How she wants it to be one of us who takes her to swim practice.

But my job—the years I've put into my career as a financial planner. I'm not sure if I'm ready to give that up.

"It won't be forever," Tripp says. "Only until she gets through middle school. She'll be older and more independent by then." He tilts his chin expectantly. "It will only be for a few years, Vanessa. That's it. Your career will be waiting for you when you get back, I promise."

I bite my lip. A few years—that's all he's asking for.

I can do this, can't I?

Because right now, the way he's holding my hand, hoping above everything that I'll agree, I'm reminded of his protectiveness of his daughter. The grief she's gone through—that they've both gone through. The way Mia clings to us.

Tripp won't be able to leave his job. He has too many cases coming up, plus he's on track for one day becoming a district judge. It will need to be me who takes some leave. I should be able to take a short break and pick back up at the finance services firm, right?

I look into those eyes of his, the soft blue-gray color that reminds me of rainwater, and feel the same wave of compassion as the day we met. How after that first date, I was so eager to fix him. How appreciative he's been ever since. I need to do this for our little family.

I squeeze his hand in return: I won't let him down.

"What are you talking about?" Janie says. We're having lunch, Thai food, although I don't have much of an appetite. The wedding is only weeks away. "You told him no, right?"

I don't speak.

"Vanessa?" Her eyes are on me. "You can't stop working." She's tearing into her food. "You love your job. He's got money. You've got money. Hire someone."

"She needs more than that."

"He wants you to be her mother."

"I'm about to be her stepmother."

"He wants you to do everything Susannah did." She waves her fork. "Did she stay at home too?"

"Yes."

"Bingo."

"It's not like that."

"A grieving husband works every day and has trouble taking care of his daughter? It's classic. That's what widowed men do. He's looking for a replacement wife. He wants someone to take Susannah's place."

I push away my plate. "I'm not going to be his replacement wife."

"Sure sounds that way to me."

"This is different."

"Oh really?" Janie says. "He's already asking you to quit your job."

"It's only for a short time. And this is for Mia."

She snorts. "Of course he says that. You sure he's not doing it for himself?"

"Me being home?"

"Yes, you being at home. He gets to go to work and can relax knowing someone is there to look after her. In-home babysitting. Someone to cook dinner. Why don't you learn how to do arts and crafts and schedule play dates too?" She makes a face.

I suddenly feel angry. I hate how insecure she's making me feel, the brutal honesty of it all. But I can't be angry with her. She's only looking out for me; I know she means well. She wouldn't be saying these things otherwise—the obvious truth when I least want to hear it, the blunt criticism that can only come from a best friend.

Janie and I have been close for going on eight years. I moved to Huntsville after a recruiter relocated me to a new bank, and she was one of the first colleagues I met, one of the first people who took the time to get to know me, which was a big relief since I was desperately looking for a friend. She'd moved from Atlanta a couple of years earlier and showed me around town, told me which neighborhood to move to, the best places for sushi.

We spent evenings talking numbers and sipping martinis at the bar, ignoring the men who circled around, acting as if we didn't want to date. Before long, Janie was promoted to senior vice president. And then I was promoted too, head-hunted by another company, financial planning this time. To this day, Janie is the one who drags me to yoga, lets me know when the local Chamber of Commerce is hosting a function. She's notorious for bringing me as her plus-one to charity events, all the while pleading with me to get involved.

She's happy for me, I know that. She's not married herself; she has one or two men she casually dates on the side, but married life is not for her—not yet, at least. She's happy for me and Tripp. She's happy I found someone. She fears Tripp is marrying again too quickly, yes, but that hasn't stopped her from helping me plan the wedding and accompanying me to dress alterations. She's sampled every slice of wedding cake.

She's just worried. I can see the alarm rising in her face.

"This won't be forever," I assure her, repeating Tripp's words. "Mia's nine. I'll take time off until she's finished with middle school, and then she'll be too busy with friends to need me."

Janie doesn't look convinced. "And then after that, there'll be something else. What about high school? Who's going to take her to those early-morning swim practices?"

"She'll catch rides. We'll get a driver."

"Vanessa, honey, wake up. *You're* the driver."

I bite my lip. She looks at me, her eyes softening.

"You can't give up everything you've worked for because he tells you to."

"It's not like that."

"She's not even your kid."

"She's my stepdaughter," I correct her. "And she's sweet. I love her. She needs someone."

But Janie isn't listening, her voice firing up in a frenzy. "And it's not just the kid. You're going to be moving into his first wife's house."

"I can change things."

"How? Everything you do will be compared to her. Everything there belonged to her first."

Her words rock me. "It won't be like that. I'll make it my own."

"I hope so," Janie says, and balls up her napkin. "Because for them, everything is staying the same. You're the only thing that will be different."

A few weeks later, Tripp and I are married. And in the blink of an eye, I have an instant family. A husband on one arm and a small child in a pink satin dress on the other. Earlier, Mia walked down the aisle in front of me, teeter-tottering in her low heels a look of immense pride on her face as she held her bouquet. She looked beautiful. I felt radiant. And the look of pride on Tripp's face as he watched us approach …

Despite Janie's warnings, I'm captivated by the joy of the wedding, the fabulous reception party, and a future I hope will be filled with happy times. I hand in my notice, telling my boss I won't be returning to work after the honeymoon, that it's only for the next few years so I can help my stepdaughter. He's never looked more surprised. By the end of the week, I've packed up my office.

I move into Tripp's house and everything is fine at first—it's wonderful, in fact. I'm discovering every nook and cranny of my new home: the windowsill with the best light for placing pots of basil; the spare closet that no one's using where I can hang my winter coats; a large open space in the front sitting room where I can install a new bookshelf.

On Sunday mornings, we make breakfast together. Mia eats everything on her plate, chattering away and asking for more syrup. And in the evenings, I weave my hand through Tripp's, the pair of us sitting on the couch, and admire the gold wedding band on his finger that matches my own.

But as the days turn into weeks and months, things start to change. Something doesn't feel right—and I realize with a start that it's me. I try to squash the feelings down, but they bubble back up again, Janie's words coming back to haunt me.

As I move from room to room, it's even more painfully obvious, and my self-doubt creeps in. In this house, I feel like an intruder. An underlying sense that there was someone else here first—and of course there was. Susannah.

Same house. Same bed. Same sheets. Her artwork on the walls. Her favorite patterns on the curtains. The vanity where she once kept her hairbrush. The same reading light I switch off every night. The rug beneath my feet the same.

Have I really become the replacement wife?

I'd never thought of that phrase until the day Janie first said it.

A divorce would have been easier. I know that sounds awful, but if Susannah hadn't died, if she and Tripp had broken up instead, gone their separate ways, it would be easier to move some of her stuff out. She would have taken most of it after their separation, and everything else I could have quietly moved around or taken to storage. But that's not what happened here.

How do you politely get rid of things belonging to someone who has died, and only a few years ago? How do you do it without upsetting your husband and new daughter? But the house screams Susannah. Everything she touched. Everything she picked out and decorated.

At first I tried to live with it, I really did, but that didn't last long. Susannah's presence haunts me every time I look around the house, consuming my thoughts, making me feel like an unwanted stranger. An imposter. I see her everywhere. Standing barefoot on the carpet. Crossing the living room wearing a soft cotton robe. Watering plants in the kitchen. Laughing in the hallway. Chasing after Mia into the playroom.

I always thought I possessed a high level of confidence. I thought that would serve me well here. But this is no longer my office or the boardroom and I am not an expert in my own domain any more—this was someone else's domain first. With everything looking and remaining the same, she is still in possession of this house. It's all hers. Even the family. The self-doubt has taken me over, and I despise myself for it.

The bed has to go first. At least that Tripp can understand … well, he tells me he does.

The dinner plates are next, Susannah's place settings, the dining room curtains, sofa cushions. I tell Tripp that I have a different sense of style, a different color palette, and hope he understands. I convince Susannah's sister to take her car and gift it to her son, who will be getting his driver's license soon—and for this, I score major points with my new nephew.

I do this slowly and carefully. I don't want it to be too sudden, so I take my time, making changes over the course of a year. Susannah's artwork from Paris is removed. Figurines are moved to another shelf, and then eventually a closet.

Every day I bring another decorative piece from the townhouse I'm selling, my paintings replacing the ones that once occupied the wall. Again Tripp tells me he understands. We don't talk about it in so many words, but he gets what I'm doing. He knows it's hard coming into a house that doesn't feel like my own. He wants this to work, our new family, as much as I do.

I'm also careful when it comes to Mia. I never want her to feel as though I'm erasing her mother. Nothing is thrown away or destroyed. The furniture is taken to a storage unit, the kitchen table draped in protective cloth, boxes stacked against one wall, hand-blown glass from Susannah's trip to Mexico secured carefully in bubble wrap. Everything is waiting for Mia to use when she grows up; she'll love the idea of moving her mother's favorite chair into her apartment in college. And Tripp can visit these things any time he wants, too. He can look at the decorations and remember Susannah picking each one out, but I don't think he ever does.

He is always saying he doesn't mind the changes, but there are certainly keepsakes I notice he's putting away on his own. He stores them in the attic. Their wedding china, for example. He says he'll want to gift that to Mia when it comes time for her own wedding day. Photo albums from when he and Susannah first met, the jewelry he'll one day give their daughter, knick-knacks and souvenirs they purchased during their honeymoon. I know those items are off-limits. I would never pack them away myself.

Mia keeps several mementos in her bedroom too. A scrapbook of flowers she and her mother pressed together. Framed photographs. A ceramic elephant Susannah brought home from India. Together we pick out a beautiful wooden trunk where she can store everything, so that she can pull the items out from time to time: wear her mother's necklace, or hold the handkerchief she was given at her engagement party.

I assure Mia I'm not covering up her mother's existence, that I would never want her to feel this way. Those pieces belonged to her mother. They mean the world to her and it's important she keep them protected. I just want to secure my own place in this family, make sure we all move forward. I also want to prove to Janie that she was wrong, and prove to myself I have nothing to fear.

I'm not the replacement wife—I'm Tripp's wife. I'm not only here because Susannah died. Tripp would still have fallen in love with me if we'd met in an alternate universe.

Together we're starting a new family. We're creating a new future. That's what I convince myself, at least.

CHAPTER TWENTY-EIGHT

Vanessa

It's early September and we've been married for a year. Tripp and I are sitting on the patio watching Mia in the backyard. She's perfecting her back handspring, something she's been working on for weeks. She tumbles in the grass before jumping up again.

Tripp says, "Not bad, Mia! Try again."

She leaps backwards, her hands pushing off the ground until she flips over, a bouncy spring to her step. This time, she nails it. She beams, triumphant.

"Way to go!" he tells her.

He has made me a vodka tonic and squeezed in the lime; the warmth from the alcohol is spreading to my cheeks. The sun is setting, the color of warm buttermilk across the sky, and I'm thinking that this evening couldn't be more perfect.

"Mia tells me she's happy," he says.

I lift the glass to my lips.

"She says you have fun together."

I smile, relishing the notion that they've talked fondly about me. After several months of working with Mia and taking care of her, I must be doing something right.

Tripp sits with me on the cushioned seat, new patio furniture I picked out in a crimson red. We continue watching her play, her bare feet kicking into the air as she attempts another back handspring, each one getting stronger than the last.

Tripp has been talking about having a pool built. I've seen the construction plans in his study and we're now waiting for the day he puts in the work order. At swim meets, people have been remarking on how talented Mia is in the water. The coach agrees it would be fantastic for her to have a home pool for extra practice.

But for now, the backyard remains flat and even, a large expanse of grass that stretches toward the fence, a clump of crepe myrtles we keep neatly trimmed on either side of the shed. We recently planted a pear tree.

I take another sip of my drink.

"How do you think the two of you are getting along?" Tripp asks.

He's been doing this periodically since the day we got married—checking in. Making sure I'm adjusting, acutely aware that he's thrown me into the deep end and that it's been a steep learning curve. Wanting me to know that he appreciates my efforts every single day.

"Good," I tell him.

"She likes you. She tells me she's glad you're here."

"I hope so. I'm trying my hardest."

Mia swoops her arms overhead. She's switching to cartwheels now.

"I'm so pleased you can pick her up. That she's not in after-school care," he says.

"Yes, she's happy about that too."

"You're getting to know each other better this way."

"I'm definitely not mom of the year."

"But you're trying. That's what counts."

"Sometimes it's hard."

"There are other moms you can talk to."

"I know, and that's been helping. But sometimes I'm not sure if I know what I'm doing." I notice Tripp shifting in his seat, his body language tightening. "But I'm trying," I add quickly. I need him to not worry. "You're right about that. We're both trying."

Tripp allows himself a small smile. "That's what I like to hear. My girls getting along and being happy."

We turn and watch Mia for a while. She's humming to herself, a tune I don't know, her ponytail hanging loose at the back of her neck. Several months ago, she asked me to style her hair in a French braid and I had to watch several YouTube videos before finally figuring it out. Sometimes I worry whether I'm doing it right. Not just her hair—*everything*. I'm making progress, I know I am, but there are days when I question every decision I make. I wonder, does she see my hesitation? The fact that I'm not sure what constitutes a good after-school snack, how I don't make silly voices the way her dad does, the way her mom used to, when we read stories before going to bed. Am I adding enough marshmallows to her hot chocolate? Do I look like I'm having fun when I sit down with her stuffed animals and drink imaginary tea?

I've never had practice and none of these things seem to come to me naturally. I'm trying my hardest—God knows I've read enough parenting books to last a lifetime. Janie sends me links for articles on parenting too, particularly the ones on navigating step-kids. Understanding the emotions of a child who has lost their mom. The bereavement process. The proper ways to discipline. How not to discipline. Links to craft websites containing Fifty Ideas for a Rainy Day. Facebook support groups. What to do when you think you're failing. The reading list goes on and on.

"Give it some time," Tripp says. "You're doing great."

But the nagging feeling is always there. I don't admit this to Tripp, but I'm almost certain Mia senses my inadequacies, the way she watches with a puzzled expression as it takes me forever to know what to say, the way I struggle. She'll never tell her dad any of this. She doesn't want to upset him. She wants him to be happy just as much as I do. But I see it in her face, the tiniest frown. The sad flicker in her eyes because I don't do things the way her mom would have done. My pancakes aren't the same. I don't use the right kind of bread for her sandwiches, with the crusts cut off. I don't always remember to pack her favorite fruit snacks in her lunchbox. I don't know how to play the card games she likes.

But I know I should cut myself some slack. There are success stories too. Like learning how to braid her hair, for example. Or back-to-school shopping, when I found a pair of Converse sneakers she loves and wears every day. Dinners when she tells me my spaghetti is her favorite.

So why is it that I still feel like I'm not doing enough? That I'm not good enough?

Because when Tripp gets home, everything he does is perfect. It's effortless. He is the center of her universe. He hangs the moon and the stars. Their relationship comes so easily—and of course it should, I remind myself. They are flesh and blood. Tripp has known her since birth. He is a natural.

Watching them, I can't help feeling like an outsider. Tripp tells me I'm not, but I can't stop thinking that I am. When the two of them are together, sharing stories from when she was little, their laughter and private jokes in the car, I feel left out—like I'm constantly trying to catch up. Tripp tries to listen; he tries to understand. Mia will often ask me to join the conversation, she'll look to me for a reaction to her punchline, but I never quite feel like I fit in. I'm late to the party. The third wheel. An interloper.

It's ridiculous, I know it is. I'm a grown-up. I should have more confidence. But I'm also acutely aware of the way I joined this family. I can't help noticing this in every subtlety.

Mia doesn't mean to do these things. She's just a young girl. She only knows that she wants to spend more time with her dad. She's with me all day and we hang out and share snacks, but when he's home, all bets are off. He is her everything. Without realizing it, she'll cuddle up next to him on the couch and stretch out her legs during movie night, relegating me to another sofa. She'll recite nursery rhymes from when she was a baby, nursery rhymes I haven't learned yet and only the two of them know. They'll discuss their favorite Olympic sports. The funny way Uncle Bill sneezes. How they both hate pickles and love French toast.

I feel like a family guest.

Only Janie listens to me, in a way that says, *I told you so, but hang in there*. She's rooting for me all the while, telling me not to be so sensitive, to give it another shot, that our relationship will click into place over time. Soon the three of us will create our own inside jokes.

I know she's right. I'm being impatient. I'm putting too much pressure on myself to be the best kind of stepmother, for it to come more naturally. I'm overanalyzing everything.

If I stopped for one second, I'd probably see I'm doing a lot of things well and not giving myself enough credit.

Because I am committed to this family. I love Tripp more than anything, and I love Mia. I want our family to work. I want Mia to have stability, for us to have a strong stepmother–stepdaughter relationship, so I'll keep trying. It means everything.

CHAPTER TWENTY-NINE

Vanessa

The workmen break ground on a custom-made twenty-five-meter pool that will not only be functional and suitable in every way for Mia's training, but also beautiful, the walls lined with blue and white mosaic tiles, a waterfall at one end made from natural cut limestone, and a nearby pool house and shower where she can rinse off.

When it's finished, on the eve of Mia's eleventh birthday, when the dust and noise have gone, the water is tested and set to a sparkling sheen, Tripp celebrates by bringing us outside for a pre-birthday celebration.

He looks so happy—so *proud*. His wife died but left him with a swimming prodigy, and he has the financial resources to provide her with everything she needs. She doesn't have to wait for the club pool to open during the summer. She can step right out of the house into her own backyard. The pool is huge, the blue tile giving it an exquisite sapphire color, the sound of the cascading fountain an extra touch of luxury as we stand on the patio and admire the view.

"Do you like it?" Tripp asks Mia.

She nods wholeheartedly, her eyes gleaming. "It's so pretty," she says.

"Only the best for my girl." Tripp scoops her into his arms, and she giggles, her face smooshed against his chest.

The two of them hug while I slice pieces of birthday cake on the patio table. The cake is covered in sprinkles, something Mia picked out excitedly at the bakery. Tripp has opened a bottle of wine for the occasion too, and poured a cup of fruit punch for Mia. There will be a birthday dinner this evening to celebrate, just the three of us. Tomorrow, a pool party for family and friends, including several of Mia's classmates from school.

"Thank you, Dad. I love it." She hugs him once more before turning to me, her eyes shining bright. "What do you think, Vanessa? What do you think of my pool?"

"It's perfect," I tell her.

She likes the sound of that, her smile growing even wider. "Yes. Perfect." And then, "Will you swim with me?"

I try to laugh. "Maybe later."

Tripp looks at me with a grin. "Come on, Vanessa, let's break it in."

I step away. "No, not right now." I'm hoping to blow them off.

"Please," Mia pleads. "You never swim with me."

"Don't be silly, guys. We don't have our swimsuits on, and we've got dinner in an hour."

"We'll be real quick." She makes a pouty face.

"Come on, Vanessa," Tripp repeats. "For fun's sake?" He drops down to meet Mia's face with his own. "Let's rush in and change. Super speed."

"Yeah!" she cheers.

"You guys go ahead without me," I tell them.

"*Please*, Vanessa." By this point, Mia's voice is teetering on whining. She is moving toward me, but I move sideways out of reach, not realizing I'm stepping closer to the pool.

"I don't want to get wet. My hair … We have dinner …"

"You're no fun." Mia looks up at her dad. "You know Vanessa doesn't go swimming with me at the club? I always want her to."

"Never?" Tripp asks. He gives me a strange look.

"Not ever." She pouts.

I take another step back. "I'd rather sit and watch," I tell him. I look down, the crystal-blue water only inches away.

"No." Mia makes a face. "You should go in too!"

And with that, she pushes me.

I fall backward, my hands catching only air, my feet kicking up, my back hitting the water first before the rest of my body drops below the surface. To my horror, my head goes under with a *whoosh*, then I am somehow leaping up for air, taking giant gulps as water streams down my face into my eyes. I can't see. My feet can't get a grip. I'm starting to believe there's no bottom. I'm kicking and flailing and slipping, and no one is helping me.

I reach up and out to grab onto something—but what? There is nothing. The wall feels miles away, and a terrifying fear rips through my head. How deep is this pool? Will I sink back under? Why isn't Tripp helping me? I can hear them standing off to the side laughing, and I want to scream, full panic pumping in my chest.

But then I hear the distinct sounds of two more people jumping in. No, someone has been pushed. Mia has playfully shoved Tripp in too, but unlike me, he is hooting and hollering. He knew it was coming. In he goes with a shout, Mia squealing as she jumps in alongside him, tucked up like a cannonball. They are splashing and shouting, their kicks causing more water to fly into the air, not caring about their soaked clothes, not caring about me in the slightest.

I reach and find concrete. A wall of shiny blue tile. *Oh thank God.* I pull on the edge of the pool, scooping my other arm in, hugging the wall for dear life. I'm safe. I can touch solid ground again. But inside my chest, my heart is pounding double-time until I feel it might burst.

I close my eyes, panting, spluttering, taking in deep breaths.

"Vanessa." Tripp swims to my side. "Are you all right?"

I'm trembling, water dripping from my face. My eyes focus on reading the black letters inches away: *5 feet.*

Only five feet, but it felt like I'd been tossed into the deep abyss.

Behind us, Mia splashes and plays.

Tripp wipes the water from his eyes. He stops to catch his breath, the look on his face changing as he realizes I'm upset. "Vanessa, talk to me." I don't answer. He looks me over, the wheels in his brain churning. "We were just playing around. She thought it would be fun. Are you all right?"

But I can't answer him. I'm too ashamed. I can only stare at the wall—my lifesaver—my chin bobbing in the water and dipping below the surface as I try to hide my eyes from him.

"Vanessa," he says again. He stops moving. Something clicks. "Vanessa, can't you swim?"

I don't want to tell him. I don't want him to know the truth. It's so embarrassing—ridiculous even.

"I almost drowned as a kid," I finally say, and it comes out as a whisper.

"You never told me that."

"A boy shoved me in and then another kid held me under. It was …" I don't finish my sentence. "I've been scared ever since."

"I'm so sorry, Vanessa."

"It's fine," I say. "I'll be okay."

Water continues streaming down my face. My shoes have fallen off and are now sunk somewhere to the bottom, ruined. My linen top and pants will be ruined too. Tripp is wearing an expensive pair of pants and polo shirt. Mia is in shorts and a tank, blissfully doing handstands and front rolls behind us.

"We built this pool and you never said anything," Tripp says. "For months you watched it go in, and you never told me you were afraid of the water."

"It felt silly."

"Why didn't you tell me?"

"I thought I could take lessons one day. Try it out nice and slow—not get shoved in." I say this a little too accusingly.

"She didn't know." He looks over his shoulder. "Is that why you never swim with her at the club?"

I nod.

But he doesn't apologize. He doesn't ask Mia to either. He thinks it was fun—a big plunge to celebrate the brand-new pool—and he wants to keep it that way. It's not Mia's fault she didn't know I couldn't swim.

CHAPTER THIRTY

Vanessa

My husband loves me, I know he does. With my whole heart I know this to be true. He is always telling me he can't imagine life without me, that we met at precisely the right time. His grief and his daughter's have been made gentler by me showering them with love and care. "You're keeping us together," he tells me.

But when I think about it, and especially now, does he mean the three of us: Mia, him, and me, the newly forged family? Or does *together* include his deceased wife too? Has he always meant to include Susannah? Because it's as if she's always been here. Even after all this time, I still feel like I'm living in her shadow. She's omnipresent. And nothing I do, no amount of redecorating the house or taking care of Mia, has made me feel like we're on our own.

Mia's thirteenth birthday is coming up, and we make plans to celebrate at her favorite hibachi restaurant. She wants to invite several of her friends, along with Tripp's parents and a few other family members too. In the days leading up to the party, I notice her talking more and more about her mother.

I miss her.

What would she say about me turning thirteen?

Would she like my dress?

Would she be happy I'm going to the eighth-grade dance?

Tripp answers all her questions. He tells her that her mother would think her dress is beautiful.

The day of the party, I hear Mia ask if she can wear a pair of her mother's small diamond earrings. Tripp fetches them from a jewelry box he keeps in the attic.

But once the party is over, she stops talking about her mother. She gives the earrings back to her dad. "For safekeeping," she says, and nothing more. And then she stops talking to us altogether. She's quiet. Reserved. She says she'd rather spend time with her friends. Her energy is focused on swimming. There are other places she'd rather be than home. I can tell something is on her mind. She's shutting me out, her father too, and we chalk it up to her being a moody teenager. She's had a bad day at school. A fall-out with a friend. A poor swim time she can't seem to shake. She takes her frustration out with laps in the pool.

She bristles when we walk into the room—everything we do is annoying. She never wants to have a conversation with us, even though we try. In the evenings and on the weekend, she stays upstairs in her room. There are periods of sulky, silent behavior that can last for days at a time. And for no reason that I can figure out, except to think she's upset about a boy, a disagreement with a friend, or increasing sadness about missing her mom.

Eventually the mood passes. And then there's something else. And something after that.

Coach is pushing me too hard.

My English teacher hates me. I got another C.

I don't want any more dinner. Can I be excused?

A roll of her eyes. *Shut my door, please.*

She's a teenager and doesn't want to be around her parents anymore. We're simply not cool.

But talking about her mom non-stop and then no longer speaking about her? That's something else—Tripp and I both know it, but we don't know what to do. Until I realize she's been writing it all down instead.

I find the journal in her room. I know I shouldn't read it; a thirteen-year-old girl is entitled to her own private thoughts. But it's sitting on her dresser. I recognize the blue leather-bound cover; it's one of the gifts her aunt Carol, Susannah's sister, gave her for her birthday.

I pick it up, telling myself I'll just flip through the first few pages before putting it back.

Blue pen. Looped cursive letters. Page upon page about nothing but her mother. It makes my heart ache.

Aunt Carol said I look just like her. We have the same eyes.

I wish she could have been at my party.

I can't stop thinking about her.

She has been writing in her journal every day since her birthday.

I hear feet running up the stairs. The steady creak in the floor as someone heads down the hall.

I drop the journal and scoot it with one finger to the position I'm almost certain it was in on top of the dresser, then jump back, but it's too late. Mia appears at the door, her eyes instantly narrowing to scowl at me.

"What are you doing?"

"Sorting your laundry."

She casts her eyes at her laundry basket, the clothes still piled in a heap. "No you're not."

"I was about to—"

"Later, okay?" She steps into the room and folds her arms.

My face grows hot. I move away from the dresser, and at the last second pick up her laundry basket, a chance to cover my tracks even though I know she's smarter than that. She moves closer to the wall and stands next to the journal protectively.

After that, she keeps it hidden, the blue leather-bound cover disappearing somewhere beneath her mattress, or at the back of her closet. Who knows, because I don't go looking.

*

Tripp has started working longer hours. To blow off steam, he tells me he's hitting the racquetball courts. He wants the exercise. Other nights he says he's meeting up with other attorneys from the firm and they're going out for drinks.

This leaves me home alone with Mia. And when she's not in her room or at swim practice, I'm increasingly becoming her chauffeur. Taking her to practice, picking her up. Taking her to friends' houses. Another party. Buying supplies for a science project. Replacing her swim cap. Quiet car rides back and forth when occasionally I manage to get her to speak. We'll talk about music—a new song she likes—or a test she needs to study for. Her responses aren't long, the conversations aren't earth-shattering, but it's something. More than a grunt and a *whatever*. She'll humor me with small talk and I'll start to relax. At least she doesn't bring up the journal, and for that, I'm grateful.

With the increased number of sleepovers and activities, my days stretch longer and more tedious, and the countdown in my head is starting to clang loudly—the day approaching for when I can go back to work. The promise my husband and I made to each other when we got married.

I didn't bring it up when Mia started her eighth-grade year—Tripp didn't mention anything either—and I told myself I could stick it out a little while longer for Mia's benefit, that we would get her all the way through middle school until she started attending Westminster High. That time is getting near.

The invitation to the mother–daughter tea has arrived. Several Saturdays in a row are booked for swim meets. The school term ends in May. No more car lines once summer begins. Fewer swim practices too. With Janie's help, I begin submitting my résumé.

Tripp is hesitant at first, and it's frustrating beyond measure. We talk in circles until, as a concession, I agree that I will go back part-time to begin with. Baby steps. A way to make sure Mia will be okay with the new transition, that she'll feel comfortable catching more rides with friends. I assure him that she will—she's already been doing it. But he remains overprotective.

In return, he tells me he'll start coming home more for dinner. He realizes he's been working a lot and wants to make a point of leaving the office on time, since I've said more than once how much I miss having him around the dinner table. We can sit down together with Mia, he agrees. It will be a good way to keep tabs on how each of us is doing.

Janie calls. There's a position at a wealth management company that she thinks I'd be perfect for and one of the vice presidents remembers me as a financial consultant. She's interested in a face-to-face meeting.

"This is great," Janie says. "You should talk to her."

"But it's not part-time," I say, a hiccup in my breath because I'm already anticipating what Janie is about to tell me.

"That wasn't the deal, remember?"

"I know."

"You can't miss this one."

"I know," I say again.

"Vanessa, didn't I warn you this was going to last through high school?"

"No, it won't. It's changing."

"Is it so you can still drive her to swim practice?"

"That and other things. She's got a full schedule."

"Look, Vanessa. Mia is an outstanding kid—don't get me wrong. She's going places. But she's already thirteen. How much longer are you going to have to cater to her schedule?"

I press a hand to my head. "She's got another swim meet this Saturday. And another one after that. Every Saturday really." I sigh and stare out the window, the pool shining brightly in the backyard. I think of the alarm set for 5 a.m., how we'll be pulling out of the driveway before dawn. "I never thought I'd get so sick of swim meets, you know? So many early mornings. So many practices before school. After school. All the time."

"It's a lot."

"I don't think she even cares that I'm bringing her. Every Saturday. My weekends, consumed. It's getting so … so tiring."

There is the sound of something scratching. A long, steady scratch—the kind that runs from top to bottom. The kind that hurts your jaw and sends pinpricks of pain scattering across your skin.

I turn my head. Mia is gripping the door frame, scraping her finger down the wood, her fingernail peeling away the paint.

My eyes lock on hers.

I'm not sure if she heard me—I'm seriously hoping she didn't. I was facing the window, my voice kept low as I talked to Janie. Surely she didn't hear what I said.

She doesn't say a word. Her hand drops from the door and she slinks away, disappearing into the darkness at the end of the hallway.

PART THREE

The Week Of

CHAPTER THIRTY-ONE

Vanessa

The Saturday Before

Another swim meet. My weekends are filled with humid air and rancid chlorine, the alarm screeching at us to wake up. The long, sleepy drives across town. Sometimes Birmingham. Other weekends Nashville. Every Saturday, the same wake-up call before dawn. But we do this for Mia. It's worth it. She's a champion swimmer and every competition we take her to is one step closer to her professional dream.

I'm wearing jeans and a light sweater to keep out the chill, as there's a hint of frost outside the window. I reach my hand and smooth a section of hair around my face, but it's unruly, and I know it's no use. In a few short hours, we'll be locked in a natatorium with enough pumped-in humidity to keep my hair frizzing in every direction.

Jesus, it's early.

I inhale deeply over my coffee. One thing's for sure: there's not enough caffeine for days like this. I rub my eyes, feeling the sting of early morning, the back of my hand grinding away at puffy eyelids.

In the kitchen, I begin the usual tasks, stuffing a bag with cereal bars and snack mix, flavored water for Tripp and myself, PB&J sandwiches for Mia. At the bottom of the bag I make sure there's cash for concessions, an extra pair of goggles in case she needs them.

I've got it down to a science now. Mia is forever digging into this bag, rummaging for another pack of gum or a towel. Sometimes she smiles at me when I catch her doing it; sometimes she'll even remember to say thank you, and I tell myself that makes all the difference.

She is sitting at the counter, a heavy stillness in the air. We both know it's too early to say anything yet; we're still in the dregs of sleep. Only the light above the sink burns. Outside, a hazy gray dawn is wrapping the front of the house in fog. Everything else is quiet.

Mia's hair is a tangled mess, a knot above one ear where I assume she tossed and turned against her pillow. She sweats when she sleeps, her body emanating enough heat through the night to make her kick off the covers, her pajama top damp to the touch. Every morning I pick up her comforter and remake the bed.

The pipes upstairs squeak, and there's a groan in the floor above as the water rushes toward the master bathroom. Tripp is getting in the shower.

I watch as Mia reviews the plate I've set before her, my coffee cup filled to the brim for the second time. She peels two bananas and cuts them with a fork, creating two evenly spaced rows. It's an unusual habit, and every time I see her doing it, I can't help but think it's a bit obsessive. But I don't ever tell her this, don't want to hurt her feelings; it's just that I've never seen anyone prepare their bananas this way—so methodical and precise—and can only imagine it's a habit she picked up from her mother. *Before-me days*, as I call them.

She pierces each banana slice with the fork and chews with focused concentration. Somewhere in her world, her thoughts are already churning, and I try figuring out what's on her mind; I'm unable, these days, to read her. She's always thinking, not sharing much with me anymore. I know I should be getting used to this by now—awkward stepmother and fickle, moody stepdaughter coexisting in the same space and revolving around one another—but it never gets easier. Lately, the distance between us only seems to be getting wider. Sometimes I worry there's something she's not telling us.

I hand her a bowl of oatmeal next. She takes it with a small nod of her head, her spoon scooping at lumps of cinnamon and brown sugar.

I note the time: twenty minutes before we need to leave, and she's not in her swimsuit yet.

Mia's practices are primarily after school, about an hour and a half of laps and timed races before I head to Westminster and pick her up. Occasionally practice will run late and Coach will send a message offering to bring the kids home. If I have plans, I'll let Mia hitch a ride.

Coach has one of those Jeep wagons, dark forest green with a slew of racing stickers along the back window to tell everyone he coaches a star-studded team. He has been teaching at Westminster for so long he's become a fixture, one of the diehards, carving out a place for himself with a power team that, lately, has become unbeatable. Records smashed. Trophies and ribbons collected. Every weekend, another headline about our school sweeping the board, another opportunity for him to have his picture posted on the school's home page. To talk about the number of college swimming scholarships.

Is he hard on the kids? Of course. But what coach isn't? He enforces extra drills, weekend pool times. As if swimming's not enough, he's been known to make them hit the track and run.

His drive to win is what also drives Mia, the determination to please him and beat her own times. She'll stand on the block, sleek muscle and sinew like a champion greyhound, long legs and defined shoulders, her black swimsuit clinging tightly to her chest. When she's nervous, which isn't often, I'll catch her chewing the end of a goggle strap, gnashing the rubber between her teeth. Other times, she twists her swim cap between her fingers, doing a slight hop and jump in place to keep her muscles loose.

But when Coach speaks to her, there's no denying it: her eyes light up, her confidence is restored; it's the only pep talk she'll ever need.

How many times have I watched Coach corral the kids after meets, his arms outstretched to loop them in a huddle, his words directed at every one of them?

"You've got to pull through that water," he tells them. "You've got this. You all do."

But for all the whistle-blowing and shouts, he also knows when to stop. In between Saturday meets, he'll give the kids a rest day. One day a week, he'll instruct them to work out on their own. That's when Mia hits our backyard pool, sometimes coming home and swimming even when she's had practice at school. Her preference is not to take a break. She'll tell the coach the same.

Upstairs, the sound of rushing water stops, the shower turns off, and I hear the padding of footsteps as Tripp crosses the master bedroom. Our house is beautiful, Southern antebellum style, but with the grandeur also comes aging infrastructure. Pipes creak and rumble when the central heating cranks on. An odd tick commences in the wall when the dishwasher runs, and a shingle on the attic will sometimes rattle at the slightest gust of wind. But it's gorgeous: antique glass doorknobs clear and smooth to the touch. A staircase carved by hand. Pedestal sinks, and a sweeping front porch made with refurbished wood from a long-ago barn. On the patio, Tripp has left part of the original brick wall exposed.

Inside, I've put a lot of work into this house too, reshaping it to become my own. It's taken several years and a lot of changes that weren't always easy, but at least it feels like my space now. I can breathe.

I watch as Mia rests her head on one hand. She's sleepy, her eyes barely open, but at least she's finished her breakfast. She's powered through. I take her bowl to the sink and fill it with water, adding coffee to thermoses next. After a few seconds, I'm aware of her watching me, her eyes carefully tracking my movements as I pass behind the kitchen counter. It's a steady gaze, the tip of her chin now cupped in the palm of her hand, the sleepiness from before drifting from her face.

"I wish my mom could see me swim," she says.

"I know you do, honey."

"She'd want to watch me."

"Of course she would."

She drops her arm. "She wouldn't complain like you do." Her face goes perfectly still.

But mine flushes red, a heat that spreads quickly down my neck.

She overheard me talking to Janie.

I can barely meet her eyes. The deeply wounded look. Her bitter disappointment at my betrayal. Her mother would never have said something like that—she'd never have thought it. We both know that's true.

I should have talked to her that day. I should have gone after her.

The heat locks inside my throat. "Mia, I'm so sorry. I didn't mean …"

But she doesn't want to hear me. She doesn't care. She slides off the stool and leaves me staring after her.

CHAPTER THIRTY-TWO

Vanessa

The Saturday Before

The drive to Florence, Alabama, will take nearly two hours. My eyes wander to Tripp's face as he drives.

His looks are straight from a magazine: chiseled jaw and gray-blue eyes. His hair is still wet from the shower; only a handful of white strands blend into the darker blonde hair along his forehead, and I'm tempted to touch him there, to reach out and stroke the skin just above his temple, letting my fingers feel the warmth of his face. But I hold my hand back, fearing he'll sense something is bothering me.

In the backseat, Mia remains silent. My remorse still smolders in my cheeks. The pain from her words hangs heavy between us, and Tripp doesn't have a clue.

She wouldn't complain like you do.

I must get her alone later. I must apologize.

Tripp glances in the rearview mirror. "Mia, you're quiet. You nervous about today?"

She doesn't answer, only stretches her legs, one of her knees jabbing the back of my seat.

"Mia?" Tripp tries again. A downturn in his eyes. He glances at me next. "You're quiet too, Vanessa."

Luckily, Mia changes the subject. "What do they grow out here?" she asks.

"Cotton," Tripp says, looking out the window. "Soybeans too."

Heading west, we're passing fields and dirt roads, the occasional warehouse and farm, as this section of northern Alabama transitions from red-tinted earth and the hills of Monte Sano to acres of flat grass, barns, and tractors.

He points to one of the roads. "There's a huge fishing pond back there. My uncle Tate used to bring us on Sundays—it has catfish as big as Cadillacs. Eyeballs the size of your head."

"No way," Mia says with a playfulness that uplifts her dad.

"Yes way," he says back.

"What do you think, Vanessa?" she asks me.

My head jerks, my coffee splashing against my mouth, and I wipe awkwardly with both hands, hoping nothing has spilled to my sweater.

"Do you really think there's fish that big?"

"Maybe as big as whales," I answer.

This pleases them both. Tripp smiles. Mia manages a laugh. I gaze out the window, hoping this is her way of saying she's forgiven me.

As soon as we arrive, we strip down from our sweatshirts from the car ride to minimal layers, long sleeves pushed up to our elbows, the humidity hitting us in the face as we step inside. A day in here is the equivalent of an afternoon in a sauna, as we fight the effects of feeling as if we're soaking in a lukewarm bath. What keeps us alert is the constant whistle-blowing and the forty-second bursts down the swim lane.

Tripp immediately moves ahead to find Coach Jacobs. He wants to confirm Mia's heats; she's signed up for four and he fears that may be too many. She might be too tired to give it her best shot. Her winning stroke, the breaststroke, won't be at its prime if she's fatigued.

I'm left alone with our thirteen-year-old elite swimmer. It's only for a moment, but for Mia, the moment lasts long enough. I hand her the bag and she snatches it from me.

"Thanks," she says, but I don't think she means it.

What in the heck just happened? I thought we were okay—that moment in the car. But I should have known she was covering up for her dad's benefit.

"Mia, I'm sorry …" I try again.

She stomps away.

"Good luck!" I call after her, a feeble attempt. She keeps walking.

I look around to see if anyone has noticed, but of course, no one has. They're too busy corralling their own kids toward the bleachers, shouting for everyone to jump in the warm-up pool. And if they do notice, the moment was so quick anyway. The body language possibly interpreted in so many ways. They'll think I'm overreacting. She's just a typical teenager who wants to grab her stuff and be on her way. She's focused on the swim meet.

She runs off to find her teammates and joins them in a group stretch, an enormous smile plastered on her face. For their benefit too, I'm sure.

I spot my husband at the other end of the pool. He's got Coach's attention, both men pointing at Mia before Jacobs is nodding, a black T-shirt tight against his arms, biceps protruding, muscles from hours spent swimming and lifting weights. He's at least four inches taller than Tripp, but my husband makes up for it with the attention he commands, the way he's standing with his chin tilted up, a smile on his face to keep Coach engaged. It's a trick he's picked up from persuading countless jurors in the courtroom. His swagger makes him appear more than six feet tall. The coach is nodding and glancing at his clipboard.

Before long, Tripp returns to the bleachers, waving to other families from school before gliding in beside me. He holds my hand, the excitement of watching Mia rippling through him. "Coach thinks it's up to Mia. She can decide."

I nod at my stepdaughter, who is now moving toward the starting block. I know exactly what she's going to do. Mia is stronger than anyone I know. She's capable of achieving just about anything. Her forgiveness for me will come soon enough, I tell myself. It just has to.

At the end of the day, with Mia winning her fourth and final heat—she didn't drop a single one—we gather our bags and unfold our bodies from the bleachers. My back hurts, my ass numb from the hours spent sitting on hard metal. The day has lasted nearly five hours.

Naturally, Tripp is ecstatic. He scoops his hand against my lower back and pushes us along through the crowd. We're rushing toward Mia, who is already beaming. She knows how much she's kicked ass. She's slaughtered the competition, beating three of her personal best times, one of her most solid performances of the year.

"You did great!" Tripp says, wrapping her in his arms.

Her hair is wet, and there's a red mark across her forehead from the tight band of her swim cap. She's rinsed the chlorine from her body and stepped into leggings and a shirt, but everything about her says *champion swimmer*: the incredible glow, the confident way she holds her head high.

"Thanks," she says, trying to act as if it's no big deal. Another day in the park. But we know better.

I must admit, standing there watching her surrounded by teammates, accepting the cheers and congratulations, Mia is impressive. There's no denying that. The hours of practice are certainly paying off—maybe she really will reach the Olympics, like people say. Certainly she'll receive scholarship offers. Hundreds more ribbons and personal records are waiting for us over the next decade.

Years more of sitting in this humid air and waiting for spurts of frenetic swimming activity. And I know it will be spectacular. In this moment, my heart bursts with pride.

Coach Jacobs pushes toward her, lifting her in a spin, her feet dangling. "Fantastic!" he says, carefully lowering her again before clamping his arm around Tripp.

I know Jacobs has a roster of other strong swimmers, a list of students he also trains, but on this day, at this moment, Mia is the star. I can see it in his eyes. He's imagining the bright future ahead.

She returns his grin with a smile. "That girl from Bishop was tough, but I got her."

"She didn't stand a chance," Coach says, pulling her close.

Several of the parents gather around to congratulate her. They shake Tripp's hand too.

"Let's not stop the momentum," Coach tells the group. "We've got another big meet next weekend, and I want to see you in practice Monday and Tuesday. On Wednesday, you're on your own. Lift weights, do a light workout." He looks directly at Mia with another rush of pride. "Mia, go ahead and hit your home pool for a few laps that day." He winks. "Let's say we shatter some more times."

CHAPTER THIRTY-THREE

Julia

The Saturday Before

I have three clients scheduled today, seniors from Westminster, all boys, two of whom will want to be photographed in their football jerseys. The other won't care in the slightest. He'll wear whatever his mother has already picked out.

When I schedule back-to-back photo shoots like today, I'll call the Tanners and ask for the extra parking space in front of their garage. Weekend photo shoots are usually no problem since the family will be at another swim meet. And this morning, right on schedule, their car left bright and early.

"I don't like leaving you alone," Thomas says at breakfast. He's folding the newspaper. My husband is one of the last remaining people I know who maintains a print newspaper subscription instead of checking headlines on his phone. He is flipping through the pages in between bites of eggs on toast, a lump of butter dribbling from the edge of his bread. The man I married had a super-fast metabolism, but not anymore. I wish he'd be more careful.

"What's that?" I ask, reaching for my glass of orange juice. I've heard him, but not heard him. It's a thing I've been doing lately: daydreaming and hardly paying attention when Thomas speaks. I'm always hoping he doesn't notice.

"You have those boys coming today. I don't like it. No one will be here," he says. My eyebrows arch. "I looked at your calendar. You left it on the counter."

Oh. My head swings to my leather-bound planner, an open page showing today's appointments.

"It's fine," I tell him.

"I don't like it," he repeats. "I won't be here. I've got those sessions with the Rotary Club, and the kids are at basketball camp until tonight."

"I've done it before."

"That doesn't change things. You'll still be alone."

"My mom is here."

"That doesn't count." He finishes the last of his toast. "What if something were to happen? What if one of the boys gets frisky?"

"*Frisky?*"

"Teenage boys. Alone in a house with a beautiful grown woman."

"Grown woman?" I snort. "Is that your polite way of saying I'm old?"

He smiles, but I haven't dissuaded him. "Julia, there's an allure to those things. Seventeen-year-old boy with a forty-year-old woman."

"How very *The Graduate* of you."

He frowns. "I'm being serious."

"I hear you," I say. "But I can also assure you there is nothing tempting or seductive about having your senior photos taken. Not a single boy I know has ever wanted to jump my bones. They only want to get out of here having fulfilled their promise to Mom that they'll come away with at least one decent shot."

"Okay, but what if one of them is violent?"

"Seriously?"

"You never know. You're in the house alone. It would be your word against theirs, since your mother's mostly asleep. If things got out of control, no one would be here to help."

"Thomas …" But I stop, seeing the look on his face. "I'll be fine," I assure him. "I've known most of these kids since elementary school. They're harmless."

But he has already put in some thought. "What do you think about installing a video security system?"

"You're kidding."

"No, Julia, I'm not." He sets aside his newspaper, his hands folding on top of one another, the way I picture him talking to employees from behind his desk at work. "It wouldn't be expensive."

"How's a camera going to help?"

"It'll document who comes and goes. We'll have timestamps of clients arriving and leaving, what happens when they come into the house. Just in case we need to know—in case we need evidence that something took place."

"Nothing is going to take place." I sit back and cross my arms. Thomas does the same. "This is a little excessive."

"No, it's not. You're gaining a bigger clientele, Julia. Inviting these people into our home at all hours of the day—don't you want to be safe?"

"Yes, but …"

"But what?"

"I'm not sure if it's ethical," I point out. "Many of my clients are underage, and I don't think you can have video rolling during their shoots, since they're also changing outfits—especially the girls."

This gets Thomas's attention. The sides of his cheeks twitch, eyes unblinking. The idea that anyone might accuse us of videotaping their children—their *daughters*—in a state of undress would be catastrophic. The very mention of a video camera at the studio could cause a dozen or more Westminster moms to freak out. I could lose clients. They would think Thomas a creep.

He falls silent and stares at his plate. The idea of a video system has run into its first roadblock. He doesn't say another word.

I look away too. It's not that I don't think the cameras are unnecessary—there's been a time or two when a member of someone's entourage, a nosy grandma or an obnoxious kid, has disappeared into other rooms of our house. They'll claim they were looking for something, or that they got lost, and I'm left wondering what they were really up to: whether they were going through my things, snooping around and opening drawers, stealing.

But there's another reason I don't want cameras installed right now, and it's something I can't tell Thomas.

CHAPTER THIRTY-FOUR

Vanessa

The Day Of: Wednesday, 7 a.m.

It's Wednesday morning, and there's the usual dash to get ready for school and work.

I'm brewing an extra pot of coffee after coming home late last night. The packet stuffing for the fundraiser took longer than expected, but we had to get through it and out of Janie's hair. She needed to pack for her flight to Orlando.

I fill my coffee mug to the brim.

Mia is in a foul mood and I don't understand why. The night we returned from the swim meet, we sat down together and had a chance to talk. I apologized for what I'd said, and told her that I never meant to hurt her, that I love watching her compete. I want to attend every swim meet. She stared at me for a long time before eventually looking away and mumbling that she understood. I really hope she does.

She is forcing herself to eat her oatmeal this morning—the one with very little sugar and loaded with flaxseed. I try making eye contact with her, but she stares ahead. Something else is getting at her. Her body is locked tight, a dark storm cloud brewing over her head.

She sits and chews.

Tripp races into the kitchen. He's flustered and searching frantically for God knows what. Strangely enough, Mia doesn't greet him, just leans over her oatmeal, her messy hair falling across her face.

Tripp tosses magazines and envelopes on the counter. He opens drawers, slams them shut. With one hand he fights his tie while the other hand digs in cabinets, coming up empty. Glancing at his watch, he mumbles something I don't understand and hustles to the next room.

"Everything okay?" I call.

I hear him circling the dining table. Another mad dash to the living area. I follow him with coffee mug in hand.

"What's going on? Have you lost something?"

He doesn't answer.

"If you tell me, I can help you look."

"It's nothing," he says, but doesn't look up.

But I can tell it's not nothing. He's checking behind furniture, pulling one of the side tables from the wall.

"Tripp," I say again, impatiently. "Tell me what it is so I can help you."

But he only shakes his head. "Something for work." And with a quick turn on his heel, he's pivoting toward Mia. "Mia, sweetie. Almost finished?"

She takes one more mouthful of her oatmeal before her spoon drops to the granite counter with a clatter. "Ready," she says. Her eyes lift as her dad approaches. "What are you looking for?"

"It's nothing, honey. Don't worry. It'll show up."

He opens one more drawer at the corner desk, a small planning area where we keep the house phone, but whatever he's looking for isn't there either.

"It's no big deal," he assures us, reaching for his briefcase while ushering Mia toward the garage. She pulls her backpack from the hook without so much as turning to say goodbye to me—neither of them does. This whole day has started off on the wrong foot.

The door shuts and I hear Tripp's Mercedes revving to life. I count the beats until it is backing out the drive and passing below the kitchen window, where a row of trimmed hedges leads toward the street. Just like that, they're gone.

I dump the rest of my coffee down the sink.

I have a facial at nine, followed by hair color and blowout, then it's back to the house to change for a group meeting downtown, a formal request with another donor. I want to look especially nice, and wear a suit I've only taken out once before.

I love these kinds of mornings, when I'm pampered at the salon, skin glowing, my hair never looking better. Philippe styles it into a gorgeous shoulder-length bob with just enough lift at the roots, the rest of it curled under with a brush. It's something I know I should do more often, and this week, I've decided to treat myself.

I'll knock them dead at the luncheon looking like this, I think. My former executive days coming back into practice, my confidence in my ability to assert our position and obtain funds restored. Slam dunk. It's days like this, with a goal in mind, that I miss working. I miss being in the office and accomplishing tasks. That power of authority.

At lunch, when the donor signs her name on the commitment form, I've never been happier. I feel important, necessary. Janie gives me a hug and winks. "You've still got it," she says excitedly.

I feel good—like a million bucks, the way I used to. But that all changes when I go to pick Mia up from school.

CHAPTER THIRTY-FIVE

Vanessa

Wednesday, 3 p.m.

I sit patiently, each car in line sputtering exhaust into the street as we wait for the kids to emerge with laughter and test papers to show. But as Mia approaches, there's a slight drag in her step, like someone's stolen her lunch money and kicked her puppy too. She tries to hide it by smiling, a forced wave to her friends, but I can see right through it. Something's off and she looks exhausted. In the excitement of this afternoon, I'd forgotten about the bad morning.

She spots me, and the smile for her teachers and friends stops short and hardens to a thin line. She gives me a cool gaze before opening the car door. No greeting. Ice cold.

"Nice suit," she says as we pull away from the curb.

So she's still pissed at me.

She faces the window and not another word is spoken by either of us for the rest of the drive. She works her jaw like she's chewing on leather.

As soon as I've parked, she flings open the door and stomps her way to the house. Halfway there she bursts into a run, ready to be away from me. I notice she's left her backpack, and I move to the other side of the car, knowing I'll have to drag it in. It's heavy, with a laptop, textbooks, and snacks she's stockpiled from the pantry, her metabolism in constant overdrive. It falls with a thud at my feet and I shift my weight in my heels.

From the corner of my eye I spot Julia at the mailbox. She shoots me a sympathetic look and I give her a small wave, then lumber toward the house, following my stepdaughter.

CHAPTER THIRTY-SIX

Julia

Wednesday, 3:10 p.m.

I feel bad for Vanessa. People haven't been able to stop talking about her since that disastrous no-show at the mother–daughter tea. I don't have kids at the middle school and I still heard about it. There's not a mom at Westminster who hasn't retold the story and said terrible things behind her back, even when I tried telling them not to. I told them it was an honest mistake, but they still want to gossip.

I watch as Vanessa struggles after Mia into the house.

My cell phone buzzes in my pocket and I read the message.

I'm home now if you want to drop off our order.

The Kirklands have been asking for their framed portraits of their daughter Makayla, the albums and extra prints too. I have everything ready in my studio, have been meaning to go by their house every day this week but kept forgetting. They've already paid in full.

They live on the other side of town and it will take me at least an hour, round trip.

I glance upstairs to the landing, the sunroom where my mom will be sitting in her favorite chair, more than likely snoozing. I head inside and up the stairs, and there she is, her eyes starting to flutter. She's about to fall asleep; I've arrived just in time. I'll be able to get her up and bring her downstairs.

"Julia?" she says, her watery eyes blinking.

"Yes, it's me, Mom."

I hate the idea of putting her in the car. It's troublesome getting her in and out of the house these days, especially when she fights the seat belt. I look at the time—I can't keep the Kirklands waiting another day. I've already texted them back and said I'm on my way.

"We're going next door," I announce, gently guiding Mom down the steps. "Just for a little while. You can stay there and rest."

She doesn't protest, just does what she's told, too sleepy to insist on staying home.

After I wrap her shoulders in a shawl, we head next door to Vanessa's. Surely she won't mind. I'll only be gone an hour, tops. I'll be back before she knows it.

CHAPTER THIRTY-SEVEN

Vanessa

Wednesday, 3:15 p.m.

In the kitchen, Mia is digging through the pantry. I've already put her backpack away and kicked off my shoes. The slamming of cabinet doors continues behind me.

"There's nothing to eat," she says.

"There's plenty."

"Where's all the good stuff?"

"I haven't been to the store yet. We could go now if you want to, honey?" I try placating her.

"I'm starving now," she complains.

"No you're not." I toss a couple of granola bars to the counter. They're fruit and nut—not bad, actually; I usually keep one in my purse—but she sticks out her tongue.

"That's it?" she asks.

"That's it, unless we go out."

"I don't want to."

I pour her a cup of juice from the V8 bottle Tripp keeps in the fridge. She slams each granola bar into her mouth—she really is that hungry—and tosses the wrappers in the trash, then drops from the stool. I can see her mind racing, the little black storm cloud still churning above her head.

"Mia, what's going on?" I try to open a conversation, but she ignores me.

"I'm heading to the pool," she says. "Coach wants me to practice." And she hurries away.

Fine. I focus on the fridge instead, considering what to make for dinner. As I rummage around for anything I can defrost, I hear a knock on the front door. I pause. It comes again.

Throwing open the door, I find Julia on my doorstep. She's not alone. She's brought her mother.

"Vanessa, hi. I have to run across town, about a half-hour there and back, nothing more." She holds Charlotte's arm protectively while the woman's eyes droop. "She was falling asleep so I'm sure she'll nap the entire time I'm gone. Is it all right?" She looks up the stairs wistfully. "I'll be as quick as I can."

Part of me wants to say no—Mia is already in a piss-ass mood, and I was hoping for some peace and quiet—but I have a soft spot for Charlotte. And Julia is right: the few times I've cared for Charlotte, she's slept most of the time anyway. She'll nap while Mia does swim practice.

"Of course," I say.

Julia has no sooner helped me settle Charlotte into the guest room than she's racing out the door. "An hour tops," she says. Her eyes meet mine. "Thank you, Vanessa."

I don't say anything in return. I'm too busy looking at Charlotte, who's sitting in the chair I've positioned in front of the window. Within seconds, her eyelids have grown heavy, with sleep sure to come.

With Julia gone, I return to the kitchen in time to hear my phone ring. It's Janie. She's at the airport, having driven there immediately after our lunch meeting for her flight to Orlando.

"What do you think we got today?" she asks excitedly. "Ten? Fifteen thousand?"

"As the presenting sponsor of the new art exhibit, I'm hoping for twenty."

"That would be amazing." I can tell she's calculating the numbers in her head. "You did wonderful, by the way. Haven't seen you that energized in a while."

"It felt good," I admit. "And I was in a great mood until I came home."

"Why? What happened?"

"Mia," I say, sighing. I lower my voice so she can't hear—I don't want a repeat of what happened last time. "She's mad about something. It's me or something at school, or both, I can't tell anymore."

"Why would she be mad at you?"

"She heard me talking to you on the phone. When I said I was getting sick of all the swim meets."

"Are you sure she heard?"

"Oh, she brought it up." I wince at the thought. "She told me her mother would never have complained."

"She'll be okay, Vanessa."

"It wasn't good. I felt terrible."

"Lots of parents get tired of driving their kids around."

"But I shouldn't have said it out loud. She looked so hurt. So angry. And then there was the tea."

"You didn't mean to miss that."

"I still feel awful."

"It was an accident."

I rub my hand against my temple. "I keep screwing up. I'm doing all these things her mother wouldn't have done."

"You've done well, Vanessa. You really have. You've got to stop being so hard on yourself."

"Tripp is talking about me working part-time so I can still be with Mia, but what's the point? She doesn't need me as much anymore. I know she doesn't. She doesn't act like she wants me around either. She's different these days, I can feel it."

"She's a teenager. We were like this when we were her age."

"The older she gets, the more she misses her mom. The more she realizes I'm not anything like Susannah. Not even close."

"You're trying your best."

I press my back hard against the counter. Another glance out the kitchen door to make sure Mia isn't around. "Something I don't understand," I say, "is if she doesn't want me around, then why did she get upset about me not wanting to be at her swim meets?"

"It hurt her feelings," Janie says. "She wants the world to revolve around her. It's not like Tripp hasn't designed it to be that way either."

I sigh again.

"She'll come around," Janie tells me. "Give her some time. You'll go back to work and she'll be okay. Tripp too."

"I hope so."

"And if it's part-time in the beginning, so be it. Maybe a consulting job where you can call your own hours."

I lift my eyes. "That could work. It could get me back in the swing of things."

"That's the spirit."

"And if I do well, I could start squeezing in extra time. Mia will become more independent, and Tripp will learn to relax too."

"Exactly." Janie gives a small laugh. "Although who's going to be my lead fundraiser?"

"I can still help with that, don't worry."

"I'm only joking. You've been amazing. I don't know many people who can take someone to lunch with a chance they'll cough up twenty K. But hey, that's why they used to pay you the big bucks. You'll do great with your new job. I'll find someone else to fundraise."

"One step at a time," I tell her.

Somewhere in the house I hear a door open and close. Mia?

I lean out the kitchen. The patio door remains closed. She hasn't gone for her swim yet.

At the same time, the sound of an airport announcement rises sharply in the background. "Gotta go," Janie says. "Time to board. I'll check back with you tomorrow. And remember," she adds. "Fight for what you want."

CHAPTER THIRTY-EIGHT

Vanessa

Wednesday, 3:26 p.m.

I hang up, still needing to settle on what to make for dinner. I take out a jar of tomato sauce, then a bottle of olive oil, and pluck basil from a small pot on the window ledge. I could make a lasagna, maybe. It's one of Mia's favorites.

I'm digging around in the freezer when I feel someone behind me. It's Mia. She's panting, her hands clenched in fists at her sides, hopelessly out of breath. But she's never out of breath. That girl could outrun me and everyone else in this neighborhood and barely feel her pulse rise. She's still in her school clothes. She hasn't been in the pool yet.

"Get out of that suit," she says.

"What?"

"You heard me. That suit. Get out of it. I don't want to see you wearing it anymore."

"Mia—"

"I'm serious! I don't want you wearing that thing."

I stare long and hard. She stares right back.

"Mia …" I try again, steadying to keep my voice calm.

"*Take it off!*" She moves forward, her eyes flaring.

What is going on with her?

"Mia, you can't talk to me like this. It's only a suit."

"No it's not! It's the one we bought for you to wear *at the tea*." I swallow. "That stupid thing where you're supposed to bring your mom, but I don't have my mom anymore. I have you. But you can never be like her. Never. Not in a million years. And then you don't even show up. You leave me standing there all by myself."

She takes another step. The only thing between us is the kitchen island. "Everyone was looking at me, feeling *sorry* for me. I hate when they do that. I hate when they look at me and say, oh, poor Mia. Her mom died, and her dad is sad, and her stepmom blew it and missed the whole thing."

Her words sting, but I must maintain the upper hand. "Mia, I've apologized. I'm really sorry I missed it, but you're out of line. And if you don't stop right now, I'll—"

"Shut up!" she screams.

This startles me. Mia and I have had our arguments—we've certainly said angry things to each other—but we've never screamed. These days she prefers to keep things low and quiet. Everything controlled. Her teenage frustration coming out moody and calculating.

But never screaming. Not until today.

She slams her hands on the counter. "You're nothing like my mom, you'll never replace her."

A flare goes off inside my chest.

I have every right to march around that counter and tell her to go upstairs, to stay up in her room until dinner, that I'll be telling her dad about her behavior as soon as he gets home. We've been keeping other things under wraps, Mia and I, trying to smooth things over to avoid Tripp getting upset. But this has gone too far.

"Mia, that is *enough*. You're grounded."

But she doesn't let up. "Dad might have married you, but you'll never replace Mom. He loves Mom the best. She's the only one that matters."

I'm stunned. The fury that's pouring out of her. I take a deep breath and slow down. I have to reason with her. I must remind myself she doesn't mean these things. She's only a kid, incapable of working through her own emotions and calming herself.

"Your mom means a lot to both of you, Mia, but your behavior is out of control. You need to stop right—"

"You know he's kept all their wedding pictures," she says. "Her dress, even her shoes. I wear it sometimes. I put on the veil and stand in front of the mirror and I look just like her. I know he misses her. He says it's the only wedding that ever mattered."

What?

"He keeps everything in the closet. The one that's kept locked. You thought he moved it all to the attic, but he didn't. Her dress. Her jewelry. I get to wear it."

I think about the closet in Tripp's study down the hall. Mia's right; it's locked, but then again, he keeps a lot of drawers locked in that room. I always assumed it held important documents from the firm.

But keeping Susannah's wedding dress there? And then Mia going in to play dress-up?

I take a step as if meaning to head down the hall. I want to see this for myself.

She pounces against the counter. "Don't you dare touch it!"

"It's just a dress."

Those few words send her into a rage. She races to my side of the counter and grabs my arm. I step back, startled. I've never seen her like this before. It's the first time she's laid a hand on me. She's staring into my eyes and digging her fingers into my skin.

I wrench away. "Mia, what has gotten into you?"

"I said, get out of that suit!"

"Let's sit down and talk."

"*Do it now.*"

"Calm down, Mia."

She looks at the counter, picks up the jar of tomato sauce. Before I have time to think, she unscrews the cap and flings it at me. Red sauce, small chunks of bell pepper, spices, and celery splatter across my legs and chest before the jar smashes against the floor, glass falling in shards. I stand motionless—shocked—the sauce coating my arms and dripping down the front of my once pristine suit. The rest of it smears down my legs.

I'm so astounded I can barely move. But thankfully it appears Mia is done. No more throwing. She is panting and heaving and waiting to see how I'll react.

I can smell the sauce across my chest, more of it pooling at my knees.

This fight is done—it has to be. She's gone way overboard. I should have understood that she's still angry about the tea; I should have apologized more. I shouldn't have worn the suit, triggering this reaction, but I could have never imagined her exploding like this.

I have to tell Tripp. How are we going to handle this? Sitting her down, asking her what else is bothering her? Do we bring her to see another counselor? Maybe she'll unload to someone else, and they'll tell us what is going on.

She needs help. Her grief for her mother has become too painful.

I step carefully from the shattered glass and tiptoe away from the mess.

"Hit the pool," I tell her, forcing my voice to stay even. "We will absolutely talk about this when your dad gets home."

I leave and head upstairs. I'm too rattled to deal with her right now. The longer I stay in the kitchen, the worse the fight is going to be. We need to separate. I'll go upstairs and get my thoughts together, clean myself up. She can stay down here and cool off—and calm the hell down. Maybe she'll stop and look around the room, realizing what she's done.

I thought tonight was going to be peaceful. We'd have dinner, talk about our day. I'd share with Tripp about the twenty-thousand-dollar gift we're hoping to get from the sponsor. He'd be proud of me. Mia would finish her dinner and head upstairs. Tripp and I could watch a show on Netflix.

But that's not going to happen—none of it. We'll spend hours talking to Mia, prodding her with questions. She might budge. She might fess up. She might cry her eyes out but not give up too many details. We'll be stumped and she'll sulk upstairs in her room. It's going to be painful.

First I'll take a shower and give myself a chance to calm down too, cleaning the stains from my skin. I'll check on Charlotte. I'll clear up the kitchen. And hopefully Mia will be in the pool, letting off more steam and taking it out on her freestyle.

At the top of the stairs, I stop, remembering what she said, her words slicing right through me.

Her dad saying his first wedding was the only one that mattered. That he would always love her mother the most.

And the dress.

Why didn't I know about this? Why didn't I know he kept it so close?

CHAPTER THIRTY-NINE

Vanessa

Wednesday, 3:52 p.m.

I turn on the shower, the steam slowly rising and fogging up the mirrors as I strip off my clothes, placing the suit into one of the sinks and filling it with cold water, my feeble attempt at getting the stains out. As I step into the shower, the water turns red, the sauce billowing down the drain in bloody curls.

The hot water pours down my back. Reaching for my arm, I wince where Mia grabbed me, her small fingers pressing into my flesh. I can't see a mark, but I know one is coming.

I rub my face and neck with a washcloth. Closing my eyes against the heat, I bite my lip to keep from crying, the intensity of the last fifteen minutes finally catching up to me. I feel winded. I've never seen Mia lose it like that, never witnessed the emotional scales of her young brain tipping out of balance.

What would have happened if I'd lost my cool too? If in some alternate universe I'd started throwing things back instead of walking away? Would we have ended up in an all-out war? Plates and cups smashing, cast-iron pans hurling, knives drawn from the block. *My God.*

I rinse the shampoo from my hair, my heart heavy. Tripp is going to have a tough time dealing with this. He won't want to believe it, his beautiful, perfect daughter going off in a way we've never seen before.

I'm already thinking of a date and time we can bring her to the therapist.

I swipe my hand against the steamed-up glass and peek across the room, eyeing the bathroom door.

Will she be coming in here any minute? After some time brewing downstairs, will she come up here, knocking gently and crying and asking for forgiveness? Will she let up and confess what's chewing her up inside?

Or maybe she's cleaning up the kitchen. That will be her way of apologizing. She won't want her dad coming home from work and seeing what she's done. He'll have to imagine the broken glass and my footsteps streaking through the sauce.

Or she's outside swimming. She's hit the pool, her demons bursting out of her so she can clear her head.

I squeeze my eyes shut and let the hot water stream down my face.

CHAPTER FORTY

Vanessa

Wednesday, 4:10 p.m.

I move slowly down the stairs. There's no sign of Mia, which means she must be in the pool. That's good; extra laps should do the trick to get her to relax again.

I've changed into a gray pullover, my hair pulled back wet, and I tread slowly into the kitchen to see what's left behind. She hasn't touched it. She hasn't tried cleaning a thing, leaving a giant mess for me to take care of.

It looks worse under the lights: tomato sauce splattered against the floor like blood, shiny bits of broken glass on the tile. It's like a damn crime scene.

I immediately get to work wiping the surfaces, scrubbing in a frenzy, trying to erase what Mia has done. One by one I wrap larger pieces of glass in paper and tie them in plastic bags, tossing the bags and wads of paper towels into the garbage can out in the garage. I take another sponge and wipe down the counter one more time.

What will happen when Mia comes back inside from swim practice? Will we talk to each other? Or will we avoid eye contact until her dad comes home? What's the appropriate length of time to ground a child who's thrown jars of food at you?

I squeeze the sponge hard, the water pouring into the sink.

I stop cleaning, my anger hardening. Enough is enough. Today she went too far. We're going to have to lay down some new ground rules.

I'm tempted to go out the back door and drag her from the pool. I should sit her down and explain the new restrictions. She'll have to listen—I won't give her a choice. I'll explain to her she cannot talk to me like that and get away with it. She'll lose privileges. I know she's going through a lot, but she cannot react that way, and so violently.

Above all, she can never grab me like that again.

PART FOUR

Mia

CHAPTER FORTY-ONE

Mia Tanner

The Night Before

I miss my mom. And I wish I didn't have a stepmother. It's that simple. My dad married her and I remember thinking it was far too quick—it's what my aunt Carol told me anyhow. It's what everyone said when Dad wasn't around. He was acting impulsively. He should take more time. And it made me mad knowing he thought Vanessa could replace Mom so quickly. She hadn't been gone that long as far as I was concerned.

Dad thinks having someone like Vanessa around will mean things will go back to the way they used to be—but they won't. Nothing's the same. And Vanessa will never be like Mom, either. She doesn't compare. Having her here reminds me every day of what I've lost.

In the beginning, I put on a brave face, at least for my dad's sake. I knew he was heartbroken and lonely—but hello, I'm here, aren't I? Aren't I enough? Why move this new person in and expect the heartache to go away?

I tried to like her. I was only seven when they first started dating, and Dad seemed happy. I thought maybe there was a chance I could grow to love her too. That it would be nice having another woman around. But that soon changed. She just didn't know how to do things right. She always looked like she was struggling. Second-guessing. Like she was trying too hard.

So I pretended I liked having her around. I'd follow her. Let her braid my hair. I told her I liked her cooking. We played board games while I watched the clock, counting down the hours until my dad would come home.

Lately, everything about Vanessa has started getting on my nerves. She's never been a mom before and she sucks at it—I know that sounds mean, but it's true. It doesn't come naturally the way I've seen other moms do it, the way my mom was. She knows she struggles but she tries to laugh it off anyway.

Funny how she doesn't laugh that much anymore.

She takes up a lot of room in our house too. Always getting in the way, never looking like she knows where she needs to be. At first, I used to hope she and Dad would have a kid together, a little brother or sister for me to play with and show the ropes. Maybe they'd be a little swimmer like me. But then Dad told me they're not having kids. That I'm the only one that matters and they're focusing all their energy and love on me. And that made me so happy.

But Vanessa has really hurt me. She's been messing up and I can't stand having her around anymore. I roll my eyes. I get pissy. I shut my door when I hear her coming up the stairs.

And can she blame me?

Missing out on the tea, leaving me standing there alone. Her absence making me realize all over again how I don't have my real mom.

What I heard her telling her friend Janie on the phone. Complaining about going to all my swim meets. How it gets so tiring.

Mom would never complain. She'd take me to every practice. She'd be at every swim event. If only she was still alive. She'd want to be with me everywhere.

I know Vanessa looked at my journal too—I couldn't believe she would go into my room and snoop. My private thoughts I didn't want her to see. These days I keep my journal nice and hidden where no one can find it. Not even my dad.

Everything inside me hurts. And lately I've been losing my cool. My anger so hot it feels like someone keeps torching my heart.

I miss my mom so much. The pain of seeing other kids with their mothers and knowing I haven't had my mom since I was a little kid. Birthdays and Christmases are becoming more difficult. I want her there with me instead of Vanessa. But I don't have her and it makes me so angry I want to scream. It's not fair.

Every time I see my dad holding hands with Vanessa, I want to look away. When they kiss, I want to run upstairs. Dad shouldn't be kissing anyone else but Mom. He shouldn't be doing any of that stuff adults do in the bedroom. He should feel sick to his stomach thinking about kissing someone else.

I've been taking it out on Vanessa, but I know I should really be upset with my dad.

After all, he's the one who's been manipulative. Lying to all of us. Hiding a secret. A secret that even Vanessa doesn't know.

But I know what he's been up to. What he's been doing behind our backs. And now everything is worse.

This evening, Vanessa has gone out to some volunteer activity, which made me hope Dad and I could have the night to ourselves. Watch a movie. Play a board game together, something we haven't done in a long time. But no. He tells me he's going out instead.

"Why? What for?" I ask him.

"I'm only going for a short jog. Just down the street."

Jogging? Dad doesn't jog. Racquetball maybe.

"Getting a little exercise," he says. He's wearing track pants.

I don't believe him, so I trail him. He heads down the street and into the alleyway. And now he's backtracking toward our house.

That's weird. Well, maybe it's a short run. He got tired and wants to come home.

But he doesn't go through our back gate. He stops and goes through someone else's.

The Campbells' house next door.

Okay, maybe he's confused. Or maybe he needs to see Mr. Campbell. Sometimes I hear them talking about money and investments, boring adult stuff. But I don't think Mr. Campbell is home. It doesn't look like his kids are either.

Quietly I creep up to the fence and press my face against the gate. Dad is knocking on their back door, and when Mrs. Campbell answers, she looks really happy to see him, like she's been waiting for him.

And then, it happens.

I see something gross. Something so nasty it makes me want to throw up right there on the spot. But I don't. Instead, I hold my breath and my heart breaks ten times over.

My dad is kissing *Julia Campbell.*

It's not just a friendly peck on the lips. It's the kind you see in the movies, all mouth and tongue and hands rubbing everywhere.

Before I can scream and tell them to stop, they're shutting the door. Dad is going inside the house with her. He's going to do that gross grown-up stuff while I stand out here alone.

My dad and Mrs. Campbell. *What?*

Doing this behind Vanessa's back.

Is this something he would have done to my mom too?

I want to scream. Leaning against the fence, I grip the wood until it hurts, until I'm almost positive I'm pushing splinters into my skin.

CHAPTER FORTY-TWO

Mia

The Night Before

The first thing I do when I go home is check on Mom's dress. It's still there. Dad keeps the key in his study, in the bottom drawer of his credenza. I've seen him take it out a hundred times before.

Mom's dress is still there, which means Dad should still love Mom. *Right?*

But he can't love my mom while doing that stuff with Mrs. Campbell. I mean, marrying Vanessa is one thing. He said he didn't want us to be lonely anymore, that someone needed to look after me. But screwing around with Mrs. Campbell? How does that help?

I touch my mom's dress and whisper goodnight to her. And then I lock the closet door.

That's when I see Dad's wedding ring. He's left it on his desk, taken it off before he went to see our neighbor, I bet. And I'm beginning to wonder if this isn't the first time Dad has done this. Maybe this thing with Mrs. Campbell has been going on for a while—he's been sneaking over whenever he can, telling us he's working late. I bet those racquetball practices are made up too.

I walk circles around the living room trying to calm myself down. I try not to ball my hands into fists. I need to stop thinking about what's going on next door—right at this very second while I'm standing here alone. And Vanessa, poor unknowing Vanessa, is across town with her friend Janie.

To punish him, I hide his wedding ring in my pocket. I'll keep it for a few days and freak him out. What will he tell Vanessa? Will she notice it's gone missing? Will he search every part of the house until he comes up empty?

Serves you right. I'll keep it hidden until I'm good and ready.

When I hear him coming back through the door, I'm still mad, but I don't want him to know I know about Mrs. Campbell—not yet. Instead, I yell at him for leaving me home by myself. I tell him I don't think he wants to spend time with me anymore.

"That's not true," he says.

"Yes it is."

"No it's not."

"Then how come you left?"

"It was only for a few minutes."

I look him over, despising the idea that some other woman has had her hands all over his chest.

Dad's eyes soften. "Mia, you know I love you, but you know I work a lot, and I admit, I need to do something about that. But sometimes I need to get out of the house and let off a little steam. Get some exercise. You understand that, don't you?"

Exercise. Is that what you call it?

"Then why didn't you come back sooner? Why aren't we hanging out?"

"We can hang out now."

"It's too late."

"Mia …"

I'm pouting and acting like a bratty child, but I don't care. "Dad, you're never here. You work all the time. You don't care about me and Mom anymore."

He looks surprised. "You and Mom? Of course I care about you guys." He steps toward me. "Mia, what's this about?"

I fold my arms. "Every day you forget more about Mom. She's disappearing and one day you're not going to remember her anymore."

"That's impossible. I'll never forget her. She was the love of my life, you know that. I don't go a day without thinking about her."

I fight the tears away, and my heart lifts. "Really? You really mean that?"

"Yes, really." He walks toward me, his arms outstretched in a hug. "I love you, Mia." He holds me close. "And I will always love your mom."

"Do you promise?" I whisper. I feel myself sink against his chest, loving this. Right now, it's just me and my dad, the way it should be. Talking about my mom, promising to always love her. Vanessa will never come close. Never mind what Dad was doing next door.

He pulls back. "Hey," he says. "You weren't spying on me, were you?"

I feel my cheeks grow hot. "No, why would I do that?"

His eyes narrow. My reddening face is a dead giveaway. "Mia, did you follow me on my run?"

"No, Dad."

"Are you sure?"

"I've been here this whole time."

He looks around. "This whole time?"

"Yes."

"Doing what?"

I shrug. "I dunno, just hanging around."

"Hanging around." He stares at me. "I don't believe you."

"What?"

He steps away. "I said I don't believe you."

"But Dad ..."

"You don't just sit around, Mia. You've never been able to." He narrows his eyes again. "Did you see me go out the door?"

"You told me you were going for a jog. I looked for something to eat in the kitchen and then came back to the couch and"—a burst of genius thought—"I finished my homework."

He makes a face. He knows when I'm lying.

His expression grows dark. "Don't do that again. Don't follow me. Do you understand?" When I don't answer, he slows down the words as if I'm dumb. "Do … you … understand?"

I count a full ten seconds before giving him the satisfaction of saying, "Yes."

"Good girl."

He turns away and I'm bursting up the stairs, tears stinging my eyes, locking the door behind me and throwing on my headphones. I turn up the volume as high as it will go.

Screw Dad.

A few minutes later, there's a knock on my door, followed by a couple more. I ignore them.

Then the first text message shows up: *I love you.*

And another: *I'm sorry you're upset with me.*

And another: *You know I still love you and your mom.*

I throw my phone to my bed, not answering any of his messages.

My phone lights up once more. This time it's a WhatsApp notification.

Looking forward to Saturday's meet! Go Westminster! Very excited for Mia and all of you amazing swimmers. You make us proud!

What the crap?

It's from Dad. He's posted a message to the entire chat group, my Westminster teammates and their parents.

Oh my God. Skin crawl.

Fine, Dad. If that's how you want to play. I pick up my phone.

I scroll down and choose Exit Group. I leave the Flippers group too. While I'm at it, I exit every chat group from school. Soon I'm gone from every one of them.

I wish I really could leave. I wish things were different.

I wish I had my mom back.

CHAPTER FORTY-THREE

Mia

The Day Of: Wednesday, 7 a.m.

Dad doesn't bother me again. I'm not sure if he knows about me leaving the chat groups, but if he does, he doesn't say anything. He doesn't ask about his text messages either, because in the morning, while I'm eating my breakfast, he is running circles in the kitchen. He's looking for something but doesn't want to sound the alarm.

"Everything okay?" Vanessa calls.

"It's nothing," he tells her.

But I know it's *not* nothing—and he does too. Vanessa would flip if she knows it's his wedding ring.

I pretend to ignore him while he's running around trying not to look panicked. Rushing to the living room next, lifting sofa cushions and peeking behind furniture.

Vanessa insists on helping him. She follows him, holding her coffee cup. "Tripp," she says. "Tell me what it is so I can help."

My ears prick up. Will he tell her? Will he come clean?

But he doesn't. I drop my spoon to the table. No more oatmeal for me. Dad is telling me to grab my things so we can head out the door.

At school I think about when I'm going to give him back his ring. Should I hold onto it for a few more days before telling him I don't like what he's doing with Mrs. Campbell? And I don't like how he saw right through my lie. I absolutely hated the way he told me to never follow him again.

How did he know? What did I do to give myself away? I thought I was better than that. I feel for the ring in my pocket—still there.

Take that, Dad.

It's a pretty boring day until the bell rings and I'm outside waiting for Vanessa. Like always, she's there to pick me up. Like always, she's at the front of the line not wanting to keep me waiting. But then I see what she's wearing, and I nearly lose my mind.

Seriously? *That* suit? The one she wore for the tea but never showed up?

I open the door, and, yes, there it is. Vanessa in all her white-suit glory. I can't believe it. I could have killed her that day, making me sit there all by myself like a complete loser, the other moms trying to hug me and tell me it was going to be all right. I had to do everything in my power not to cry in front of them, when deep down I was begging and screaming for my real mom.

She humiliated me.

And now she shows up today of all days wearing the suit. As if I wouldn't notice. As if I'll think it's okay. She shouldn't have worn it. Not when I'm already angrier than hell about Dad and Mrs. Campbell.

At home, it only gets worse. I see Mrs. Campbell standing in her driveway and I want to yank the wheel from Vanessa's hands and run her over. But I don't. Instead, I only glare at her. I guess she's prettier than Vanessa, but there's no way she's prettier than my mom.

I throw open the car door and fly across the yard, not caring about Vanessa as I leave her behind and run for the house. The faster I get inside, the better. If that awful neighbor talks to me, I might snap. Vanessa will want to know why I'm being so rude, and then all holy hell will break loose.

*

I'm in my room putting on my swimsuit when I hear Mrs. Campbell at the door. She's got her mother with her—that old lady who's always watching and staring but hardly ever speaks—and can you believe it? She wants to leave her here. She says she's got to run across town; can Charlotte stay and take a nap?

Unbelievable. You're screwing around with my dad and then you have the guts to show up at our door?

And of course, the always clueless Vanessa says yes. At my window, I watch Mrs. Campbell pack a bunch of stuff in her car, several boxes and picture frames. And I think: this is my chance. I can creep over. I can find a way to get back at her.

If there's anything being an athlete has taught me, it's about being lightning fast. And when I hear Vanessa on the phone, my plan becomes even more perfect. She'll never know I've gone.

In the garage, I grab two cans of spray paint left from a science project and sprint as fast as I can across the Campbells' front yard. The side door is unlocked, the one where Mrs. Campbell brings her clients, and I rush inside. Her studio is exactly how I remember: weird pieces of furniture, big lights, and a bunch of backdrops hanging from a rod. Dozens of senior photos hang on the wall, her own shrine to Westminster school.

I pop open a can and shake it.

At first the paint comes out in small spurts, but then I press my finger down steadily and it comes out nice and even, solid black. I make big looping swirls across her desk, criss-crossed lines over her computer, spraying the floors and walls next. No words, only zigzags and circles. Her couch, ruined. The rugs, an ugly pattern. Her wood floor, covered in black paint.

I spray until the first can runs empty and then I pop open the second lid. I go to town on the backdrops next—big up-and-down lines that look like the ones on those machines at the hospital, the kind you see in the movies when someone is about to die. Up and down goes the spray, my design mimicking heartbeats, and then a straight line.

EKG flatline. Sorry, folks, but Julia Campbell is dead.

And then I see it—delicate and silver, with a single charm. My mom's bracelet.

She received it the year before she died, a gift from the art museum for serving on the fundraising committee. I've seen it among the things Dad and Vanessa saved for me when I was young. Mom's jewelry and other treasures, carefully stored in a small wooden box on my dresser, waiting for me to wear when I grow up.

And now that bracelet is here.

I can't believe it. It hurts so much. The thought that Dad was in here last night, kissing the neighbor—and giving her Mom's bracelet to boot.

I scoop it up and press my fingers around it tight. This bracelet is mine, and I'm never going to give it back.

CHAPTER FORTY-FOUR

Mia

Wednesday, 3:26 p.m.

Back in the house, I find Vanessa standing in the kitchen still wearing the suit. Why hasn't she changed? She can't be comfortable. And I can't stand to look at her anymore.

"Get out of that suit," I tell her.

"What?"

"You heard me. That suit. Get out of it."

What happens next is out of control—even I have to admit that—the adrenaline running through my veins so fiercely after what I've just done to Mrs. Campbell's house. I'm on a roll. I tell Vanessa about my mom's wedding dress. I throw a jar of sauce at her. *Dad is going to kill me …*

To my amazement, she doesn't fight back. She takes it. She says we're going to sit down with my dad and talk about it later. And then she goes upstairs to take a shower.

I run to my dad's study, unlocking the closet, wanting to see Mom's dress. The sight of it always comforts me, pristine and beautiful and white. I touch my hands to her veil, running my fingers along the lace and watching the way it drapes to the floor. What's that fancy word they call it again, the stuff it's made of? Chantilly lace, that's right. Beautiful lace and a line of crystals along the edge.

I suddenly want to wear Mom's dress again—to feel her—so I step in and pull it over my swimsuit, the straps looping over my shoulders, a balloon of material at my waist. I try not to trip on the fabric as I locate her shoes on the closet floor and slip them on. They're still too big—one day I'll grow into them—but when I glimpse my reflection in the mirror, I look really pretty, and I feel my breath calming. I can't hear the blood raging in my ears anymore.

I try twirling in a circle, but it's hard. The skirt weighs a ton, the dress wide and heavy. I love knowing my mom was wearing it the day she married Dad. The best day of her life, I imagine. I feel her with me now as I stand there looking like her, loving the feel of the satin material against my arms, everything soft and silky. I place the veil on my head and slip the comb into my hair.

Turning to the side, I can see the veil hanging down my back. The material is so long it bunches at the floor, but that's fine. I stand on my tiptoes.

I've never done this: tried on Mom's dress without Dad around. He would flip; he doesn't like me coming in here without him. He says we must take care of her dress. "We don't want it to get ruined, Mia," he always says.

Don't worry, Dad. I won't let anything happen to it.

For extra effect, I put on his wedding ring. It's far too big for my skinny little fingers, so I end up sliding it on my thumb instead.

Just as I have the ring set in place, I hear a gasp at the door.

CHAPTER FORTY-FIVE

Mia

Wednesday, 4:15 p.m.

It's Vanessa. I'm caught. *See, I was telling you the truth. But crap, now you've found me.* She drops a wet cleaning sponge to the floor.

The dress is heavy and I shift my weight quickly, regaining my balance and facing her head-on. "Do you like it?" I ask.

She looks shocked—confused. And then comes the recognition of knowing this is my mother's wedding dress. That I was telling the truth all along.

"You play dress-up in this? And your dad knows?"

"Yes," I tell her.

She bites her lip and slowly backs from the room. "I didn't realize he kept it right here …"

I slam the closet door and chase after her into the hall, but I'm wobbling in my shoes, trying my best to keep up. "What's wrong, Vanessa?"

She's moving fast and heading for the patio door. "I need air."

This is probably where I should stop. I know I shouldn't wear my mother's dress outside; I don't want to risk ruining it, but I'm too angry, out of control. Part of me is having fun. Relishing the fact that Vanessa can't stand seeing me this way. I'm so hurt, I want to hurt someone else.

I follow her.

"Don't you think I look pretty? Don't you love my mom's dress? Don't you wish you'd worn something like this on your wedding day?" I'm astonished at my own words. I sound so mean, but I don't know how to stop my fury.

She's moving quickly, looking once over her shoulder to see me coming after her. "Mia, go and take that off. *Please.*"

I watch the sunlight playing off the water in the pool, knowing how this will shine on my dress too, how the crystal beads will shimmer, how every part of Mom's gown will be radiant.

I take a few more steps, careful not to trip on the satin material.

Vanessa stops. Tears are forming in the corners of her eyes. "What's wrong?" she asks. "What did I do? Is someone hurting you?"

Without a second's thought, I say, "You came into my life."

"Mia." She's pleading. "I didn't want to come into your life that way. But it happened and your mother is gone—"

"Don't talk about her. I don't want to hear it from you."

"All I've ever wanted is to make you and your dad happy. I only wanted to make everyone feel whole again."

"We were fine the way we were."

"Why can't we try to be a family?"

"I have a family. It's me and my mom and my dad."

"Mia—"

"Dad wishes Mom was here and not you. You're really only around to be my babysitter. The truth is, I don't need you anymore and neither does he. And it's not like you want to be around me anyway. You're sick of my swim meets—you said so yourself. You didn't even show up to my tea."

"Mia, I don't know how many more times I need to apologize—"

"You're always apologizing."

Her face hardens and she folds her arms sternly. "Well you need to start apologizing too."

A lump lodges itself inside my throat. "Don't tell me what to do."

"Mia—"

Hot, angry tears come next and I force myself to blink them away. "I want my real mom instead of you. My dad wants my mom too. Can't you see?" I hold the skirt out in front of her, my hands reaching into the satin folds. "He keeps her wedding dress. In his office. A secret from you." I hear my voice shaking. "You must think that's weird."

"It's sentimental. Your mother means a lot to both of you … but yes, it's weird. It's different." Her chin trembles. "I don't like it, but we can work through it. Your dad and I can talk about it. In time we'll get through this together, this grieving process. Maybe we can go away together, take a vacation—"

"A vacation? Do you even hear yourself right now?" I hold out the skirt once more, but I wobble again. I'm too close to the water's edge, and I fight to keep my balance, the weight of the skirt pulling at my upper body as I dig deep with my legs. "Look at me," I tell her. "Look at what I'm wearing. He will never be able to get over my mom. She's the only important person in his life. Not you. *Never* you."

This last comment stings her. "Don't say that."

She turns her back. She's walking toward the house but I'm not ready for this to be over with, so I blurt it out fast. "He's with Mrs. Campbell!"

Vanessa halts in her tracks. "What?"

"He is," I tell her. "I saw it with my own eyes."

She turns to face me. "Mia, this isn't funny."

"I'm not joking."

"These aren't things you can just make up."

"I'm not making it up. I saw it. You just don't want to believe me."

Her face drops. "What exactly did you see?"

I don't know why I tell her, but I need to tell someone. It's been eating away at me all day. Every hour at school, it was all I could think about, and now I'm ready to burst. I lash out at her.

"I saw my dad go over to her house, last night. They were kissing and hugging, and it was gross."

"How? Where did you see them?"

"I was in the backyard. I saw him go right up to the back door."

Vanessa pauses. She's folding her arms and thinking. She doesn't want to believe me. She's trying to hide the hurt on her face.

She glances across the yard to Mrs. Campbell's house and then stares back at me.

"Are you sure that's what they were doing? Maybe you were confused and it was something else."

"What? I think I know what kissing and hugging looks like."

"Not the friendly neighbor kind?"

I roll my eyes. "No. Not even close."

"Last night?" This time her voice is barely a whisper.

"Yes, last night. While you were out, Dad was next door with Mrs. Campbell." The heat blooms in my face—my anger and my shame. I can't believe I'm ratting out my dad. But the need to hurt someone else keeps growing stronger.

"Don't say that," she says. "You don't know that's what you saw."

"It's true. It happened. I don't think it was the first time either." And I add, knowing this will wound her more than anything, that I'm being especially cruel, "I don't think my dad loves you anymore."

Vanessa snaps. Something in her eyes flashes, and she rushes forward, her hands reaching out. I flinch. But it's too late. I try moving away, my balance shaken, my ankles betraying me at the worst possible time.

I think I'm falling, Vanessa's reaction coming from out of nowhere. At the last second, I wonder if I might be able to grab hold of her and pull her into the water. I can tug on her arm. I know she can't swim.

PART FIVE

After

CHAPTER FORTY-SIX

Detective Angela Blakely

Mia Tanner was missing. And then she was found.

But it's not what we wanted.

We find her body five days after she goes missing. Five days of interrogations and news conferences, dead-end leads, search teams coming up empty. We've never worked so hard in our lives.

It's frustrating when a heavy storm moves across Huntsville, the rain pouring down for days, and the search slows down. But then the skies clear, and I get a call.

"Hikers," dispatch says. "Reporting a body." I wait, the dread rising in my stomach. "A teenager." The adrenaline hits my brain so hard I'm dizzy.

The drive to Monte Sano takes ten minutes, but I can't reach the top of Embankment Drive fast enough. I'm white-knuckling every turn, tires screeching until I reach the trailhead. Half a dozen patrol cars have beaten me to the parking lot, lights flashing.

My door flies open. "What have we got?"

Officer Donahue points to a group of hikers huddled against a car. "They came off the main trail."

One of the men—wearing a plaid shirt and dirt-stained jeans, eyes as wide as saucers—is nodding with the frenetic energy of a jackrabbit, his words pouring out. "We had to cut around because there was water all over, and then we saw … We had no idea …

never thought …" His eyes dart around nervously. "It's the only reason we found her."

"Show me."

A fence post marks the entrance to the park, the light dropping the instant we set foot beneath the trees, the trail littered with fallen branches and leaves, remnants from the storm. Officer Donahue stays close to me as we walk, several more officers behind us. He doesn't say much—doesn't need to—but I know what he's thinking, can see it in the way he's silently keeping pace. He feels it in his gut the same way I do, the telltale signs of what we're about to find, the missing girl we've been looking for around the clock for the past five days.

Ten minutes in and we reach the flood the hiker was telling us about. Water gushes across the trail and drops into a ravine. The man motions up a hill and we follow. My boots slip at the top and I grab hold of a tree.

"Not much farther," he tells me. Another fifty yards and his steps slow. "She's over here."

I peer into the clearing—searching, scanning the pine straw, the shadows and rocks—until my eyes settle on something low to the ground. A patch of yellow among the leaves.

Blonde hair.

I take a step closer.

Petite body. Black swimsuit.

Another step.

The face of Mia Tanner.

My stomach drops.

Shit, I knew it—I knew it the moment dispatch called—but now, out here in the woods, her body mere feet away, the reality of the situation rockets its way through me and fear takes hold in my chest.

Mia Tanner. My missing persons case turned homicide.

I move toward her, then stop. Someone else's prints are visible in the mud; they halt ten feet away, circling to where the hiker is standing now. I check his boots, retrace the prints, and look up to him again. "Is this as close as you got?"

"I didn't want to go any closer," he tells me.

I order everyone to stand back so we don't contaminate the evidence any further. I slip on a pair of foot covers and gloves and approach. Twenty more paces and I'm standing over her body.

She's tiny—I knew she would be—about a hundred pounds, her small form tucked against a log. She's been dumped. Someone has tried covering her body and failed, the dirt washed away by the rain until her arms and legs are exposed. Her skin is a bluish-gray color, her hair wet and matted with leaves. She's wearing nothing but a swimsuit. No shoes, no jacket. Her body is curled to one side, face tilted up, eyes closed.

I crouch beside her and find no strangulation marks or bruising, no injuries to the skull. Nothing to indicate external trauma, no immediate cause of death. Every fingernail is intact, not a trace of dirt underneath. She didn't fight, or she didn't fight for very long. The bottoms of her feet are untouched too, not a scratch. She didn't walk here, and she wasn't bound. My guess is she was carried. She was dead before someone brought her here.

The perpetrator was hasty too, not bothering to dig a hole but piling her with dirt, layering her with leaves and earth in a rushed attempt at hiding her. Whoever dumped her needed to get out of here as fast as they could.

Stepping carefully, I find nothing on the ground beside her. The area is virtually untouched.

I scan the woods next. We're nearly three miles from the Tanners' neighborhood, without a cleared walking path. The killer must have driven up the mountain, parked their car, and carried her to this spot. But they didn't come from the main trail. That would have been too risky—someone would have remembered seeing them. They had to have come in from somewhere else.

Over my shoulder, I ask, "Where's the next closest road?"

"Besides the trailhead?" Officer Donahue thinks for a second before lifting his arm. "That way, about a quarter-mile. Nolen Street."

I follow his gaze: a dark shadow of space between the trees. Another forty yards to where kudzu vines twist tightly around rocks. "They came from that direction."

Officer Donahue frowns. "There's a lot of overgrowth."

"But it wouldn't be impossible?"

"No, not impossible."

"We need to find out who was seen driving on Nolen the night Mia disappeared. Question hikers, people who live up here, anyone who may have noticed something between the hours of five p.m. and six a.m."

His eyebrows shoot sky-high. "What makes you think it happened that night?"

"She's still in her swimsuit. They took her from the pool, killed her, and dumped her before the rain came on Thursday morning." I tip my chin toward the ground. "And you see those tracks? The hiker's prints and our prints are the only ones coming in from the main trail. Whoever did this was here before everything turned to mud." I pivot to the other officers. "Search the woods from here to Nolen and another mile in every direction." To Officer Donahue: "Return the hiker to the trailhead, will you? Get his statement. Find out if anyone else was seen driving up here."

He dips his head. "Yes, ma'am."

I watch as everyone nods in turn and splits out. Then I face Mia once again, the panic creeping under my skin. I'm trying not to let it show as my mind runs in a hundred directions, thinking of what lies ahead. Searching the crime scene. Finding the killer. Telling the parents. Facing the media. The firestorm that I know is coming. My ass on the line if we don't find out who did this—and fast.

In the beginning, as I sat in the dining room of one of the more elite families in Huntsville, I was convinced this was textbook runaway, that she'd be home by dinner, and that the fire was unconnected.

I gave the parents a hard time, the stepmom especially—I'll be the first to admit it. I tried poking holes in their relationship, looking for a wicked-stepmother scenario. I didn't like the fact she'd gone outside to check on the fire first.

And in the middle of everything, I made a mistake: not asking about Mia's phone sooner. There were a few odd messages from her dad, but then the lead came in about the swim coach and we were on the hunt. Tracking down the coach to see if he had her.

I felt so sure—we all did—that this could be it. He would have her and we could safely bring her home.

But we found Coach Jacobs more than two hundred miles away at the Gold Strike Casino, a charge on his credit card putting him at a gas station outside Tunica at the same time Mia was coming home from school. Security video showed him at a blackjack table for seven solid hours before cashing out at 10 p.m. It had been excruciatingly disappointing. He had been outraged to think we had considered him a suspect in the first place, but his anger quickly turned to panicked grief. By the early hours of Thursday morning, he was on every news station pleading for help, desperately asking people to look for her.

And the allegations by those parents, the ones who said he'd been inappropriate with the girls? They changed their minds, admitted they'd jumped to conclusions when they first heard about Mia. They apologized, and without any other suspects, I was back to square one.

The shoeprint in the alley turned into nothing too: a neighbor walking his dog the day before, the size thirteen print matching a pair of loafers he'd packed in his suitcase for a business trip to Atlanta. He'd left town a full eight hours before Mia went missing.

Five days slipped by, and around I went with more interviews. More visits with neighbors and teachers asking them what they knew. But nothing turned up and it felt like I was beating my head against a wall.

And throughout it all, what bothered me most was *how* she was taken. The absolute brazenness of it, someone kidnapping her in broad daylight without fear of being caught, the stepmom only feet away on the other side of the house. And the fire—another complication. Either ridiculous timing, or the murderer had the balls to set the blaze themselves, an enormous gamble as dozens of first responders rushed to the scene. People running to the front of the Campbells' house instead of paying attention to what was happening in the back next door.

Mia, taken in a five-minute window where no one remembers a damn thing.

CHAPTER FORTY-SEVEN

Vanessa

"No."

Tripp doesn't want to hear it. He's backing away, taking one step and then another, widening the gap between him and the detective, as if the space he's creating will make what she's saying less true.

"I'm so sorry," Detective Blakely tells him.

Tripp shakes his head. "No, not Mia." And he makes a choking sound, a discernible gagging at the back of his throat, his body trembling, eyes staring wildly, begging for her to tell him she's made a mistake, that she didn't mean to come to our house and tell us Mia is dead. But when the detective doesn't say anything of the sort, and the truth finally hits, it's unbearable to watch. He falls to his knees, a wail emanating from his mouth, fists pressed against his face so hard the space around his forehead turns white. I kneel on the floor beside him, pain ricocheting across my own head.

Mia is dead.

What in the hell went wrong?

Yes, we were fighting. Yes, I was furious. But I never wanted her to go missing—I sure as hell didn't want her to die. We've been looking for her everywhere, for days; it's been constant. Friends and family, all of us searching and praying and hoping.

With the full-on search and non-stop media, I've had no choice but to force everything else to the back of my mind: Tripp's wedding ring, the dress, Julia. I couldn't talk to him about any of it. I mean, how could I? *Honey, I know we're looking for our daughter, but …*

The last few days our lives have been consumed by nothing except finding her. Tripp has no idea what I know, no clue as to how much I'm keeping inside. Mia putting away the dress. The ring now hidden in my dresser.

Before this happened …

And I only turned away for a few minutes.

I've been so afraid that the other stuff will come out. I don't want Detective Blakely to know about my fight with Mia, the things we said to each other before she disappeared. She'll demand information about that last hour—what really happened—and I can't risk it. The focus needs to be on who came into our backyard and stole her, nothing else. No spotlight on me, the stepmother.

When I found the ring in the pool and started panicking about my own husband, I was furious again. The chance he'd been cheating, the very woman he was having an affair with staying at my house—sitting with me, for heaven's sake—while everyone was out looking. Can you imagine how hard that was? To listen to Julia while she pretended to help? I was heartbroken. I hated her. And I was furious with him. Because I believed Mia. Despite everything, I didn't think she would lie. Not about something like this.

But I couldn't accuse them of the affair—not yet, not until I knew more. And not while Mia was missing. Finding her was the only thing we were focusing on.

Before I knew it, Tripp's family had filled the house and there was hardly a moment for the two of us to speak in private. The cops camped out in our living room, with reporters blocking the street. Tripp and I made joint statements to the media. Press conferences were set up in our front yard. The two of us, side by side, a unified front. Anxious and heartbroken, searching for our daughter.

CHAPTER FORTY-EIGHT

Detective Angela Blakely

I barely sleep, unable to get the vision of Mia out of my mind. Over and over again I see her pale blue lips, her small hand curled against the ground. A flash of the school photograph her stepmom gave me, the sweet smile and the crinkle above her nose. Full of life.

As soon as the coroner's report hits my desk the next day, I'm pushing aside my coffee, doing a double-take as soon as I read the first line. I didn't see a single mark on Mia's body, no signs of trauma, and now I know why.

I head directly to the Tanners' house and find a bigger mob on the front lawn than the day before, reporters shoving mics in my face as soon as I exit the car, a photographer almost tripping me with a tripod until I push him out of the way. Shouts come at me from every direction: *How did she die? How close are you to catching the killer?* I clear a path to the porch, my arm sticking out in defensive mode as I cut through the crowd to the front door, which is opened by an officer.

Inside the house, I hear hushed conversation. The lights are dim. Several members of Tripp's family are clustered in the living room, and I can hear the soft sounds of someone crying. I find the Tanners seated on the couch, Tripp's parents beside them, his mother and the former judge understandably grief-stricken, their shoulders hunched.

Vanessa has her face buried in a wad of tissues as Tripp sits motionless, staring into space.

"I'm so sorry to trouble you, but I need to speak with you both." When the Tanners don't look up, I clear my throat. "Somewhere private."

Vanessa's eyes meet mine and she drops her tissues to her lap. Tripp slowly lifts his eyes to my face too, several seconds passing before he unfolds his body from the couch, releasing an anguished exhale as he stands before me. The pair move slowly toward Tripp's study and I follow them, Tripp's father watching as we enter the room. Once inside, I close the door.

"How are you both holding up?" I ask.

They look at me bleakly.

"I received the coroner's report," I tell them. "Mia's death is consistent with drowning."

A long pause. It takes an eternity for them to realize what I'm saying.

Vanessa sinks into a chair. When Tripp speaks, his voice is garbled, constricted. "What do you mean?"

"Her lungs were filled with fluid."

"But how? She's a champion swimmer." He's still using present tense.

"The fluid found in her lungs combined with the fact she was still in her swimsuit leads us to believe she drowned." I slow my words for this next part. "It makes us think she drowned here. In your pool. Before someone carried her away."

Vanessa returns the tissues to her face, her nostrils flaring pink. But Tripp is silent—stunned—his eyes traveling across the room in the direction of the backyard, happier memories of Mia possibly entering his mind, along with the brutal understanding that that was where she died.

"She may have only gotten a few laps in before someone forced her underwater," I tell them.

His eyes swing back to me. "But if she drowned, then why not pretend it was an accident and leave her at the bottom?"

The thought has already crossed my mind. "My guess is they wanted to get rid of her."

"But why?" His voice cracks on those two words.

I raise my shoulders. "Maybe they were covering something up. If they took her away, everyone would be out looking. They could buy themselves more time."

"To do what?"

"To throw us off—to throw everyone off."

"But she's a champion swimmer," Tripp repeats. "She's not supposed to drown."

"They took advantage of the situation," I say. "We believe Mia drowned suddenly and without a chance to cry for help. She didn't suffer."

Vanessa sucks in a breath. "That's why I didn't hear her," she says.

I nod. "That's why no one heard her."

CHAPTER FORTY-NINE

Julia

Our house is an active crime scene while the fire is being investigated, the police still trying to work out if it had anything to do with Mia's kidnapping and death—and I can't believe I'm using that word: *death*. It's unbelievable, too horrific to think about. Poor Mia, that poor child, stolen from her backyard and killed.

I wander from room to room of the Embassy Suites, our new home that Thomas promises won't last long, walking past bags of clothes, some of them donated by friends, others bought brand new, Thomas dutifully itemizing each receipt for insurance purposes. Stacks of stuff are piled on the floor and scattered across beds: books and movies, a PlayStation for the kids, blankets, flowers, and meals. Dozens of friends have dropped off care packages telling us how sorry they are—*how truly sorry*—how devastated they are for everyone involved.

But none of these things will bring Mia back.

Thomas is worried about me. He doesn't say it in so many words, but I can see it in the way he's constantly hovering, taking a leave of absence from work to stay at the hotel. In his words, to help take care of everything. And the truth is, I know he will and I'm thankful for the security, but when he's not looking, I do something I know I shouldn't. I sneak into the next room and call someone else—the man I was once sleeping with.

I need to know he's okay. I want him to know how devastated I am about Mia.

Tripp doesn't answer, and it's not like I expect him to; we haven't spoken since the night his daughter disappeared. I leave him a message and tell him how sorry I am, how I'm thinking about him, realizing it's the same message my friends have been leaving me, everyone meaning well but not quite knowing what to say, all of us on repeat: *If there's anything we can do …*

I feel terrible about the affair, I really do. And I'm glad it's over. We both know it's done. The search for Mia has consumed everything in his life and I'm almost positive he hasn't thought of me for one second. What has happened to his daughter has put a stop to everything, as it should.

But I still remember the last night we were together, the night before Mia disappeared, before our world went to hell. We'd had an unexpected opportunity: my kids had gone to practice, Thomas was downtown smoking cigars with friends, and Vanessa had gone to Janie's to help with a fundraiser. It was our chance to be together.

Tripp texted around six, confirming that he'd come over. When he showed up, I jumped to my feet and sprinted down the hall. He came in through the back gate from the alley, where hardly any of our neighbors venture. It's a place we know he won't be seen.

I threw open the door to see him standing there, and with one arm scooped at the small of my back, he pulled me in close for a passionate kiss. His foot kicked back and shut the door, and we were against the wall, barely two feet into the hallway, his hands tugging at the robe I was wearing, the silk slipping down my shoulders.

"Tripp," I whispered in his ear. "We have to sto—"

But he kissed me hard, I remember that, mouth and tongue against mine. He knew we didn't have a lot of time. These were borrowed moments when we hadn't expected our families to be gone, and on a school night too.

I'd been seeing Tripp behind my husband's back for almost a year, going back and forth between feeling downright terrible and then telling myself—telling Tripp—*this will be the last time.* It should have never started in the first place.

We were drunk—a dinner party at the McMillans' house that carried on far too late. Thomas had to work early and offered to drive Vanessa home. Tripp said he wanted to stay behind and talk with neighbors and I offered to help clean up. One by one, our friends left. The front door closed until it was only the four of us, and eventually, the McMillans stumbled upstairs. One thing led to another with Tripp, and we should have stopped. We shouldn't have ended up in that back room together. We should never have taken off our clothes.

My neighbor, Tripp Tanner. The man I've known for years and who I consoled after the death of his first wife. For months we've been telling each other it needed to end. But we couldn't seem to stop. Maybe we were bored with our marriages. Maybe we were just bored with life. Maybe we loved the excitement too much. And we kept finding ways to be together. The concept of *the last time* broken repeatedly.

To this day, it's one of my biggest regrets. My deepest, darkest secret.

Vanessa would lose her mind if she knew. We'd never speak again. Her marriage, ruined.

And Thomas? How would he react? He'd waste no time packing my bags and tossing me to the curb. He'd hate it, but he'd have no choice. He'd never stand by and let something like this happen to him and to his family name, the public shame of it all only helped slightly by my punishment. He would be devastated. I'm not sure if he would ever marry again after suffering such a deceit.

That night when Tripp came over, I told myself once again that we needed to stop this nonsense before we got caught. But

Tripp was in my house and my family was gone and his mouth was doing things to make me moan …

After leaving my message for Tripp, I hang up the phone. When I emerge from the bedroom, Thomas encourages me to sit beside him so he can show me house listings online. He pulls up house after house for consideration. He says we'll move somewhere new, somewhere grand, filling it with new furniture. I can rent my own studio space downtown and make a proper business of my photography; I'll no longer need to bring clients to the house. He does all this in the hopes of cheering me up, and it works for a short while—at least it gets me thinking about something else. Every one of the houses is beautiful, each one a place, he says, for us to start over.

Laptop perched on his knee, we're looking at one of the more promising houses that we'd like to try and see this afternoon when Detective Blakely calls from the hotel lobby: she's asking to come up. I glance anxiously at my husband and his eyes catch mine. Doesn't she know how much we've been through? Can't she leave us alone? We've told the fire chief everything we know. There's nothing more to share with the police.

But Thomas, always the obliging one, tells her, "Of course."

Within minutes, the detective is at the door. Gently she breaks the news about how Mia died.

"What? How?" I hear myself stammer as Thomas puts his arm around my already shaking shoulders.

But Detective Blakely looks past us into the hotel room.

"I need to talk to your mother, Mrs. Sinclair," she says, and I flinch. "Now that we know Mia drowned, this one very important detail could have her remembering something new."

I hesitate, but Thomas holds the door wide open. "Anything you need."

She brushes past us and makes a beeline for the sitting area. I follow closely on her heels, wanting to reach my mother before the detective can startle her with her questions. I drop to my knees, patting Mom on the arm, hoping to gently pull her from her latest daydream. I watch her blink once, twice, before she turns her face to me.

"Mom," I say. "Detective Blakely is here to talk with you."

Her eyes shift upward. My words take several seconds to register, and when it does, she gives the detective a small nod.

Blakely takes that as her cue and sits opposite. "Mrs. Sinclair," she begins. "I'm sorry for what you and your family are going through. I'm also sorry to tell you that Mia drowned."

I wince, Thomas clutching my hand.

"She *drowned*, Mrs. Sinclair," the detective repeats, gentle but firm. "Do you understand what I'm saying to you?"

A pang hits my chest as I watch tears fill the corners of my mother's eyes, noting the tremble in her chapped lips.

"I need to ask you if you remember anything else about that day—anything at all. Can you help us, Mrs. Sinclair? Can you help us find out who did this to Mia?"

"Mia," she whispers, her voice hoarse.

"Yes," the detective prompts. "You remember her swimming?"

A slow nod, followed by a steadier, more lucid one.

"Do you remember anyone else in the pool?"

Her expression is pained, the words sinking in. "Mia drowned?"

"Yes, she drowned. Did you see her struggling in the water?"

"Mia doesn't struggle. She's a good swimmer."

"Yes, but something happened to her in the pool that day. Did you see who did this to her?"

Mom doesn't answer.

"Did you see her fighting with anyone? Was someone forcing her underwater?"

"Mia in the pool …"

That's when it hits me, the first lurch in my stomach. And I'm reminded of the ring we found—Tripp's ring—shining gold at the bottom and very much out of place. Vanessa and I have not spoken another word about it since that night, since I told her that the ring being there was a coincidence.

But that was before we knew Mia died there.

I steal a glance at Thomas and he's listening intently, a concerned look stretching across his face. He has no clue about the ring—how can he? I've never brought it up. And it seems Vanessa has never told the police either.

"Was anyone else with her?" the detective asks. "Was anyone else in the pool?"

I hold my breath. Is this it? Is this when my mom will suddenly remember? She'll say something about Tripp being there, a struggle with Mia, and Vanessa's fears will be confirmed. She was right to wonder about the ring; I just didn't want to believe it at the time. But it can't be right, not Tripp. He would never hurt his own child. There's got to be another explanation.

"Only Mia …" Mom says. "Only Mia swimming."

I try not to let the air rush full force from my mouth.

"Mrs. Sinclair, are you sure Mia was alone?" Detective Blakely persists.

"She's a good swimmer."

"Yes, but did you see something happen? Did someone take her?"

"Mia in a wedding dress."

The detective's face twitches. "What wedding dress?"

"Beautiful and white."

Blakely's look bounces from me to Thomas. "What is she talking about?"

I press a hand to my mother's arm. "What are you saying, Mom?"

But she keeps her eyes on the detective. "So pretty. Such a pretty dress."

"Mrs. Sinclair, Mia was found in a bathing suit, not a dress."

"Beautiful and white," she repeats.

Again Detective Blakely looks to us for help.

"She might have dreamt it," Thomas suggests. "That happens sometimes. Somewhere in her mind she's thinking about something else."

"But a dress?" the detective asks.

"It's hard to know," I explain. "She could be thinking of me in my wedding gown. Or a movie she saw, or—"

"No," my mom says suddenly. "I saw Mia."

A nagging feeling wriggles its way between my ribs. I kneel closer, squeezing her hand. "A car," she says.

And all three of us jolt.

Detective Blakely is breathless. "A car, or a truck?"

I remember reports about the beat-up truck driving around the neighborhood.

But my mom answers, "A car."

The detective says, "Black? White? Big or small?"

Mom lifts a shoulder. "Just a car."

Detective Blakely moves to the edge of her seat. "Whose car?"

Mom's shoulder lifts again.

"Where did you see the car?"

"In the alley."

The detective's eyes snap wide. The hairs on the back of my neck do a slow march north.

"Who was it?" she asks. "Did you see them stop behind the Tanners' house?"

But Mom is rambling again. "Mia … a beautiful wedding."

"There was no wedding, Mrs. Sinclair," the detective insists. "Only Mia swimming." She tries again. "Did you see someone get out of the car? Did they come into the backyard?"

"Mia on her wedding day."

"Please think about the car." The detective's patience is waning. "Please, Mrs. Sinclair. I need to know what you saw. This could be the person who hurt her."

"Such a happy day," my mom says. "Until Mia fell down."

CHAPTER FIFTY

Detective Angela Blakely

I want the whole pool checked. I don't care if we've already done it once before—we're missing something, I know it. Mia drowned in this pool and I want to go over every square inch. Have the whole backyard re-examined.

A pool vacuum is dropped to the bottom, the filters inspected, the surrounding landscaping torn apart. Workers pull baskets from skimmer drains; another crew checks the pumps. Patio furniture is systematically flipped upside down and swept.

I'm standing next to a worker from the pool cleaning service, a man in coveralls whose name tag identifies him as Dan. I'm trying my hardest to be patient as I wait with hands on hips, the stress coursing through my veins, the distinct smell of chlorine pool bleach in my nose as at last Dan pulls a basket from the deep end.

"The skimmers should have picked up anything else," he says, sifting through soggy leaves, a chunk of pine straw. His hand scrapes bottom—nothing.

At the shallow end, another skimmer basket is lifted, this one containing pieces of insects, arms and legs and wings, more soggy leaves, and a hair band, a black scrunchie kind, strands of blonde hair wrapped tightly around the fabric. I'm almost certain this belonged to Mia, but I want it verified just in case, so the hair band is labeled and dropped in a plastic bag.

The vacuum pulls sediment from the floor, and water samples are poured into containers. Chemicals, suntan lotion, nail polish, cleaning agents, every type of shampoo the family has ever used will be matched to whatever might show up. Every sample will be taken to the lab and tested, nothing missed.

And then, the oddest thing.

Dan brings me a metal strainer, water dripping through the bottom and splattering inches from my shoes. "From the main pool pump," he says, running his hands through the muck.

I peer into the container and get another whiff of overpowering chlorine. All I can see is more leaves—*dammit, Dan, I don't want more leaves*—but then he fishes three shiny objects from the bottom of the basket and places them carefully in his palm: three tiny, sparkling beads sitting in a row. I look closer. They're not beads, but something else: clear and professionally cut, each one blinking in the sun.

Dan looks them over. "What do you think these are?" he asks. "Some kind of jewelry?"

I pinch one of the specks and hold it up to my eye.

I can't believe what I'm seeing. *No way*. The old lady might have been making sense after all.

"Crystals," I say.

"What?" Dan asks. "Like the kind you see on costumes?"

"No." I keep a steady gaze on my hand. "The kind you see on wedding dresses."

"Was there ever a wedding in your backyard?" I ask the Tanners, and they shake their heads. "Where did you get married?"

"First United Methodist Church," Vanessa tells me. "The one on Clinton."

"Mr. Tanner, your first wedding?"

I watch as he shifts uncomfortably in his seat. "Same church."

I pull out a plastic evidence bag. "We found these in one of the strainer baskets of your pool. Any idea what they are?" Vanessa leans forward against the table. Tripp reaches out to touch the plastic. "They're four-millimeter faceted Swarovski crystals. Expensive, the kind you find on designer clothes—and, more interestingly to me, on wedding dresses." Vanessa's head jerks in response. "Do either of you have any idea how these ended up in the pool?"

Tripp's eyes swivel between us. "Crystals?"

"Did Mia ever play dress-up? Did she play pretend weddings?"

"She had grown out of that," he says.

"But is there a wedding dress she would try on sometimes?"

Vanessa shrugs. "Not mine. I don't have my gown anymore. I donated it."

"Could she have tried on something else then?"

She looks to Tripp.

"Mrs. Tanner," I say. "Can you think of any dresses Mia would have played with? Something crystals might have fallen off?"

Tripp doesn't let her answer. "I don't understand what this means. What does this have to do with my daughter?"

"On the day Mia went missing, Mrs. Sinclair talked about seeing a wedding in your backyard. Mia in a wedding dress. Guests coming into the yard. It sounds far-fetched, but she tells this story and then we find these in your filter. It's an odd coincidence, don't you think?"

He blinks rapidly.

"Mr. Tanner, do you know anything about this? Have you seen crystals like this before?"

Tripp frowns. "No. And I don't understand why they would end up in the pool."

"That's what we're trying to figure out." I shift my eyes to Vanessa. "Mrs. Tanner, is there anything about that day you want to tell us?"

She doesn't say anything.

"What was Mia doing?"

"You already know that. Swim practice."

"Did she wear a gown?"

"Why would she do that?"

"Did you see her wearing a gown?"

"I don't think so …"

My eyes narrow. "What do you mean, you don't think so?"

"I don't know why she would."

I sit back, unconvinced, my brain churning. Thoughts moving ahead.

Sliding the crystals into a container, I close the lid with a click. "Okay, thank you both. We'll be in touch."

CHAPTER FIFTY-ONE

Vanessa

After I see Detective Blakely out, I go looking for Tripp. He's already in his study. The door is locked when I try turning the knob. "Tripp? Let me in." I rattle the door against the frame. "The detective. What she said …"

But he doesn't answer. There is only the sound of a desk drawer opening, rolling smoothly against the track, the clinking of metal as he locates a key. A click.

He's checking on the closet. After what Detective Blakely found in the pool, he needs to make sure the dress is all right. He'll realize that maybe Mia has been wearing it without us knowing. *A dress you should never have kept.*

"Let me in, Tripp," I say again. "We need to talk."

It's time to ask him about the dress. Why he kept it from me. Why he didn't tell me he was showing it to Mia.

And above all—and what has been burning me alive since that day—how he could have betrayed me with Julia. The secrets he's been keeping.

"Tripp, open up!"

Still no answer. Only the sound of something being pushed aside.

I beat my fist against the door until it hurts.

There is so much Tripp has kept hidden from me. My husband, who I once trusted and loved with all my heart, who I thought told me everything, is not the man I thought he was. How long has he been cheating on me with Julia? When did it start?

How could they do this to me?

When he showed Mia the dress, did he tell her no one could replace her mother? Is that why she was acting more resentful toward me? I admit, I made mistakes, I hurt Mia, and I absolutely regret that, but no wonder she lost it that day; no wonder she lashed out and said those terrible things to me by the pool.

The shock and outrage at what she knew about her own father.

"Tripp!" I beat the door again.

We so desperately need to talk. We need to come clean. He can finally tell me the truth about Julia. He can explain to me about the dress. And I'll tell him about my fight with Mia, why I didn't want anyone to know the terrible things that were said.

Yes, Tripp, I'll tell him. *She put on that dress. She told me about Julia. There is so much explaining for you to do … but I didn't hurt her, I promise.* I was upset, but that's not what happened. She went outside. The crystals must have fallen when she walked along the edge of the pool, but that was it. The last time I saw her, she was putting the dress away. She was going swimming.

I hear Tripp's hurried footsteps as he rushes across the room and I pull my fist away from the door. He yanks it open.

"*What?*" he says.

I try looking past his shoulder. "Tripp, we need to talk."

But he takes off, walking at a fast clip down the hall.

"Wait!" I shout.

I hear him grabbing his keys from the table, the door to the garage opening and closing with a slam.

"Tripp!" I call again.

The car engine starts.

I head back to the study and my eyes land on the closet door he's left wide open, expecting to see Susannah's gown, long and white and layered in lace, the one Mia showed me.

But the closet is empty—one look across the room and I see only an empty hanger.

Susannah's wedding dress and veil are gone.

CHAPTER FIFTY-TWO

Julia

Thomas finishes his call with the fire chief, his arms folded as he stares out the window across the parking lot.

"What did he say?" I ask.

He pulls his eyes from the glass. "The fire started in your studio. That was the point of origin. Our house fire has officially been declared arson."

Arson. It's what we thought, what we've been expecting to hear, everything in the investigation pointing in that direction. But my studio? Why? Why would someone start a fire there?

I feel the wobble returning to my knees, the unease shooting through my belly. "Are they sure?"

"They used gasoline. The fire started in the studio before spreading to the rest of the house." He slips his hands in his pockets, his eyes tracing a pattern on the carpet only he can see. "They used gas containers I kept in the garage. The fire chief says they found what's left of them near the back door, melted to nothing." He gives a small, frightened cough.

And this is how I know—that one sound, the clearing of his throat: it's his way of concealing his fear, trying to protect me, to keep me from connecting the dots.

But it's too late. My heart is pumping so fast and I feel the first shiver.

"Thomas, whoever did this knew where to look."

"We don't know that."

The words are rushing out of my mouth. "They went straight to the garage. They knew where to find the gasoline, they didn't bring their own. They knew where to go." I feel the terror snaking its way through my skin. "They've been to our house before." And the truth hits me so hard, I gasp. "Thomas, *we know this person*. We've welcomed them into our home, the kids have met them before—"

Thomas puts out his hands. "You need to calm down."

But I'm pacing. "No, don't do that. Don't try to protect me."

"Julia—"

I whirl around. "Someone deliberately set fire to our house. Someone we know. They picked the studio."

"It could have been any room."

"It was the studio," I repeat.

"It doesn't have to mean anything."

"This was directed *toward me*. You know it was. You were right about those cameras."

He folds his arms. "Someone burned our house down to get to Mia—not to get to you."

"Then why pick the studio?"

"They came in the back. It's the first room they found." He raises his voice. "They *did not* pick on you on purpose."

But I'm no longer sure about that.

CHAPTER FIFTY-THREE

Detective Angela Blakely

I find Fire Chief Sam Hendricks in his office. My double tap on the door gets his attention and he glances up. One look at me and his mouth twists. He knows I'm not here for small talk.

"What's the latest on the Campbell fire?" I ask. "You officially ruling out insurance fraud?"

He curves his hand, ushering me to sit.

"I'm fine."

"You look like you haven't slept in days."

My face burns. "Because I haven't."

"No shit." He sighs. "Angela." He waves his hand again—this time an order. "Pop a squat."

We've known each other since I started my career. Sam was one of the first people to congratulate me when I moved from burglary to narcotics, and then, eventually, homicide. He's always asking me why I've never settled down. Got married. Had children. "You're making a mistake marrying the job," he says, but I don't take any notice.

Today, when he tells me to sit, I relent, but only because he's right. I *am* exhausted. My feet shuffle and my legs bend until I'm settling deep into one of his sagging chairs, two metal coils digging in my back as I adjust my hips.

More than twenty years on the job and he has yet to get new office furniture.

He studies me with the same analyzing look I know I've been giving everyone else for the past week. "How are you holding up?"

"I'm not here for counsel—"

"Stop being so tough," he snaps. "This is me you're talking to."

I startle, glancing anxiously over my shoulder, not wanting anyone to walk by and overhear. I reach out an arm to swing the door closed.

"Better?" he asks.

I nod, taking a deep breath. I can relax with him, I know I can. I can tell him the truth. I can fess up.

"It's a mess," I admit.

"No shit."

"The parents are hiding something."

"They always are."

"Something is off."

"And you're running yourself ragged trying to figure it out."

"Wouldn't you be? I've got a dead thirteen-year-old girl, and these crystals we found in the pool—"

He waves a hand. "I heard."

"None of it makes sense," I say. "*None of it.* This family …"

"What's your hunch?"

"I don't know, but something's not adding up."

Sam stares at me, waiting for me to say something more, come up with some ingenious clarity. But I feel like I'm grasping at straws in the dark—blind, awkward jabs—and just when I think I've got something, the answer drops quickly out of reach again.

Frustrated, I haul another deep breath. "Can you just tell me about the fire? The reason I came here in the first place?"

He takes a long look at me before shaking his head.

"Insurance fraud," I say again, starting from the top. "Are you ruling that out or not?"

He fishes for a file on his desk. "We're ruling it out. Everything checks out with the family." His reading glasses return to his nose.

"But we already anticipated that. They're loaded. There's nothing to be gained by torching their own house."

"And you know for a fact the fire started in Mrs. Campbell's studio?"

"Yes, absolutely. Arson without a shadow of a doubt."

"And the family's alibis hold strong?"

Sam flips open the file, his finger dropping to a line on the page. "Julia Campbell wasn't home. She made a delivery to the Kirkland household just after three thirty; got stuck behind a wreck on Hughes on the way home. It was another thirty minutes before she saw the fire."

"And Thomas Campbell?"

He flips to another page. "He took his son's car to work, went to get it serviced around four, but the wait was too long so he headed back to the office. We've got him badging in at four fifty-one before his wife called screaming about the house." He turns another page. "Both kids were at practice until they were sent to friends' houses. And as you know, Mrs. Sinclair was at the Tanners' next door."

"So no chance any of them started the fire?"

"Nope." He peers over his glasses. "The Campbells are clean. Someone else started that fire to get to the Tanner girl. Someone who had time."

"Time, I know." My eyes shoot up. "More time," I say.

Sam gives me a puzzled look. "Yes. More time to start the fire."

"And kidnap the girl." A strange feeling takes root in my stomach. I jump from my seat. "That's it."

"What is?"

"Time," I tell him. "That's what I couldn't figure out before."

He looks confused, but then clarity comes. His eyes lock with mine.

I reach for the door and race down the hall.

CHAPTER FIFTY-FOUR

Detective Angela Blakely

Since the moment Mia went missing, I've been concentrating on a five-minute window—maybe ten, tops—when she was taken, a narrow window of time when someone stole her from that backyard.

But I've been approaching it all wrong. The timeline is off, I see that now. The realization dawns on me the second I leave Sam's office, the prospect tunneling its way through my brain until it's staring me smack in the face.

I call the Tanners and ask them to meet me at the police station. I've never asked them to the main precinct before, always discussed Mia's case in their own home, and when they arrive, the fact is not lost on them, the apprehension apparent on both their faces. They sit in metal chairs, the squeaking sound of a chair leg causing Vanessa to jump. She's skittish and trying not to be, the space below her left eye twitching, a splotch of makeup smudged beneath her lashes. Tripp's shoulders sag and he wears the same crestfallen look as earlier, but something is bothering him—something new. His eyes are strained and he won't stop tapping his foot against the floor.

He reaches for a glass of water and takes a long sip, the water going down in a noisy choked swallow. He doesn't offer a glass to Vanessa, which I find odd. Her body is angled away from his, the tension between them palpable. She looks like she hasn't taken a full breath of air since she entered the room.

"Mrs. Tanner, I'd like to ask a few more questions," I begin, and watch as her shoulders stiffen. "A kidnapping scenario was risky before, with you being in the front yard. Whoever took Mia didn't have a lot of time to grab her—not with the fire trucks, and you coming back to the house. But now that we know she drowned, this changes things." I look at her curiously. "Don't you think this changes things, Mrs. Tanner?" I try reading her face. "Because the thing is, drowning takes more time—more time than we previously had to consider. The idea that she was taken in only a matter of minutes?" I shake my head. "I'm not so sure about that anymore."

"What do you mean?"

"You were home with Mia for nearly two hours before she went missing. Julia Campbell saw you return from school just after three p.m. She dropped off her mother ten minutes later."

She nods.

"What happened after that?"

Her eyes flit from me to Tripp. "But we've already gone over this."

"I want to run over things once more."

Vanessa proceeds. "Mia had a snack, then she went to her room."

"And then?"

"I was on the phone with Janie. Mia started practice."

"What time did she go to the pool?"

"Around four."

"Four p.m.? Are you absolutely sure?"

"It was around that time, yes. She swims for an hour before Tripp comes home."

"What were you doing?"

"I was going to make dinner."

"But you never made it."

"No."

"And why was that?"

The corners of her eyes round slightly. "I still don't know why I have to keep repeating myself."

"Please continue, Mrs. Tanner."

She holds my stare.

"Mrs. Tanner," I prompt.

She clears her throat. "I took a shower. Came downstairs to make dinner but saw the fire. I ran out front, got scared. Went upstairs to check on Charlotte and—"

"Mrs. Tanner, did you leave the house?"

Her face freezes. "What?"

"Before the fire. Did you leave the house?"

Tripp spins in his chair.

"Why would I go anywhere?"

"Did you leave?" I repeat.

"No, I couldn't. I had Charlotte upstairs. Mia was in the pool."

"Were you home the entire two hours?"

"Of course I was."

"How do we know she was in the pool at the time you're telling us?"

"She swims from four to five."

"But did she that day?"

"Yes, she always swims that hour."

"Can anyone confirm you were home?"

"Charlotte …"

"She was sleeping," I remind her. "When you finished your phone call with Janie Roberts, it was three-thirty p.m. That leaves another hour."

"I already told you. I took a shower and then I was in the kitchen. Mia was home. *I* was home. She was swimming. I never left the house. You can ask anyone. My car never left the garage."

"Mrs. Tanner," I say, "the truth is, Mia didn't have to be swimming at four. She could have gone into the pool earlier. Or you could have taken her from the house."

Her face turns white. "Taken her ...?"

"You could have returned to the house before the fire."

"Returned? What are you talking about?"

"Before Mia disappeared," I continue, "did she play dress-up? She wasn't listening to you, wasn't doing her swim practice and—"

"But she *did* swim."

"She put on some sort of gown."

Vanessa's voice is trembling. "Why are you saying these things?"

"She wasn't doing what you asked. She wore a dress—"

"Susannah's dress," Tripp blurts out, and I stare at him, unblinking. It's my turn to hold my breath.

"What was that, Mr. Tanner?"

"Susannah's dress," he tells me. "It's missing."

Vanessa puts a shaking hand to her mouth.

"My first wife's wedding dress," he says. "I didn't say anything yesterday—I didn't want to believe it." He whirls on Vanessa. "That day, did she try it on? She knew where it was and she put it on for some reason and it upset you. She put on the dress and now it's gone." His eyes are bulging. "What happened, Vanessa?" He recoils in his chair. "Did you do something?"

"No, I never touched her!" Vanessa says.

"You were angry," I tell her. "You got carried away. The pool was right there—"

"I would never go near that pool!" Her breath rushes out.

"And why is that?"

"I'm terrified of the water." She glances anxiously at Tripp. "I can't swim—tell her. Tripp, tell her I never swim."

But he doesn't say a word.

I shake my head. "Mrs. Tanner, you could have done it in three feet of water. You could have held her down."

"No, I don't go in."

"Did someone help you then?"

"What?"

"Did someone else drown her? If you didn't go in the pool, did someone else do it for you?"

"No." Her eyes are frantic.

"If you didn't leave the house, did someone else park in the alley and help you move Mia's body?"

Her shoulders heave. "No."

Tripp is crying too. "Vanessa … what happened?"

I turn on him. "What about those text messages to Mia?"

He swipes the tears from his eyes. "What text messages?"

"The messages you sent the night before she disappeared. What was she so upset about?"

"But we've already gone over this."

"Remind me," I say.

"She wanted us to spend more time together. She was missing her mom."

"Yes, that's right." I nod. "You were pretty insistent on apologizing, weren't you? Is there something you didn't want her to tell your wife?"

"No, of course not."

"Did you come straight home from work the day Mia disappeared?"

"This is unbelievable …"

"Answer the question, Mr. Tanner."

"I was driving when Vanessa called."

"You said you were coming home from work, but now"—I pause—"now we know you left the office earlier." He shifts in his seat. "We took another look at your phone records. You made two phone calls that day just after four p.m. The problem is, the cell phone tower you pinged is the one at the entrance to your neighborhood—not the one downtown by your office. You also sent that same number several messages."

Beside him, Vanessa stops crying, her chin lifting as I pull a sheet of paper and read, "*Can you get away? Somewhere that's not your house.*

I've only got an hour. Then a follow-up message: *We need to be more careful about Mia.*" I glance at Tripp for a reaction. "At four fifteen, a response that says: *Stuck in traffic. Haven't moved an inch.* Last message from you: *I'll be thinking of you.*" I place the document on the table. "The person you were texting is Mrs. Julia Campbell."

Tripp's face turns bright red. Vanessa is taking in deep breaths through her nose.

"Can you explain any of that, Mr. Tanner?"

He doesn't hesitate. "I'm having an affair."

"Is that what this is?"

"That's *all* this is."

I look to Vanessa, wondering what her response will be to this blatant admission, but she is sitting and listening, taking it all in. And I realize: she already knew.

I stare again at Tripp. "What did you mean by being more careful about Mia?"

He can barely look me in the face. "She was starting to suspect something—suspect us."

"How?"

"I think she saw me the night before. I went to Julia's while everyone was out, but I think Mia followed me." He lowers his head, as though he's ashamed, but it's short-lived, because his eyes snap open. "I tried talking to her about it, but she didn't want to. She went to her room. That's when I sent those messages." He sucks in his breath.

"Were you worried she was going to expose you?"

He shakes his head. "No."

"Did you think she was going to tell everyone what you were up to?"

"I would never hurt my daughter." He grits his teeth. "If that's what you're implying."

"Mr. Tanner, after you tried meeting with Mrs. Campbell, what were you doing in the neighborhood for the next forty minutes?"

"I wasn't in the neighborhood. I went back to work."

"Because Mrs. Campbell wasn't available?"

"No … Yes …" He gives me a disgusted look. "I went back to the office."

"Can anyone verify this?"

"Yes, my admin."

"But before you returned, did you stop at your house?"

"No."

"The extra forty minutes would have given you time."

His eyes pop open. "To do what?"

"Mrs. Sinclair remembers seeing a car. Mia in a wedding dress." I hold his stare. "Did you drown your daughter? Are you the one who took her body away?"

Tripp slams his hand on the table. "You think I killed my own daughter so she wouldn't rat me out about Julia?"

"Something happened, Mr. Tanner."

He stands abruptly. "That's it. This has gone way too far. I'm not saying another word." And he moves toward the door, pulling Vanessa by the arm.

CHAPTER FIFTY-FIVE

Vanessa

Outside the police station, I'm shaking; my first impulse is to throw up. The sobs are jammed in my throat, a vice closing around my lungs so tight it's hard to breathe. I'm having trouble walking straight, with the very real possibility I might hyperventilate and collapse right there on the asphalt.

Tripp latches his hand around my elbow, and I balk. My first instinct is to call Janie and ask her to pick me up, but my feet have turned to slush, my muscles useless, and Tripp is navigating me through the parking lot before guiding me inside the Mercedes and slamming the door shut.

We drive the first few minutes in silence, both of us reeling from what just happened, staring ahead blankly. I press my hands to my chest, willing my heartbeat to slow down, to get my breathing under control, gasping at the dozens of accusations we just heard.

Everything is out in the open now.

Everything.

It's what I wanted—just not in front of the police detective.

"I didn't drown her," I tell him.

He cuts the wheel.

"I never left the house. She was there and then—"

"What happened to her?"

"I don't know."

"What happened to the dress?"

"I don't know that either."

"How can you not know?"

"She had it on, but she was putting it back."

"Did you see her do it?"

"No. I went upstairs."

"So what happened to it? It just *disappeared*? Just like her—it fucking *disappeared*?"

I shake my head, temples throbbing.

Tripp stomps his foot on the gas. "They found her in a swimsuit. There was no dress." He whips his head at me. "Why didn't you say anything before about her wearing it?"

"I was terrified. We were fighting, I didn't want anyone to know. They would think I did it—that I had motive."

"Well you look guilty as shit now."

"I wanted to tell you. I tried telling you yesterday but you took off."

Another jerk of the wheel, and my hand braces against the window as we turn a corner.

"You should have said something to the police," he says. "From the very start. We needed every piece of information—all of it. Dammit, Vanessa, this could have told us more. I would have known about the dress."

"And then what? You'd know your daughter decided to show it to me?"

"I don't know what that was about," he says. "But I think you did something."

"I told you I didn't."

"Then what the hell happened?"

"Someone else killed her."

"I don't believe you. You've been lying. To all of us. To me."

"You're the liar! You're the one who's been seeing Julia. Jesus, Tripp, you've been cheating on me this whole time. When Julia couldn't meet up, you stopped at the house. You saw Mia—"

"Don't you dare make it seem like I did something."

"Then where were you?"

"I did *not* go to the house."

"Did you really go back to the office?"

"Yes."

"Can you prove it?"

"Of course I can. Stop turning this around on me."

My voice shakes. "Detective Blakely is questioning you about taking Mia. There's a forty-minute gap where you're missing."

"I wasn't missing. You know that's not what happened." Tripp presses hard on the gas. Up ahead, he makes another sharp turn. "Don't forget the detective is also accusing *you* of leaving the house. Of having all the time in the world to take Mia." He cranes his neck. "Is she right?"

"No, of course not!"

"How do we know? It's only your word against Mia's. And now … Oh God …" He takes his hands off the wheel, the car veering. "She's gone … Mia …"

"Tripp!" I stare ahead at a car approaching. A van. A truck next. The front of it—a bumper, a flash of metal—comes too close. My heart leaps in my throat. I lunge for the steering wheel. But the driver swerves with only seconds to spare—horn blaring deafeningly, the driver's face contorting and cursing us as we pass. Our car rocks too, an abrupt side-to-side motion as Tripp struggles to regain control, swinging the Mercedes right, then left, before slamming to a stop on the side of the road.

He shuts off the car and I hear the ticking sound of the engine, both of us breathing heavily, a relentless pounding in my ears. The seconds pass, the two of us grappling with what to say next, and

I look out the window. We're a half-mile from the house. I can walk the rest of the way if I have to.

"You did this," he says.

And I feel the rage roaring through my heart. Everything I wanted to say to him yesterday in his study and didn't get to. The deceit.

I thought our marriage had been solid, that our years together had meant something. But he's been cheating on me. And with Mia's tragic death, he is finding ways to blame me. He's turning things around and making it seem like it's my fault when there is still something he's hiding. Something I haven't brought up until now.

"What about your ring?" I ask.

He doesn't move.

"It's missing," I tell him.

"I know." He moves to cover his bare hand.

"Do you have any idea where it went?"

He doesn't answer.

"No idea at all?"

Still no answer.

"Because I have it," I tell him, the anger burning inside my lungs.

A strange look comes into his eyes. Am I imagining that it's panic?

He stares at me. "What do you mean?"

"I've had it since the day Mia went missing. And now I'm wondering if I should tell Detective Blakely. Tell her how I found it in the same place our daughter drowned."

CHAPTER FIFTY-SIX

Vanessa

The day of the funeral, our families arrive, aunts and uncles crying and hugging by the staircase, the same painful scene as the day after we found out about Mia. But this time, one thing is different. Tripp and I are no longer side by side on the couch. I avoid him and sit alone, every nerve ending in my body on fire, the sound of his voice making my skin crawl. I hear him sobbing; someone tries comforting him but I don't go to him.

I'm faintly aware of one knock after another, someone else opening the front door and letting people into our house. One of Tripp's cousins approaches me cautiously, offering her condolences but then quickly stepping away. It's just as well; I have trouble knowing what to say in return.

Soon fewer people are walking over. My parents remain steadfast at my side, but I'm growing increasingly nervous and wring my hands in my lap, noticing the surreptitious looks in my direction, followed by the more obvious stares, hushed talk coming to a stop the second they think I've overheard what they're saying. Susannah's sister Carol turns away when she sees me. My mother leans over periodically to tell me to ignore them.

But I hear their words: *She wouldn't do something to Mia, would she?* And it hurts.

Janie is at the door—thank God she's here—and my heart pounds in my chest as I watch her push across the living room.

She clutches my hands as she sits. "Vanessa," she says. "What do you need—"

I turn away from my parents. "They think I did it."

Her eyes zip around the room and she lowers her voice. "Don't say that."

"It's true." My mouth is trembling. "Detective Blakely came right out and accused me. She accused Tripp too. But he's only telling his side of the story. Everyone's going to think …"

She grips my hands again. "But you didn't do it, Vanessa," she says forcefully. "Someone else took her."

"Then why is everyone saying it? Tripp …" My voice shakes when I say his name. "He's going to let them think it's me."

"You can't talk like this. The police are questioning him too, remember?"

"Yes, I know."

She leans in close. "Vanessa, they will find out who did this. They'll clear your name soon enough." She squeezes my hands again. "You've got to hold tight. Don't let them get to you."

"I'm trying." But the tears are spilling from my eyes. "I just don't know how much more I can take."

CHAPTER FIFTY-SEVEN

Detective Angela Blakely

I'm walking the length of the alley behind Ripple Lane. It measures a quarter-mile in total, but I only want to go as far as the two houses. Two crime scenes: one burned to the ground, the other temporarily vacant while the Tanner family is attending Mia's funeral.

The gate to the Tanners' backyard is closed. The shed blocking any view. Moving further down the fence, I press my face through the wooden slats and can make out the pool beyond. Above, the second-floor window where Mrs. Sinclair sat and dozed, gazing down on a crime scene and not knowing that was what she was taking in.

There was no wedding like she claimed—only Mia in her late mother's gown. And a car in the alley. If the old woman is right, the car was parked right where I'm standing now.

I walk next door to the Campbells' residence, what's left of it anyway: blackened brick, toppled chimney and beams, a large section of burnt grass spreading from the perimeter of the house to a wrought-iron gate at the back of their yard. With one slide of the latch, the gate swings open and I'm in.

The killer came through this gate, arson the first part of the agenda. In and out, gasoline poured, the blaze starting at the back of the house before spreading.

Next up, Mia.

I return to the Tanners' fence. Reaching over the top, I unlock the gate and leave it open, the way we found it the night she disappeared. The killer entered this way, crept to the pool and drowned her. Either that, or someone else was waiting on the other side of the fence to let them in.

Vanessa Tanner.

I asked her point-blank if she'd drowned the girl. Did she make up that nonsense about being afraid to swim? Or could she have stood perfectly in three feet of water and held her under? She couldn't leave the house, so she had someone else take the girl's body instead, dumping her on Monte Sano, trashing the dress too.

But who would do something like that for her?

I already checked: her best friend Janie was on a work trip in Orlando. Who else would have helped?

Or am I wrong? Perhaps Vanessa is innocent of everything and Tripp Tanner is the one behind it all. He burned down the studio to cover up his affair with Julia. Maybe he'd left something behind, evidence that would give them away, so he torched the place. Mia caught him out, and when she confronted him, things went disastrously wrong and he silenced his own daughter.

I step away from the fence and count thirty paces between the two gates, not far for someone needing to dash between houses. They could have taken cover behind the Tanners' storage shed, where a willow tree also provides cover with its branches. Next door, the Campbells have their own storage shed too, but on closer inspection, it's different from the Tanners': older, and more like a garage, a throwback to when the neighbors all had garages in the alley.

I try lifting the latch, but when I pull the handle, it doesn't budge. Locked. I rise on my toes and cup my hands against a row of windows. Nothing inside but lawn equipment, a weed eater, dozens of potting buckets piled high on a shelf.

My eyes scan a large empty space in the middle. A patch of oil on the concrete.

A space where a car used to be.

"Just a car. In the alley," Mrs. Sinclair said.

Just a car.

Another shot of adrenaline to my brain.

No wonder she thought nothing of it—she'd seen this car before. She knows who this person is too.

CHAPTER FIFTY-EIGHT

Detective Angela Blakely

I call Officer Donahue and demand a search warrant. "As fast as you can," I tell him before dropping the phone to my lap, my car veering out of Twickenham and joining the rest of the traffic, the Embassy Suites several miles away.

I've been targeting Vanessa and Tripp, what with the timeline, the wedding dress, Vanessa home alone with the girl. I've been zeroing in on Tripp Tanner for the fire too, and the possibility he would harm his own daughter. But this new hunch—whatever this is—I've got to follow. Perhaps I've been considering the wrong person all along.

I take the sharp turn on Madison.

Julia Campbell wasn't home, the fire chief said. *Stuck behind a wreck on Hughes.*

And Thomas Campbell?

He left around four … but he didn't badge in until 4:51 p.m.

I drive the lanes of the hotel parking lot until I find the dark green 4Runner the Campbells have been driving since the fire.

I peer through the windows and spot an empty Starbucks container in the cup holder, sunglasses on the dash, a back seat covered with bags from retail stores, files brought home from work. I'm not sure what I expect to find—something painfully obvious?—but I know it won't be that easy. There won't be a wedding dress sticking out among that mess. No veil stashed beneath the seat or one of Mia's hair ties dropped in the trunk.

No one would be that stupid.

And without the Campbells unlocking the doors, there's nothing I can do.

I wait patiently for the search warrant to arrive, Donahue texting me updates. Within the hour, he's pulling up in his patrol car, the document freshly signed by the judge. I snatch the warrant from his hands, reading it over to make sure we're cleared before pressing my phone to my ear and asking the Campbells to meet us in the parking lot.

"We've only just returned from Mia's funeral."

I don't care. "We need to check your car."

Thomas sighs. "This isn't the best time. The kids borrowed Julia's car. And you know mine burned in the fire."

"I'm talking about the other one. The one you had serviced for your son."

His voice rises. "The 4Runner?"

"That's the one."

There's another beat before he says something about coming down, and hangs up the phone.

I watch as the Campbells appear from the hotel's sliding doors, Julia keeping her head close to Thomas's shoulder as they move toward us in the parking lot. She loops her hand around her husband's arm with the look of someone wanting to be protected, and I think, *Wow, these people are incredible.* Julia Campbell was having an affair with the next-door neighbor; she's been lying to her husband's face, but she continues to cling to him—her ultimate hero for getting the family through the ordeal of a house fire and piecing them back together. The man she's depending on to fix everything when in the end she has no clue. No idea what he may be capable of.

I remind myself that no one does.

"How can we help you, Detective?" Thomas asks.

I display the search warrant.

Julia looks anxious. "Why do you need to check the 4Runner?"

"Please unlock the doors."

The pair of them look confused, mouths parted. They want to argue—I can see it in the way Julia's eyes are flicking back and forth. But beside her, Thomas is taking the key fob from his pocket and double-clicking the button.

At the sound, I immediately open the trunk. No wedding dress, of course, but shopping bags, cookware, bath towels and sheets, all similar to the things I saw from the window. At least now I can rummage to the bottom, pushing aside piles of clothing with tags and receipts.

"We lost everything," Julia says, as if this needs to be explained. "We had to buy it all new."

I ignore her. I'm lifting a pair of brand-new tennis shoes when I detect a distinct smell. I lean my head farther into the car—the odor is sharp and piercing.

I know this smell.

I throw open the back door. More shopping bags. But on the floor, several small stains in amoeba-shaped patterns across the mats.

"We had to get the car detailed," Julia says. "Whatever they used ruined the seats." She turns to her husband. "Isn't that right, Thomas? It's unacceptable. We must say something."

"Yes," he says.

I lift my head and stare. "When did you have the car cleaned?"

Julia looks to her husband again for an answer.

Thomas takes a couple of seconds to think. "Sometime last week."

"After Mia disappeared?" When neither of them responds, I close the car door. "My guess is it wasn't the cleaners who ruined your seats."

"Yes, it was," Julia insists. "They weren't like that before."

I stare at them. "This is chlorine bleach from the Tanners' pool." Julia and Thomas's eyes open wide. "How much do you want to bet we find Mia's DNA in this car too?"

PART SIX

The Drowning

CHAPTER FIFTY-NINE

Mia

It's funny how you're not sure how things will end for you, until they do. I'm only thirteen, and apparently my end is going to come way too soon.

I'm at the edge of the pool, holding my breath. Here we go. Here's where Vanessa is going to shove me right into the water. It will shock the hell out of us both. I didn't think she had it in her.

And she doesn't. Instead, she takes a step back, and finally there's space. Whew. I look sideways, the water only inches from my feet. That was close.

She opens her mouth, then shuts it, and before I know it, she's storming toward the house. "You're lying," she says. "You're making this up."

"I'm not! I know what I saw—Dad and Mrs. Campbell."

She spins at the door. "I don't believe you." She's crying and looks away. "Take off that dress, Mia. Please."

I follow her inside the house but struggle to pull the satin behind me, the dress dragging and sweeping across the floor. I stumble, fighting to regain my balance, my hands pushing against the wall. Quickly I feel for Dad's wedding band and press the metal against my finger—she hasn't noticed it yet. With everything else I'm wearing, she hasn't spotted his ring.

"I'll take it off," I tell her. "But you have to promise not to go near it."

She gives me a hurt look. "I don't even want to see it."

I glance toward the study. "Dad will be home soon and I need to swim my laps."

She nods faintly and turns for the stairs.

But I stop, my eyes wide. "Please don't tell Dad I told you about Mrs. Campbell. He can't know that I know or that I told you."

She only nods again, tears spilling down her cheeks. Then she quickly runs up the stairs and I hear her bedroom door closing as she locks herself inside.

I can't help but feel shaken. That fight between us was super intense, my mind jittery about everything I said out loud. The trouble I've started.

I lift the skirt and head to Dad's study. I'll put the dress away and hopefully Vanessa will stop crying. Dad won't know anything either. And in a few minutes I'll be swimming the butterfly.

As I look in the mirror one last time, loving the way the veil falls past my shoulders—I really do look so much like Mom—I feel someone standing behind me.

I can't believe it. Vanessa wants to talk some more.

But when I turn my head partway, I make out the outline of someone else, and a creepy feeling runs up and down my spine, a twisted hollowness in my tummy. The person standing there is bigger than Vanessa—much bigger—and I don't like it, not one bit. I want this person to leave me alone.

CHAPTER SIXTY

Mia

"Mia," Thomas Campbell says, watching me. "What have you done?"

He takes up most of the doorway. His shoulders squared. His arms folded firmly against his chest.

My nerves rise like hard spikes inside my throat. "What are you doing here?"

"I came to find you. No one answered the back door."

"Well you can't be here."

"I know what you did."

"Me?" I protest. "I didn't do anything."

His face hardens, his jaw setting in a grim line. "Oh yes you did. I have proof."

He's about to say something else but stops short. Perplexed, he looks me up and down. "What are you wearing?"

"My mom's dress."

He clicks his teeth. "You look ridiculous."

My eyes snap wide. "Don't say that!"

"Well you do." He sighs, but waves his hand, deciding not to argue about it. "I need to know what happened to my house. Where are your parents? I called for your stepmom but she didn't come to the door. I need to speak to them now."

"They're out," I lie, hoping I can deal with him without Dad and Vanessa finding out.

"Then tell me, why did you do it?"

The studio …

"I don't know what you mean," I say.

A dark shadow drops over his face—he's done with stalling. And I glance away, knowing there's a big chance I'm about to get into trouble. Super big trouble. He'll call the cops. The police will show up any minute at my door. I'll be grounded for life. They'll kick me off the swim team.

"Mia, I know it was you."

Play it cool.

"There are security cameras. I've got you on video."

Crap.

He raises his eyebrows. "Oh, you didn't think I had cameras? Well I do. They're brand new."

Oh boy. My mind is swirling. I've been caught, and I'm mad at myself for not thinking things through and checking first. I should have looked for cameras. I should never have gone over there … I shouldn't have lost my mind like that.

"I want to know *why*, Mia. I mean, my God, my wife's studio—it's trashed. What did she ever do to you?"

"Nothing."

"It's *not* nothing. What's going on?"

"Nothing is going on."

"It's on video, plain to see."

I stare at the floor.

"I had to stop by the house," he says. "I needed the extra keys for Robert's car and that's when I saw the spray paint. When I checked the video, I found *you* heading into the studio. Ten minutes later, you came back out."

I shrug. "You saw me go in. Doesn't mean I did anything."

"You walked in with two cans of spray paint. Looks pretty suspicious to me."

"I went to your house but I didn't do anything."

He makes a spluttering sound. "You looked around, is that it? Someone else painted the place?"

"Maybe."

"Who did it? Julia? Granny Charlotte? *Me?* It was you, Mia. Face up to it."

I hear a sound somewhere in the house, and my ears prick up, listening for Vanessa. Did a door open and close? Is someone on the stairs? But no, there's no one. She isn't coming down. She has no clue Mr. Campbell has me trapped down here. Now that I want her help, she's nowhere to be found.

An idea comes to me—an idea from out of nowhere.

"It was Vanessa," I tell him.

He blinks.

"She made me do it." I feel the shame reddening my face, but I don't back down.

"Stop making excuses."

"I'm not."

"It was you. I know it was you."

"She wanted me to do it."

The look on his face suddenly changes. "You're some piece of work, you know that? I thought you were a good kid."

This situation is quickly going from bad to worse. And two things I know for sure: I don't like the way he's glaring at me, and I don't like the way he's blocking the door.

I lift my skirt and push past him to the hallway. I've got to get out of here. He grabs my arm and I yank hard to shake him loose, stepping away as fast as I can. But he's following me—he's close on my heels—and my eyes dart right, then left, seeing there's only one way to go. The patio door is wide open after my fight with Vanessa. The same door Mr. Campbell walked through into our home.

I rush outside, the dress dragging as I move. He's following me toward the pool.

"Go away," I tell him, looking over my shoulder. I stumble, my feet tangling in the material around my legs, the beaded edging of the skirt catching on the concrete.

"You can't blame Vanessa. You can't throw this on someone else."

I whirl around. "I'm not!"

"*She's* not in the video. You're the one caught red-handed."

"But she made me do it," I repeat.

"Stop saying that."

"It's the truth. I'm telling you, she forced me."

"And why would she do something like that?"

"Because she hates your wife." And with these words, I almost gasp at myself. I'm so desperate to get out of trouble that I'm throwing else everyone under the bus.

His face twists—pure shock—as if he's never imagined anyone would speak horribly about Mrs. Campbell. I take a step back.

"Why would she hate her?" he asks.

And I despise myself for what I'm going to say, the lies I'm mixing with the truth. "Because she's jealous."

He makes a face. "Of what?"

"Her life. Everything. She wishes she could be like her."

"This is ridiculous. Why would she do something like that? You have to stop lying."

"I'm not lying!"

"You know," he says, stepping toward me, "this is very disappointing, Mia. I always thought better of you. Everyone says what an amazing young lady you are, what a talent at swimming, how we're going to see you in the Olympics one day. But" —he shakes his head—"this was a really bad thing to do. You've hurt a lot of people."

His words sting. He can see right through me. "I'm a good person! Don't blame me. Vanessa is the one who's not good."

He reaches for his phone. "I'm calling your dad."

"No, don't do that!" I lunge forward, but he swipes it out of reach. "Don't call him," I plead. "Don't tell him."

But he's scrolling for his number. "He needs to know. We can talk it over, assess damages." He looks at me. "Figure out your punishment."

And all I can think is: *Stop! Don't do that.* I was supposed to get away with this. No one was supposed to know I spray-painted his house. I didn't know there would be cameras. I've really messed up this time. I did something big and got busted, and now someone is on to me. Someone who's smart and has evidence.

Think, Mia. Think. Get his attention on something else—anything other than what you've done.

"Mrs. Campbell is screwing around with my dad!"

His finger freezes in mid-air.

"Dad and your wife," I tell him. "They've been kissing and hugging. I saw it."

He shakes his head. "Just stop."

"I mean it. They're together."

I can't believe what I'm saying—giving up my dad like this, telling Mr. Campbell these things when I've barely spoken to him my entire life. But now it's out; for the second time today I've blurted about my dad. The first time was on purpose. I wanted to hurt Vanessa because I was just so mad and needed someone to yell at, but now I'm desperate to come up with the one thing that could get Mr. Campbell off my back, point him in a different direction, make him think about something more terrible than me and my spray paint.

"You're unbelievable," he says.

But I can't stop. My brain is taking on a maddening beat of its own.

I lift my arm. "You see this?" I say, and he glances up from his phone. "This is my mother's bracelet. But my dad gave it to *her*—to your wife." The words are spewing from me. "I found it in your wife's studio—in your house." I shake my arm. "This is proof they were together."

He doesn't buy it. "That's my wife's bracelet. All the ladies on the fundraising committee received one."

"It's not. It's my mother's!"

His face tightens. "Why would your dad do that? Why would he give my wife something?" But then his face drains white and his expression changes, like he's thought of something else and is about to be sick to his stomach. "That can't be … He wouldn't…" He grimaces, struggling to fight the thoughts from his mind. "*She* wouldn't …"

But then he shakes his head. Any chance of my story ringing alarm bells in his head has disappeared.

"You're wrong," he says firmly.

"But I saw them last night. You weren't home and Dad went over."

"Last night?"

"Yes."

A spark in his eyes. "Then I should have it on video. And when it's not there, I'll know you're making it up."

I startle—the cameras would have been rolling last night. He'll have a recording and then my dad will be caught red-handed too. *Crap, what have I done?* I didn't want him to actually check the video, I only wanted to get him to leave me alone. He can raise hell with Mrs. Campbell later. She can lie and cover it up. If he asks my dad, he can deny the affair. And if Dad questions me about it, I'll tell him Mr. Campbell is making it up. That I never spoke to him.

But if there's video—

"I'll rewind the tape," he says. "I'll tell your parents about everything you've lied about today."

My tummy flip-flops. "Don't watch the tape! Don't tell him!"

He shoots me a disgusted look. "What? You're backtracking now?"

"I just …" I stammer. "I don't want you to see—"

"*Mia!*"

The way he says my name makes me jump. His eyes are wild, his patience gone. I'm scared, my nerves shaking and rattling, and I feel my weight shifting again, the heavy drag of the skirt pulling me to one side.

"You can't make up stories like this and not imagine there will be consequences. Words and actions have consequences, Mia. *All the time*. You're old enough to know that by now, right?" He takes a step forward, edging me toward the pool.

"But my dad can't know …"

"What? That you're lying about him and saying horrible things about my wife?" His face rages red. "You can't make this kind of stuff up and think you can get away with it."

"I'm sorry. I …"

I take a step back, but my heel gets stuck. I can't move, the material caught beneath my weight, one leg held firm while the other struggles against the fabric.

"Saying things like this ruins people's lives, Mia—ruins marriages. How could you say those things? How could you do that?" And he raises his arms and shoves me right into the pool.

I plunge in sideways with a splash, the satin and lace pulling me down immediately. Swinging my arms in giant loops, I try keeping my body upright—anything to stop my head from dropping below the surface—but nothing's working. I'm only grabbing air, water rushing past my fingers. I kick, but that only makes things worse. My feet are stuck, tangled in a web of petticoat.

Panic rises fast in my stomach. Why isn't Mr. Campbell helping me? Why isn't he pulling me out?

He's not even moving; he's standing frighteningly still, staring at something that's caught his attention, something over the fence.

I can't tell what it is at first, there's too much water clouding my vision, but then I see it: an orange glow above his head. Clouds of black too.

A fire. *Flames.*

He's watching his house burn.

And that's when I realize he doesn't care about me. He's pushed me into the water and doesn't care that I can't come up on my own.

I struggle. My feet stretch out but it's no use, I can't touch bottom. The heavy satin swirls around my legs, the gown taking on more weight in the water until its sheer volume tugs me down.

I'm sinking, my face slipping beneath the surface until all I can see is wall-to-wall water, a beam of sunlight darting through the deep end, the blurry outline of Mr. Campbell continuing to look away from the pool.

I want to scream: *This isn't a joke! I'm not playing. This is for real!* But I'm underwater and he can't hear me.

I hold my breath for as long as I can, but this time it's different. It's not like any swim meet I've been to. It's not like those times when I've purposely sunk to the bottom, hanging out in the deep end and enjoying the quiet. This isn't fun and games. I'm scared and alone while the water swirls around me.

Dad's wedding ring slips from my hand and drops into the water, a gold shimmer gliding toward the bottom. I try reaching for it but it's too late; I can't see it anymore. The ring sinks to the floor.

But something silver shimmers at my wrist. Mom's bracelet. I've still got that, at least. I've got a piece of Mom with me.

Blue and white light surrounds me—beautiful shades of water, except right now they don't look so pretty anymore. I glance up again, but Mr. Campbell doesn't turn. It's final: he's making no effort to jump in and rescue me.

My mouth opens, the water rushing down my throat into my lungs, the bubbles rising from my face, and I'm so desperate for air, I take another gulp. And that's when it happens. Everything suddenly goes quiet, until I can no longer feel the pain. It feels like I'm dreaming, the need to take another breath soon fading, my strength draining away until I can no longer kick, my arms stretching out instead, fingers pointed, my hands shuddering one last time until the rest of my body comes to a stop.

I feel my eyes closing. Everything about me feels as if it's going into a deep sleep. My heartbeat slows. The pool, the water, the bubbles disappear. All that remains is peace and quiet.

Everything goes still.

Except my thoughts.

I'm sorry, Daddy. I'm sorry for everything.

I think about my stepmother.

I'm sorry, Vanes …

But I don't get a chance to finish her name.

CHAPTER SIXTY-ONE

Detective Angela Blakely

We arrest Thomas Campbell the following morning, the lab confirming that the stains we found in the 4Runner are a match to chlorine bleach used in the Tanners' pool. And despite the cleaning, we found traces of Mia's DNA in his car.

"You got him," Sam says.

I nod, letting my body sink into the fire chief's chair, this time not caring about the metal coils digging in my back. I'm still riding the high from the arrest.

Sam shakes his head. "Damn, who would have thought? Did he say why?"

"He says he didn't kill her—that she accidentally drowned while he was distracted by the fire—but I think he's lying. He says he never touched her except to dump her body on Monte Sano. He stripped the wedding gown off, burned it with the veil, carried her out into the woods, and left her against a log. Covered her with dirt. Then he went to his office and changed into a spare suit he kept there. Left the burnt pieces of the dress in a dumpster, along with his ruined clothes. He says the whole thing was an accident."

Sam whistles. "No jury's going to believe that."

"Of course not."

"Why did he burn the dress?"

"He said it was too heavy to carry her wearing it."

"And why was he there in the first place?"

"He was picking up something for his son's car. Said he left it in the garage out by the alley."

He scratches his head. "No, why did he end up in the backyard with the girl?"

"His story? He saw her in the wedding dress and it got his attention. He unlocked the gate and came in through the yard. He claims he called out for the stepmother but she didn't answer."

"Horse shit," Sam says.

"Agreed." I lean back in the chair. "I think Mia told him about his wife's affair with her dad, and Campbell lost his ever-loving mind. He was afraid she was going to blurt it out to everyone." I click my teeth. "He took it out on the girl."

Sam makes a face. "He drowned Mia to cover up his wife's infidelity?"

"It's messed up," I agree. "And something else. He's fighting the arson charges. Says he didn't start the fire—something about security cameras he had installed without his wife's knowledge because of her photography business, and that we'd see the evidence there, except nothing was backed up to the Cloud. It all burned."

"Convenient. So who did set the fire?"

"No idea." I grin at him. "That's *your* job."

He doesn't respond.

"You said it yourself," I say. "The point of origin was the studio—a place where he knew Tripp Tanner had been with his wife. He took gas from his own garage and started the fire. He couldn't stand to look at that room anymore, so he burned it, the fire distracting everyone while he fled the scene and hid Mia's body."

Sam peers over his glasses. "So it turns out the girl's parents really are off the hook? All those fears you had about them earlier and they're clean?"

"Looks that way," I say.

"Unbelievable. And the stepmom never saw or heard anything?"

I shrug, feeling the familiar satisfaction that comes with closing a case. "Turns out her only crime was not being in the right place at the right time."

CHAPTER SIXTY-TWO

Detective Angela Blakely

Something still bugs me about Thomas Campbell's story. I can't shake the feeling I've missed something.

If he really did drown Mia so she wouldn't tell anyone about his wife's affair, then why not just leave the girl in the pool, then call 911 and say it was an accident? The weight and bulk of the dress sinking her to the bottom would have been enough to back up his story.

The fire was raging, his house burning, and he was in turmoil about his wife. He pushed Mia into the pool to silence her, and then realized that at any moment, the stepmother would be coming back out to the yard. Fire trucks were going to show up. Instead of leaving her and lying to us about how she'd drowned, he'd taken her body and run.

Of all his mistakes that day, that one was his biggest.

But the man must be smarter than that.

I visit Thomas Campbell in his jail cell, wanting to know the truth. He's pale, a doughy, pasty white that's taken over his skin. It's a familiar look; I've seen it plenty of times on the faces of people struggling with the fear of prison, cell doors slamming, shouts from other prisoners, the harsh reality of what this will mean for the rest of their lives.

He'll be staying in this solitary holding cell until his arraignment, several weeks away. Then a guilty verdict, I'm sure of it, followed by a bumpy, cold van ride to a larger facility several hundred miles away.

I look him over, the white button-down shirt and slacks he was wearing the night he helped with Mia's search long gone and replaced with a gray jumpsuit.

And to think I let him get in my patrol car. He rode along with us even though he knew where the girl's body was. While Tripp Tanner was in the front seat panicking, his daughter's killer was riding in the back, suggesting ways to help. He cut through vines and bushes with the rest of the search team, all the while making sure no one was getting near his hiding spot. And when the rain came, it washed away everyone's footprints, including his.

He sits before me, slumped against the wall, looking shell-shocked.

I don't waste any time.

"Why didn't you just leave her at the bottom of the pool?" I ask.

But he doesn't answer, only lifts his eyes to me, the eyelids and the skin around his cheeks puffy.

"Why go to the trouble of pulling her out of the pool and dumping her body?" I insist. I wait for a response, but there isn't one. "Mr. Campbell? Why would you do that?"

He gives a small, pained cough, a gurgling sound as he clears his throat, taking forever to speak. "I don't know," he says.

I wait another beat.

Is that it?

But no, it's not. I know it's not. He's lying again.

I narrow my eyes, wanting him to come clean.

Something made him pull Mia out of the water. There's a reason he carried her away, why he didn't want to be caught next to the pool.

"Mr. Campbell?" I repeat.

He stares at me, shoulders sagging, for an infuriatingly long time, and I glare right back until it feels unbearable—for him, not me. And then something in his face shifts. A resolution. A new breaking point.

"The bracelet," he says, wincing.

"What bracelet?"

"The one on Mia's arm."

"She wasn't wearing a bracelet."

"No, I pulled her out of the pool so I could take it off."

My heart thumps loudly in my chest.

"Why would you do that?"

He sucks in a rattled breath. "Mia said it was her mother's bracelet, that she'd gotten it from my house. That her dad had given it to my wife as a gift."

"Mr. Tanner gave away a piece of his late wife's jewelry to his mistress?"

Thomas shudders at the word *mistress*.

I continue. "Mia showed you the bracelet to prove they were having an affair?"

"I didn't believe her," he says. "I thought she was making it up, along with everything else she was saying. All the ladies on the fundraising committee received that bracelet years ago, her mom and my wife included. But when she drowned, I realized I had to get the bracelet off her arm—it was the only thing that would connect her to us. I mean, why would Mia Tanner be wearing my wife's bracelet? You'd jump all over something like that, wouldn't you? You'd find out about my wife's affair, what she'd been up to with Tripp. It would be out in the open, and I couldn't risk that."

A vision of Thomas Campbell diving into the pool flashes into my brain. But not to save Mia—he'd lost that chance when he didn't realize she was drowning. No, he jumped in after the fact. To remove a single piece of jewelry.

"I wanted to get rid of it," he says. "I pulled her out but couldn't get the damn thing off. The clasp was too tiny, too delicate, and my hands were shaking. I was petrified. Time was ticking and ..."

His face drops. "I freaked out. I couldn't leave her like that, not with Julia's bracelet still on her arm, so I grabbed her and ran."

"What did you do with the bracelet?"

"I tossed it somewhere in the woods … I burned the wedding dress and dumped her body."

"You did all of that to get rid of your wife's bracelet?"

"Except it wasn't," he says. "It wasn't hers." He stares hard at the ground and his face goes slack, the grief taking over his body.

"What do you mean?"

He doesn't meet my eyes. "In the woods, when I finally got it off her wrist, I realized it really was Susannah's. It had her initials on it. Julia must have lost her own and Tripp gave her Susannah's as a replacement. I couldn't believe it." He splutters. "Julia had left it in the studio exactly where Mia said she'd seen them together. It was all true and it was all going to come out."

I watch Thomas bring a hand to his face, his palm pulling from his forehead to his chin.

"Did you push her, or did she fall in on her own?" I ask.

His eyes flick up. "I told you already. She fell in on her own."

I glare at him. He's lying, I know he is. He's given up every detail except this final one. The one that would mean he'd killed a child.

"I should have just left her at the bottom of the pool," he says.

CHAPTER SIXTY-THREE

Vanessa

Janie helps me pack my things, my clothing folded in several suitcases, while a moving team carries boxes and furniture out to a truck.

I'm only taking what I brought to this house five years ago, nothing more. The rest can stay behind and get covered in dust for all I care. Nothing is coming with me to remind me of Tripp.

In the end, my worst fears about my husband came true, our marriage unraveling with the disastrous accusations and the ugliness of the affair. I should have known he wouldn't hurt Mia, though. I should never have accused him.

But you know what? He shouldn't have accused me either.

It's too late now—what's done is done. The trust between us erased. Our marriage over. And it hurts more than I ever believed possible.

I've told Janie everything about that last day with Mia. She listened as I described the wedding dress, the argument we had beside the pool, the fact that I ran upstairs to hide, not wanting Mia to see how heartbroken I was that her dad had been unfaithful. I cried about Mia being gone, the sobs shaking my shoulders so that Janie had to hold me tight to calm me down.

I was so afraid of that pool, so wary of going near that water; what happened to me as a kid, the panic I'd felt, never leaving my mind. And to think that's what happened to Mia. She'd been an elite swimmer, and yet that pool is the place she drowned.

Throughout all this, I do wonder about Julia, my next-door neighbor, my friend. I know I should tell her to go to hell—she sabotaged my life with Tripp, she did those things behind my back—but I'm not the one who's married to a killer, who'll have to contend with that ordeal. I get the chance to pack up and leave, while she's picking up the pieces a monster left behind. Testifying at her husband's trial.

Janie is helping me carry boxes out to the driveway when I see someone parking their car on the street. A woman gets out.

Julia.

At first I think she's here to check on her house, chunks of it bulldozed and cleared out in the weeks since the fire, since the horrible tragedy with Mia. But she's closing the car door and walking toward me instead. I hold my breath. Everything in my body locks tight.

Janie watches her approach as I shove a box into the backseat. Finally I turn and stand my ground to look at her.

Her face is drawn. Eyes pinched. Not a stitch of makeup, her shirt loose and dwarfing her shoulders. She looks if she's been to hell and back. Because she has.

And so have I.

"I know you don't want to see me or talk to me," she begins, "but I want you to know how sorry I am. For everything."

"And what is everything?" I ask.

She fumbles nervously with her keys. Behind us, the movers load another piece of furniture into the truck, but I keep my eyes firmly trained on Julia. I'm so angry I'm not sure I can stand still long enough to hear her apology.

"What I did to you," she says. "What *we* did. Me and Tripp. We deceived you." Tears choke her throat, but then she recovers, her voice rising a hitch. "If we hadn't done what we did. If Mia hadn't seen. She wouldn't have told Thomas—"

"Don't you dare blame this on Mia!"

"And Thomas wouldn't have done what he did—"

I stomp forward. "I said don't blame this on Mia!"

Julia shrinks back.

"No one had to kill her." My face is now inches from hers. "Thomas didn't have to lie."

She's crying now. "He didn't mean to … He didn't know …"

I don't want to listen to her anymore. Whatever else she has to say isn't going to make a difference—not to me, at least. She's not sorry about her affair with my husband. She's only sorry she got caught. And what Thomas did to my stepdaughter? She'll make excuses for him too. She'll say Mia fell in the pool, just as he keeps insisting. It's what he'll say in court too.

Janie slams the trunk closed. My cue to leave.

"Please go," I tell Julia. "I don't want to see you again."

The front door of the house opens and Tripp emerges. Julia glances at him, then back to me, before turning away, stumbling and knocking her ankle against one of the sprinkler heads as she rushes to her car.

I face my husband.

Closing the gap between us, I walk one last time to the front porch, to the house where we both thought we'd live happily ever after. My eyes never leaving his, I dig my hand into my pocket and pull out the ring—his wedding band. He hasn't asked for it since I told him about it after we left the police station.

I drop it into his hand and he stares at it, the gold metal shining against his palm. But it doesn't look shiny to me anymore.

I make him meet my eyes. "Goodbye, Tripp," I tell him. And this time, he doesn't get a word in. I turn on my heel, telling myself that part is done. It's over with.

I join Janie at the car, and she waves her hand to tell the movers to head out. Tripp can only stand there and watch us leave.

He's lost his daughter. He'll be living in that big house alone.

Thomas Campbell stands accused of drowning Mia and hiding her body. He's accused of setting fire to his house too.

But they've got that part wrong.

I know this because it was me. *I'm* the one who set the fire.

After the fight with Mia, what she told me about her dad, I found a way to get back at my husband's mistress. I went to the place I knew she loved best—where she had placed her sticky, dirty hands all over my husband's body—and I torched her beloved studio.

Could it have been simply an accumulation of that day, my emotions already running high—Mia grabbing my arm, glass shattering in the kitchen, the discovery that Tripp kept his dead wife's wedding gown in a closet, Mia telling me he didn't love me? Yes, all of that took its toll. But the final straw was when Mia blurted out what she'd seen.

They were kissing and hugging, and it was gross.

And then came the visuals: the way I imagined Tripp and Julia fumbling and falling their way inside her studio, all tongues and hands and sweat and groans. It made me crazy.

Did he think of me? Did he compare us?

Did he stop to think about Susannah?

When I got to the studio, I couldn't believe what I saw. The place was wrecked, stuff knocked over and nearly every surface covered in paint. Black lines drawn over the walls, zigzags covering the monitor and keyboard, the Persian rugs ruined. Someone had gotten there first.

But who?

I didn't have time to think—or care. I had left Mia home alone to swim and was pouring gasoline on Julia's desk. I lined up her candles, the ones she liked to use during photo sessions, then knocked each one over ceremoniously.

I let it all burn.

A LETTER FROM GEORGINA

Thank you so much for reading *The Stepdaughter*. I had so much fun coming up with the story idea and letting the action and suspense kick off from the very first page. I hope you enjoyed the roller-coaster ride as much as I enjoyed writing it.

If you did enjoy the book, and want to keep up to date with all my latest releases, please sign up at the following link. Your email address will never be shared and you can unsubscribe at any time.

www.bookouture.com/georgina-cross

One of the best parts of writing comes from seeing the reaction from readers. Did you work out the next twist? Did you see what was coming? Were you able to feel the emotional struggle and pull between stepmother and stepdaughter, the father too? If you enjoyed the story, I would absolutely love it if you could leave a short review. Getting feedback from readers is amazing and it also helps to persuade other readers to pick up one of my books for the first time.

Thank you so much for reading!
With much appreciation,
Georgina

 GeorginaCrossAuthor

@GCrossAuthor

@GeorginaCrossAuthor

Georgina-Cross-Author.com

ACKNOWLEDGMENTS

There are so many people I'd like to thank for helping me launch my first book into the world.

My amazing agent, Rachel Beck. Thank you for taking a chance on me that day at the writers' conference in Chicago. I'll never forget sitting across from you during the author pitch session and us instantly connecting over our love for suspense books. You always work tirelessly on my behalf and your reviews have made me a stronger writer. Thank you for being my agent and for never giving up on me! Big thanks also to my literary agency, Liza Dawson Associates, for your help and guidance. It's so greatly appreciated.

My brilliant (or, as they say in London, "brill") editor, Maisie Lawrence at Bookouture. Thank you for seeing the potential in my writing to sign a two-book deal. That phone call with you continues to be one of the most exciting days of my life. I look forward to working with you on the next book too.

My very first beta reader, Michelle Hammett Ortakales. Thank you for taking the time to read my work. Your words of encouragement were the boost I needed to keep writing. I love that you are the Will & Grace in my life and thank you for always making me laugh.

My sister friends who cheer me on, the Unicorn Mafia. Thank you for accepting the times I went M.I.A. for entire weekends in a row so I could write. My Susie's Wish crew, especially my vice president, my rock, Letricia Ogutu. We've been through so much together. Thank you for helping keep Susie's memory alive through the work we do. I know Susie is smiling down on us. My best friends from Louisiana State University. Thank you for encouraging me to follow my dreams from the very first days we met as teenagers. Geaux Tigers!

My author friends, Rea Frey, Nicole Angeleen, and Jenny Hale, for showing me the ropes and cheering me on too. Your feedback has been incredible—especially Nicole, who continues to be one of the most amazing beta readers and editors for my work.

My sister, Davinia Troughton, who said she always knew I could do it. Goodness knows how many pages you've seen me type when we were growing up. My brother-in-law, Joshua Howes, for being someone I can talk to about writing and for inspiring me with your writing projects too. My beautiful nephews, Leo and Elliot: your E-E loves you! Sending big hugs to my aunties Rosie, Liz, and Beryl from "across the pond". You remain my #1 fans on social media.

I am indebted to my parents, Cecilia and Kelvin Troughton. You always believed in me and hoped I would publish a book, and now it's finally here! Thank you to my mom for saying you love every sentence even when I know the paragraph needs work. You are my biggest cheerleader. And to my dad for being the first officially published author in our family. We're so proud of your memoirs. I love you both.

My husband, David Estacio. I couldn't have done this much writing without you. You came into my life and brought me the love and support I needed. You have been so patient and kind, especially those weekends and mornings when I continue to hunker down over the keyboard, unwilling to break away for hours. Thank you for believing in me and for being the first person I tell when I receive publishing news. I love that you come up with some of the best plot twists and turns too. I love you so much.

My stepsons, Andrew and Matthew. Thank you for welcoming me into your life with open arms. I love watching you grow into the smart, confident men you are today and that we are together as a family. Thank you for tolerating my attempts at cooking.

And most of all, my sons, Reece and Liam, to whom I dedicate this book, and every word I commit to the page. Reach for the stars, boys. Chase your dreams. Go after them. Work hard, stay true, and you can achieve anything you want. The sky is the limit and I can't wait to see what you will accomplish. I love you.

CPSIA information can be obtained
at www.ICGtesting.com
Printed in the USA
FSHW021408040920
73572FS